# HARMONY
## Interrupted

THE DRAGOON THRONE

## TANYA STEVERDING

Magic Twinkle Books
ESCAPE INTO THE PAGES

# HARMONY

## Interrupted

### THE DRAGOON THRONE

# CONTENT TRIGGER WARNING

This book is intended for adults only.

Please understand this paranormal adult romance
novel may not be everyone's cup of tea.

I just want to advise that while I try to write a world
that is accepting and diverse, the journey of good
prevailing over evil may have moments that could
cause some to feel triggered. Please be mindful of
your mental health. Read only if you are emotionally
prepared for triggering content.

Childbirth, blood, violence, kidnapping, childhood
trauma, slurs, and other potentially triggering
language. Attempted sexual assault/rape insinuated
in a few scenes.

*Tanya Steverding*

This book is dedicated to the memory of:


Brandi Buckley

Jo Kirksey

My best friends and loved ones
who were avid fellow readers.

And to my sister, Tarin Yesko.

Three beautiful mothers who died too young.
Our sisterhood lives on in my heart.

My niece Paige Hill.

I am ever grateful for their influence and
continued inspiration.

Rest in peace, forever in my heart dear loved ones.

# CHAPTER 1

## (Earth)

## Kayla

"Again, my name is Kayla Grace Garcia. I am twenty-one. As I have said before, I am an empath with other so-called "gifts." I reiterate this to the cop interviewing me.

"My best friend and foster sister is Brooke Elaine Baker." I flick my finger toward the notepad the cop was scribbling his notes on. "I gave you her number already too. She is also gifted and is probably sensing my trauma right now. I need to call her back." My phone begins to buzz and bounce on the car's hood that I was leaning against. Brooke's face smiles up at me from the screen.

"See?"

"Ma'am, I don't need to know all this. I only need the facts to write my report. Now, tell me how and why you knocked this dude out." His head tilts toward the ambulance, where a grim figure lies on the stretcher.

What a dick! I roll my eyes and begin reciting the whole

episode again, slower so the officer can keep up. I even add some larger-than-life hand motions to keep his attention.

"I was on the way to work. I transfer buses here. That creep jumped out when I walked passed the alley there and grabbed me! He tried to pull me into the alley. I could tell he planned on raping me and keeping me as his plaything." I shudder as I remember the images that played in my head when he touched me. The things that he did to his playthings were vile. I take a deep breath and slowly breathe out to calm myself.

"Fearing for my life, I fought like hell. I reared my head back and busted his nose. I bit his arm and stomped his toes before dropping my body to escape his grip. The second I got loose, I turned and nailed him in the nuts!"

"You fucking bitch!" His evil screams are still echoing in my head.

"He grabbed my ankle when I tried to run. I ended up falling. I could barely hold my face away from the concrete. I could feel him crawling up my body. Thinking he had me, I was certain I would die a horrible death! I grabbed anything I could get my hands on to defend myself." I struggle to fight back my tears. This is too raw, so soon after it all happened.

"I felt around me in a panic and found a brick under a plastic bag. I smashed that bastard with it until he was limp and finally let me go." I glare at the asshole as he is loaded into the ambulance, and another wave of disgust makes me want to vomit.

"We have been telling you cops the same damn thing!" a woman calls from the corner of the street. "We have been telling you that something like this would happen! He has been taking our girls, and you have ignored the problem! What is one less sex worker? Am I right?"

Murmurs of agreement rise from the small crowd of sex workers surrounding their outspoken leader.

The sex workers are kind to me tonight. People who are

stigmatized tend to be the kindest in my reality. I hope they stay safe.

"I am begging you to check out the third door on the right, down the alley." My desperation and continued efforts finally get to the cop because he sends his partner to check out the door . . . The young officer freezes in his tracks as he looks into the third doorway.

"Yo, Joe! We have a huge problem back here!"

Joe, the cop I'm talking to, stares me down and sternly points at me.

"Stay here! Do not move a muscle. Do you hear me?"

My smile is sickeningly sweet as I salute him. "Not a muscle."

I know what they're going to find. I want to see the look on their faces when they realize I've been right all along. I'll probably see fear.

Joe and his partner's expressions turn horrified. They gaze back down the alley at me. No one ever believes me until they see the proof with their own eyes.

Joe reaches up to his radio and calls for the detectives and the coroner before directing two officers to move the onlookers back away from the scene. He reads over his notes as he walks back to me, clearing his throat softly.

"You are lucky, Kayla. Things could have ended badly tonight. I will call you to come down to the station on Monday. I have your information in case we need you sooner. I can have an officer take you if you need a lift home."

I reach over and pick up my phone. "I could use a lift to work instead. I can't be late again."

The phone buzzes again. Brooke's smiling face fades to black after the second buzz. She must know I am safe for now, though this event has triggered me. As I climb into the patrol car, I begin thinking back to when Brooke and I met in the foster system.

As children, we ended up in a foster home that cared for children with mental health issues. In our case, we were there to be psychic. It really freaked people out most of the time. I remembered looking out the window and seeing this blonde girl grab her trash bag of stuff from the trunk of the social worker's car.

I felt drawn to her the moment I noticed her. I knew she could not see through the dark screens covering the windows, but as I looked at Brooke, she tensed, her back going straight, and I felt a zap of some kind in my soul.

Brooke turned and looked directly up at my window, making eye contact even though she could not see me. She dropped her bag and ran into the house. I ran too and met her halfway down the stairs.

" Hi, I am Brooke," she said with happiness as she gave me a bear hug that felt like home to me. Usually, when I touched people, I felt their emotions and thoughts, but I never once felt any side effects or psychic triggers from Brooke's touch.

We were inseparable from that moment on, which made it safer for us both. The foster parent's sons were disgusting and had tried to prey on me when I first arrived, but I was too mean for them to get easily. The bigger brother once tried to grab me from behind, and his energy and disgusting intentions instantly ambushed me. I screamed and kicked, fighting like a wildcat. They Stayed away from me when I told them I knew exactly what they intended to do. They were scared of me, and I was happy that they thought I was a freak.

When Brooke arrived, I was watchful and did not want those boys near her. But one time, when Brooke went to the bathroom, I felt her fear. I barged my way into the bathroom, and I fought the boys away from Brooke. The foster mom was livid at me for hurting her sons. She claimed I was crazy. The state sent counselors that talked to us extensively, and a new social worker placed us into a new home just hours after the fight. Brooke and I worked the system after that so we could stay close to each other.

I adore her softness and her ability to be what I cannot be. I love her goofiness and free spirit. She is a breath of fresh air in a world where I am constantly tuning into negative emotions. Brooke and is a ray of hope, a daily reminder for me to have faith in humanity. I can feel people's true selfishness and intentions, and often the scales fall heavy on the wrong side of things. I have only ever felt warmth and acceptance from Brooke. She really is a light in my dark. Today has been dark for me, but I know Brooke will always have my back, and I will always have hers, no matter how opposite in personalities we may seem.

"Brooke, I am okay, I promise!" I say as I finally answer her call.

"Kayla, I think you should just come home for the night."

"We need the money. I am not missing work tonight." Brooke is worried and thinks I am putting myself through too much stress trying to keep my job. She believes the universe will provide, and she never cares if she is the one who is pulling more weight than I am. But I am the one who keeps burning through jobs. We have government housing, but we still pay rent and bills. I don't want us to live in the slums forever, and I need to be fair to Brooke and carry my share of the financial responsibilities. It's not her fault I am so broken with this gift.

"Kayla, don't be stubborn. I know something awful happened. Stop worrying about the money; tonight, you can make an exception."

"Don't worry your pretty little head about it, Brooke. I will explain everything tonight after my shift. Love you, bye, I am almost late." I feel bad for hanging up and cutting her off.

Brooke is the sunshine in my world of dark and gray. Her energy calms me and restores my faith in humanity. She has her hippie grounding techniques, meditations, chants, and positive vibes. They all make her an optimistic, quirky person. She is always trying to convert me to her calmer ways. I doubt she will ever succeed, but I envy her positivity.

I know she sabotaged her own opportunity to be adopted so she could stay with me. Brooke would act out for the doctors that evaluated us. Often, potential adoptive parents would see a blue-eyed blonde girl's photo and arrange to meet Brooke. Brooke would have meet-and-greets where she would bite them or lash out wildly. She became a crazed hellion so that they wouldn't adopt her. I feel selfish because I am so thankful she stayed. I don't know much about the meaning of life, but I do know it's not worth living without my best friend by my side.

When we aged out of the system, we got issued a small apartment that the government assisted us with. We live in a shit hole, but I try to believe in our ability to dig our way out of this rotten life to build a quality one. I wish I could believe in us as much as Brooke does.

The alarm on my phone cuts through my thoughts. Glancing at the buildings blurring past the patrol car, I realize we are five blocks from the dive bar where I work. The all-too-familiar ball of chaotic energy builds in my chest, and my leg starts a rapid staccato that grabs the officer's attention.

"Is there a problem?" The officer glances back at me in the mirror with a crook of her brow.

"Yep," I rub my hands down the front of my jeans. "It appears that I am late again and need this job. The rent is due, ya know."

The officer's brow arches higher as she pulls up to the front of the bar, sending the more questionable patrons scurrying into the shadows.

"I am not sure losing this job would be that bad," I mutter, getting out of the car and rushing inside. Who needs to constantly have strangers' issues rattling around in their heads all the time? Some people's thoughts are seriously sick. I tend to get angry after I get a glimpse of the horror.

Along with that, I am not a good flirt. I am not great at being social and faking being nice, which hospitality servers are supposed to excel at for large tips. So, I despise it here.

My people meter is like a gas gauge, and I am usually on empty before I even leave my apartment. I crave solitude, so this bar is a nightmare on every level. Tonight, I am feeling raw and violated.

Not long into my shift, work begins to get rough, and I am already out of patience. A drunk man grabs my ass as I walk by, and I am overwhelmed by his grimy thoughts.

*"This bitch is curvy. I bet she can take it hard. I will follow this skank later and show her what a real man feels like."* Not this shit again! The man's eyes glaze over with a sick lust as he stares at me.

*"I will yank on her long brown hair and make her call me Papi. Sweet tits. She's all mine, and she doesn't even know it."*

I sense his history of cornering women and assaulting them. My mind spins with the vision of a cashier locking up the store late at night. The disgusting lust this man feels towards this lady swarms my body. He grabs her at her car and slams her head down hard on her hood. She wakes up to being raped, and he punches her repeatedly, getting turned on at the sight of her blood and teeth coming from her battered mouth. He tortures her until life fades from her eyes. Slowly, the bloody horrid vision dissolves from my mind.

Startled by what I'd seen, I dropped my tray of shots. The grimy invasion of his evilness makes me sick, literally sick. No, I don't feel bad that this creep ends up drenched. He doesn't deserve the air he breathes. The nasty man stands up and towers over my five-foot-two frame. I feel his rage and see hate in his dark eyes. My fear turns to anger, and I can't help it as I lash out at this repugnant fuck!

"Well, get on with your bad self! Bring it!" I take a fighter's stance. I challenge him, wanting any excuse to fight this asshole. I want to rip his throat out. Such a disgusting wave of rage consumes me. I am not a talented fighter by any means. I just let my temper get the best of me.

The bouncer, Derek, recognizes my icy glare and knows I am about to attack. Hell, he knows the drunk is about to attack too. That man raises his tattooed fist to punch me. As

Derek steps between us, I read the word 'hard' in capital letters on his knuckles.

"You are an evil murdering rapist. I know what you are!" I scream as Derek turns his back to that guy and hauls my ass out back.

"Get that bitch out of here. You need to train these waitresses up better," the ass-grabbing punk yells as the owner, Mike, offers him free booze.

I am the one getting dragged out, seriously?

With Derek's hand on my arm, I absorb Derek's heartache over his girlfriend and his kid. He is sick with worry—way too many sensations for me to take in. Sometimes I feel like I am on a roller coaster. No, more like I am in a kaleidoscope of emotions. It is too much all at once. Derek is heartbroken. His girlfriend took his two-year-old daughter to California to be a Marine's wife.

*"Derek, you're a loser! All you care about is your motorcycle club. You don't even make enough to support us. You're just a bitch boy for your crew, and that's all you'll ever be. I found a real man! He will take care of us the way we deserve."*

Derek is contemplating getting his boys together and going after his girlfriend. He pushes that thought aside, believing he is a loser and utterly defeated. He isn't in the mood to fight for me tonight.

"Don't touch me, Derek! You know I don't like to be touched!" I yank my arm out of his grasp.

I sink to the asphalt in the alley at the back of the bar and reach for my phone. I try to center myself and get my bearings emotionally. That rapey, violated, and ready-to-fight feeling shifting into feeling heartbroken blurs my ability to focus and calm down. I try to focus on feeling my own genuine self over others.

"Kayla, that man was going to do god knows what if I didn't drag you out there. You can't punch every customer you don't like. You are nothing but trouble, and I can't handle another bar brawl right now."

Mike, my boss, sticks his head out the door. "Derek, get in here and handle this mess!" he yells. "Kayla, you're fired! You just aren't working out. Here's your shit." He throws my purse at me. "Go home."

Mike finally hit his last straw with me. I shrug it off as my cell phone rings. I guess I lost this job after all.

# CHAPTER 2

## Kayla

"Kayla, we need a getaway," Brooke says when I answer her call. I want to cry. The last thing we need to spend money on is a getaway. I ignore her and explain my night to her while pacing back and forth near the dumpster that is giving off a sharp odor of old beer and rot.

"Damn! It's starting to rain, and I need to catch the bus. I'll see you soon. Love you, bye."

I make my way to the sidewalk and climb the hill toward the bus stop. The rain and night air makes the cold seep into my bones as my tears fall freely. I am just glad the rain camouflaged them. I am feeling particularly sorry for myself and guilty about losing another job.

I need a reset, a chance to regroup, do better, and maybe learn some of Brooke's barrier-building. The Zen stuff she's so adept at. I am not sure I will have time, though. I have to hit the ground running and search for a job.

I step into a convenience store to get a cup of coffee. The cashier glares at me as I drip water all over the floor. I do not want to touch this cashier. Her angry energy radiates toward me as it does every time I shop here. I am too raw for her crap right now. I breathe in a deep breath, trying to stay calm and do my regular shopping without any more tears.

I get my usual large cup of coffee and hot chocolate for Rita, the homeless lady who lives at my bus stop. I take advantage of the "buy one, get one free" hot dog deal, ketchup on mine, and mustard and onions for Rita.

I pull out what little cash I have to pay the cashier. She gives me my change without saying a word, but her body language and her angry, indignant breathing tells me she isn't going to change her disdain for me.

As I reach the door to exit, I hear her proclaim, "They are like stray cats. Once you feed them, they never go away."

I roll my eyes as the rain pelts down on me again. I look up the hill and see a familiar figure lying on the bus stop bench. A blue tarp is draped over her tonight to repel the rain and cold.

Shame fills me. Here I am, feeling so upset about losing a job and being miserable in the cold, but there's Miss Rita, homeless and trying to get comfortable to sleep out in the rain.

The cashier is cold-hearted. She is overly entitled with her judgy ass. I despise people like her.

I walk up to Rita's bench and raise my voice to be heard over the rain. "Miss Rita, I got the usual."

The tarp starts to shuffle, shaking the water off, and Rita's beanie-covered head pops out, giving me a gap-toothed, gummy grin, reminding me of a piano missing a few keys. She wiggles one hand out of her sleeping bag to unzip her cocoon.

The bus stop has a cover and sides for advertisements, but it does little to prevent the rain from getting us wet. I carefully place her hot chocolate and hot dog on the bench and hold the tarp up to shield us from the rain while she sits up to eat. Her grateful expression seems exaggerated by her leathery, worn, wrinkled face, but her energy is innocent and pure.

"You are here sooner than I expected," Rita says with a mouthful of hot dog.

A while ago, I made the mistake of offering Miss Rita coffee and a muffin the first night I showed up to catch the bus home. Miss Rita scoffed at me and said, "What makes you assume I'd want that junk?"

I stood there awkwardly holding two cups of coffee and said, "I'm cold and love coffee, so I figure you might be cold and want a cup too. My bad. I won't offer again."

Miss Rita looked one way then the other before she leaned in toward me and whispered, "The aliens brainwash us with coffee. Don't drink it, or they'll get you too, and you won't like the butt stuff they do!"

I almost spat out my coffee, laughing but tried to control myself. I understood she had some mental health issues, and I could relate. Most people treated me like a nut because of my psychic ability. I could tell she genuinely feared for me, so I pretended to be shocked.

"Thank you for letting me know about the brainwashing." I made a significant gesture by throwing the coffee away as if it stung me to hold it.

Then I asked her, "So, what is safe to drink and eat?"

She told me about hot chocolate and a hot dog with mustard and onions. Now no matter how late I got off work, I went to the twenty-four-hour convenience store and brought her those items. I let her think my coffee was hot chocolate. It was a lie I could live with since I loved my coffee.

"About that, Miss Rita, I got fired tonight, so now I won't be catching the bus home from here anymore."

Homelessness is so rampant here. It's overflowing the area, and there doesn't seem to be an answer. I always feel I myself am one paycheck away from this fate. If I had the power to help, I would try to change things.

I can only do the little things, like hot chocolate and a hot dog. Plus, I have been drawn to Rita. I like her sass and purity, even in the haze of her mental health delusions.

Rita glances up with mustard on her cheek and takes a sip of her hot chocolate.

"I'll miss you, Kayla, but you shouldn't be out here anyways."

I laugh as Rita lies back down.

"Please throw that tarp back over me, will ya? And don't drink the coffee."

I see a twinge of sadness in her eyes and feel the same, knowing this is goodbye. As the bus pulls up, I take the rest of my cash out and stuff it in the jar in Rita's cart.

"You take care of yourself, Miss Rita," I say, choking back my sadness as I cover her with the tarp and then take my bus home.

I have always liked that Rita was mindful and never touched me. I will genuinely miss our nightly exchange, and I will have to come by to check on her from time to time.

# CHAPTER 3

## *Kayla*

"Honey, I'm home!" I say as I come through the door, in my best Ricky Ricardo imitation. I need to hide my trauma from Brooke. She is already worried about me.

Brooke is chanting while sitting cross-legged on the floor. She ignores me until she stops her chants and rings her bell three times. Brooke evaluates me, grabs a towel, and hands it to me.

She says, "I know just what you need. I am taking you camping."

She hugs me, not caring about my wet clothes, and I instantly calm down and start to warm up.

"You need a hot shower and a pleasant night's sleep," Brooke insists in her bubbly, bouncy way.

"Don't worry about a thing. We got this," she maintains as she shuffles me toward the bathroom, where she has a diffusing mister already releasing a calming aroma.

"You're too cheery after I just got fired. I'm worried here. We can't get by on our good looks alone," I insist.

"Have a little faith," Brooke says confidently as she leaves me to my shower. "The universe will help us."

In the shower, I let the hot water soothe me. "Faith!" I say, looking up.

"Come on, if there is a god, goddess, or anything out there in the universe, give a girl a break already. Give me a world worth living in," I whisper in prayer, finding it hard to have faith in anything much more than my friendship and sisterhood with Brooke.

I cry, letting it all out. I scrub my body, then sink to sit in the tub, letting all the scummy feelings wash away.

After my hot shower, all I want is my bed. I am so exhausted from falling apart in the bathroom. I fall asleep when my head hits the pillow.

I wake up to the smell of food and coffee. Brooke has already started organizing and packing.

"You should have woken me up. I would have helped," I say, staring at Brooke, who is sitting on the floor with our packs.

"You know I like to organize things a certain way. Besides, you needed to sleep well and recover." Brooke zips up the pack and sets it by the door.

"I made eggs and coffee. It would be best if you ate while I pack up the PB and Js. We are poor-boying it this weekend, but it will do us good to get fresh air." Brooke radiates excitement.

I want to look for a job, But I do need a reset after yesterday. Brooke somehow knows I need this. Just being around her, I am instantly at ease and looking forward to our camping trip.

We can't afford it, but we choose the cheap route and give a little gas money to a neighbor willing to drop us off at the trailhead and pick us up in a few days. The trees always seem to refresh me. Brooke is right. I need this. She knows me so well. Next week I will hunt for another job, but for now, I can daydream of a life like this.

"I need to go off-grid and live here forever. This is paradise, don't you think?" I say. "It is quiet and beautiful. Maybe we can become forest rangers and get the dream job with a cabin somewhere in the middle of nowhere. Learn how to live off the land, be self-sufficient, and all that jazz."

I have to duck under a tree branch, but Brooke, who is taller than me, walks right into it.

"You, okay?" I ask, worrying about her pretty face.

Her blue eyes roll, and she laughs it off.

"Yeah, I'm okay. I am just trying to figure out this trail map. I think we're off the trail."

I break through a thick batch of branches, ensuring they don't snap back and smack Brooke again.

"It's okay. We won't get lost. I want to be where the people aren't," I reassure Brooke.

We take a water break and sit in comfortable silence, simply enjoying the forest around us.

"Listen, Brooke. I'm so sorry I lost another job. I hate that I am so broken." Brooke's blue eyes stare at my own with softness.

"Kayla, stop it," Brooke demands in her gentle way.

"You know I understand. We're in this together and will always find a way. You help me when I need it. We balance each other out. Last night was not your fault, Kayla. None of it was." Brooke insists. "I will chant, and the universe will give us a path. I'm not worried one bit. We will eventually get a cabin somewhere and live the dream," Brooke promises me, meaning it too. "Kayla, I feel an immense change for us. I know it's near, and I know things will finally turn around and put us where we need to be."

"You are too chill sometimes. I worry you don't realize how much trouble we are in if I can't start paying my share."

Brooke shrugs, waving me off. She taps her compass three times and shakes it.

"What?" I ask while she is staring at her compass and the trail map.

"Oh, it's nothing. The compass is going wild. See?" Brooke

holds the little thing in front of my face, so I can get a decent view of it spinning frantically.

"Great! Now I got us lost trying to go off-trail," I say, throwing my hands up. I feel like I failed us again.

Brooke sits crossed-legged and starts to chant. She claps three times, stands, and gracefully dusts off the seat of her pants.

"Kayla. We are here, and this place is magic. It's nature at her best. We need to be here. It would be best if you were here too. Let go of all your worries for the next couple of days and get back to the basics. Remember when we were kids and got lost? We used our intuition and found our way. Here, grab my hand and feel the way with me."

Brooke reaches for me, and I take her hand, immediately feeling calmer and eager to explore.

We hold hands and close our eyes. I hear her chant softly, and we both have the urge to hike and go with it. My anxiety about work and responsibilities washes away, and I can be present now.

Brooke works almost religiously on the gifted side of herself with daily meditations and grounding exercises. Being gifted is her spirituality, whereas I usually try to fight my ability. Over the years, I have become comfortable with small moments of "embracing my nature," as Brooke would say.

Alone in the woods, I want to keep us both safe. I am calm enough to indulge the link she and I discovered as children. I trust it, as we always seem to find our way when we use it.

"Brooke, I wish we could live here out in the middle of all these trees," I announce, as I enjoy this place. Brooke smiles sweetly at me. "I would need my creature comforts, though. A garden and some chickens would be cool. A hot tub, Netflix, my Kindle, and fast food. I have my fair share of vices, so not completely off-grid living for us." I dream of having a life out here in the woods.

"We can make this happen. We have our goals, and we will find a way." Brooke says confidently.

"Thanks for this, Brooke. I needed to cleanse myself of all the crazy lately." I breathe in the trees. I love the smell of pine—it makes my dark, moody soul much lighter.

I glance at the wooded path and all around. The green is so intense that my eyes almost hurt from looking at it. The smell of the forest and wet moss melts my stress away.

"So, where should we set up camp?" I ask, turning toward Brooke.

Brooke retakes my hand, and we close our eyes and focus on our other senses. I feel the familiar pins-and-needles sensations going up my arm. They turn into a hum I can feel and almost hear. The humming sounds like whispering in my ear, but I struggle to make out the words. I get the feeling that if it had a voice, it would be female. Still, some communication is made because my intuition gives me a direction to go, and I always trust this inner part of myself.

As I open my eyes, they lock onto Brooke's. We grin at each other, knowing we both amplified our intuitive abilities and came up with the same destination. I turn off the path we had just made and start carving another way through overgrown brush and trees.

Brooke always loves it when I do this stuff with her. She feels I am accepting and evolving with my true nature, and she gets a bit triumphant.

I love that she has this connection with me and that it makes her happy. Without Brooke, I would never deliberately try to use any of this. I worry that the more I embrace this side of myself, the more susceptible I will be to the ugly side of it.

"I hope we don't find poison oak." Brooke laughs. I stop, my back to her as she follows me.

"Girl! Don't put that juju out there like that." I scan around to inspect the growth we are tramping through and don't see anything suspicious. I continue in the direction my intuition had told me was best.

About dusk, we end up standing outside a primitive cave entrance against the mountainside. It is hidden behind a boulder. I face Brooke with excitement and see the joy in her eyes.

"Did we discover a new cave?" Brooke asks.

"Should we go check it out?" We are being drawn in, but I still wonder if we should.

Brooke closes her eyes and holds her hand to the boulder to sense any dangers. Her palm draws a circle three times on the stone.

"I don't sense any dangers. I feel pulled to go in."

"I always say, follow your gut. Our intuition never fails us." After all, Brooke confirmed it was safe.

I open my eyes when Brooke grabs my shoulders to stop me from walking into the cave. I didn't realize I was walking into the cave. I feel hypnotized and disoriented. The buzzing in my head is on full blast, and I feel something trying to take over.

"Not without me, Kayla. Slow your roll," Brooke insists.

I laugh out of nervousness and shake my head to regain myself. The humming, the whispering female in my head, distracts me incessantly. I don't usually get this much nudging from my gift. This is annoying me. I am fighting to control my own will.

It's like a child ringing the doorbell relentlessly. It feels like it should be a simple thing to get this connection right. If I could turn the dial on a radio over just a bit, it would all sound clear. I want to understand as much as the pushing in my head wants me to make sense of it all. I don't like losing control, but somehow this feels like a need to communicate, not so much a need to take over.

I recognize an outside source, a familiar presence. This energy is usually subtle and doesn't harm me. It's kind of like how Brooke's energy doesn't harm me. I never seem able to understand anything other than a sense of direction. I can't make out the words, but it has never hypnotized me like this before. I can't believe I am walking into the cave with my eyes closed. I feel an unease now that wasn't there before.

I need a minute to think and shake off this intense urge to enter the cave.

"We need wood. It's almost dark," I mumble, turning to go gather firewood.

When I return, I feel a bit more level-headed and myself again, so we get our flashlights out and head into the cave.

# CHAPTER 4

## Brooke

"We go in the direction of the universe," I muse aloud. Tingles of goosebumps sprinkle down my arm. It's another affirmation to my soul that the universe wants me to go this way.

We step into the dark cave and find the sounds of the night in the forest seem to disappear. I notice that Kayla has calmed down on our hike in the forest, but something upset her just outside the cave. Kayla seems okay now. I know she is trying to block her concern from me. But I have been able to tell her moods since we were kids. I let her keep her secrets. Last night she was terrified, and her emotions were assaulted by what happened. I hate that she suffered through that. I know sometimes she feels like she is burdening me, but even after all the years we've been best friends, I can never convince her that she is never a burden to me.

I remember when those two boys had me cornered in the bathroom. They wanted to do bad things. Kayla and I were friends at this point, but she still kept to herself, drawing or writing in her little notebook with her pink pen. A loner who liked it that way because almost everyone stayed away from her. I felt her gift and knew there was more to her than she let on.

I didn't think Kayla had noticed where I was or what was happening to me, but when those boys locked me in the bathroom with them, I was scared. I automatically screamed for help in my mind, but my body was frozen in fear. The next thing I knew, that tiny, feisty girl crashed through the locked door, stabbing her pink pen at the boys until they ran away. Kayla got into trouble for attacking them, and I was angry that no one listened to me about how she helped. We were both kicked out of that foster house because the boys were the foster mom's biological children, and we were deemed unsafe and crazy, according to her.

I heard Kayla in my head say, *"I got you, girl. Those nasty perverts deserve worse."* I knew Kayla was unique, and I was grateful she saved me. We've been together ever since. I haven't heard her in my head since then, but I feel her. I am connected to her, and she empathetically sends me her energy, so I know when Kayla is upset.

"I feel warmth, an invitation to go farther," Kayla says with her brows furrowed in that way of hers.

I know she is questioning her gift. Kayla doesn't trust the universe and her gifts, at least not without encouragement.

I shrug in nonchalant agreement as we venture deeper into the cave because if I am nervous, Kayla will bolt. Something significant is happening here, and we both need to figure out what this means.

What is drawing us in with a psychic invitation? It feels wonderful and safe. I am more eager than ever to seek the answer behind the most potent physic call I have ever felt, aside from my soul-deep connection to Kayla.

Still, I am worried. Something is unusual about tonight.

After quietly making our way through the cave's tight

passage, we come to a wall with a tiny crawl space for an opening.

"We have to crawl through this opening," Kayla says. "Our packs are too bulky, so we must leave a few things here. We will need to push our packs in front of us. This will get tight, and who knows how far down this will go." She crouches on her hands and knees to shine the light down the hole in the wall.

"Well, we can't stop now. Let's move," I eagerly encourage Kayla. I pull some things out of our packs, glad Kayla wanted to take the lead.

"You are way too happy about this." Kayla shimmies into the dark hole. "But you're right. There's no way I can stop myself now," Kayla whispers more to herself than to me.

I get it. Kayla's nerves are up. I am proud of her for going with it this time. Usually, I am the one to go with the flow of the universe. Right now, I am drawn in just as much as Kayla, and I must go farther, even though I don't like small spaces.

Kayla kicks dirt at my face as I crawl into the hole to follow her. I push my pack in front of my face to catch Kayla's dirt. I hear her struggle with her own pack and the bundle of firewood. Kayla mumbles to put my flashlight into my mouth as she has. As we squeeze through the jagged path, I start praying my intuition will take us to a safe place.

It feels like hours of struggling to navigate the tight twists and turns of the tunnel. We are both feeling the walls close in. My energy tenses with anxiety. That rarely happens with my happy-go-lucky self. I am starting to worry as we come to a corner on a downward angle. It seems particularly complicated to navigate.

"It's all fine, Brooke. I won't let anything bad happen. You're safe. I'm here," Kayla tries to reassure me.

I must be letting my shields down too much that Kayla can sense my anxiety. I usually do the reassuring. I normally try to overcome anxiety through my chanting and coping techniques, but the claustrophobia I am suffering in this tight space makes it hard for me to stay calm. I feel something huge is happening—something life-altering—and I don't know how to be at ease with the unknown. This is highly unusual for me. I need to be clear-headed for Kayla.

Conflicting emotions are like a storm inside me. Logically, I should have never allowed us to crawl into a cave. I know there is no way back at this point, but this tunnel is beginning to feel confining. As I get to the corner, I pull the light out of my mouth and flex my jaw to relieve the ache from my face cramping. I taste dirt, and the air feels stale.

The dirt Kayla stirs up is like a tan fog in my flashlight beam. I feel a cool sensation hit me like a wave and know that Kayla and I need to maneuver downward through an even tighter squeeze of a hole.

"No way for us to be able to go backward from this point," Kayla says over her shoulder. The dirt around us muffles her voice. "Brooke, honey, it gets awkward. It's twisting downward. I'm heading down now."

"Be careful," I say as I hear Kayla's pack drop.

"The wood got stuck. Don't worry. I got this. Just follow me carefully," Kayla grunts as she pushes on the wood blocking the way.

A wave of odd energy washes over me, causing goosebumps. I wonder if Kayla is feeling something similar.

."I got it!" Kayla says excitedly. I hear her yelp as she falls away from me.

I try to grab her, but my bag is in the way.

My flashlight zaps me, and the light goes out. "Shit!"

I break out in a nervous sweat. My ears start to ring, and the darkness, with its strange energy, has me scared. I begin to cry.

"Kayla! Tell me you are okay," I beg as I move farther into the hole, feeling for a safe path. My bag drops too, and it isn't long before I fall. Sliding downward, I break through and find myself hanging by a ledge I grabbed blindly in the dark.

"Please don't be dead. Please don't be dead," I repeatedly say like a chant, willing Kayla to be okay. I blindly grab another ledge and find my footing on the wall.

I move one ledge at a time and feel confused about whether I'm going up or down. I allow gravity to reassure me that I am going down. I slip and fall in the dark, thick air. Terrified, I scream just before I land. My ass hit the ground hard, but thankfully, it was a shortfall.

I crawl on my knees and feel around in the dark to find Kayla. My hands come across the wood.

"Kayla!" Frantically, I search my pockets for a lighter. "Don't do this to me, Kayla, please! Answer me." I sob and wipe my snotty nose and tears away. "Okay! Calm down, Brooke. Think! Think! Think!" I say out loud to try to help get myself together. I find my small notebook in my pocket and tear the piece of paper off to light a fire.

"Please burn, please light!" I cry over and over, willing the wood to burn as my shaky hands hold the small flame. I blow on the wood until it lights. The fire burns, slowly building and getting brighter.

I close my eyes and take a deep breath to steady myself.

"She is okay. She is going to be just fine."

I give myself a pep talk and attempt to gain the courage to seek Kayla. I open my eyes and look up, away from the flame. I jump and fall backward as giant fangs are in my face, about to eat me—my heart pounds in my chest and ears. I stare up at the teeth. It takes me a moment to realize they are the old bones of a giant. *Is that a dragon?* I realize whatever it is. It's long dead. I need to find Kayla.

I scan around and see Kayla slumped over the remains of a fossilized egg. She is bleeding from her head, and her blood is black under this light, dripping over the stone egg.

"Oh, my God! Kayla!" I rush to her.

I feel for a pulse. "Oh God, no! No! No! No!" I panic, still crying. My heart starts beating again, and I am calm when I feel her steady heartbeat under my fingertips.

I roll her off the egg and lean her up against it. I check her over and see if there are any more injuries. She hit her head and cut her forehead well. I find the pack and grab a bottle of water and a towel.

"Please, wake up, Kayla," I beg, wanting to see her eyes bright with life again.

# CHAPTER 5

## Kayla

"Kayla! Kayla!" I hear Brooke cry out my name. I feel her gently moving me, and I turned to lie against the rock instead of slumping over it. I open my eyes, expecting darkness. Brooke must have found a way to start a fire because a small flame burns, lighting up the cavern we've fallen into.

Brooke's dirty face is full of concern and stained with tears as she looms over me, using her fingers to gently probe at the top of my head to investigate my injury. Brooke's scared and concerned face stares into my eyes.

"Your brown eyes are as mean as normal," Brooke says as relief lights up her dirty face, and she smiles.

"You look awful, Kayla. Don't ever scare me like that again," Brooke says, fighting a sob.

Brooke holds a towel to my head. I roll my mean brown eyes as I hold that towel to stop the bleeding. I feel dizzy and sad that I scared Brooke.

"You may need a stitch or two. You're always so accident-prone. I swear, I almost had a heart attack when I saw you." Brooke says with worry in her tone.

I groan as my headaches. I sit up straighter trying to find a comfortable position.

"Thanks for always taking care of me. I'm sure it looks worse than it is. Head wounds bleed a lot, not to mention I have a thick skull," I say.

When Brooke steps away to gather something from one of the packs, I take in the cavern for the first time.

It is a dead end, a tall room with no holes or openings that I can see. Brooke has managed to start a fire since her flashlight zapped out too. Our phones are dead as well. The cave is empty except for the fossilized remains of a dinosaur lying curled around me. I watch the ground and notice ancient, fossilized eggshells.

"Wow!" I utter in a whisper of awe, forgetting my injury as I take it all in.

I assume the giant bones were dinosaur remains, but after my blurry eyes adjust in the firelight, I see the remains of a dragon skeleton. It could be some unknown dinosaur, but something inside me screams, "Dragon!"

Brooke glances at the dragon, as calm as ever, handing me a bottle of water and taking it in herself.

"I know. I was so focused on you that the dead dragon had to take a back seat. I was frantic to get the fire started so that I could find you. When the fire lit, I turned around and saw teeth before anything else came into view. It took me a second to realize it was old bones. You were hurt and needed me, so I focused on you." Brooke scans me over, worried.

"I think you need to be careful. You probably have a con-cussion."

I take a deep breath and try to stand up on shaky legs.

"Maybe you should sit a bit longer," Brooke suggests as I turn to take in the whole scene.

*A dragon,* I think. *How tragic for the mother and babies.* I examine the mom's remains and broken eggs around her bones.

I notice the smooth rock I landed on is intact, an unhatched egg—a whole dragon egg. My blood stains the smooth surface.

Dizziness and confusion hit me. Energy from out of nowhere swamps me, and I am heartbroken over the unhatched egg and the momma dragon losing her babies, leaving only the fossilized cream-and-white marble stone egg, whole and beautiful. Grief infuses me as if I had lost my own babies.

"You're right, Brooke. I don't feel like myself."

Brooke grabs me and helps me to sit again. I mourn for the loss of the momma dragon, and I have the urge to curl myself around the unhatched egg to send it soothing energy.

*How is this even a thing?* Brooke calms me, but I doubt she's sending me soothing energy. *What the hell is happening to me?* I ask silently, like a desperate prayer.

The momma dragon is a skeleton with broken rib bones from falling on the floor. The energy in the dirt and petrified egg is palpable. I am drawn here for a purpose. It feels right to be here.

*Mine!* my inner voice demands, and I wonder, H*ow hard did I hit my head?* I feel crazy and foolish for wanting to comfort my egg.

"My egg?" I say out loud. Brooke has an odd expression.

"Okay, if you want it, I doubt we can move it an inch, much less out of this cave." She gives me a "you're silly" look with her eyebrow raised, and I could see the lingering concern behind her eyes.

I'm seeing Brooke in double vision when she starts to speak.

"Dragons are real!" Brooked giggles and hugs me.

She is oblivious to my internal struggle. I settle down again and get comfortable for the night. I lean back against my egg, resisting the urge to spoon it. I can't help but send it warmth and soothing energy.

I feel so foolish. I must have a concussion or something. I am doing weird things, well, weird for me, which is saying a lot. I don't understand any of these odd things. Why was it so important to have come here? What drove us in this direction?

"So, now that we are in a deep, dark cave with no light source other than our small bundle of wood for the fire, how are we getting out?" Brooke questions, which brings me back to reality a bit.

"Shit!" I say loud, and all I can think is, *Houston, we have a problem!*

How could I have trusted my intuition? How could I have thought that going into an unknown cave like this was somehow the best idea? I must have been traumatized more than I realized by last night's event. Maybe all my senses are jumbled after all that. I hope Brooke can't sense how frantic I am feeling in my head.

"We should be kind of panicking right now," Brooke says in an almost singsong voice. "This is so cool, right, Kayla?" Brooke smiles, but her eyes have a tightness to them.

I love Brooke. She is a gem, and I adore her optimistic personality, but sometimes I worry that she never takes anything seriously enough, even when it's called for, like now. We have plunged into the deep, dark bowels of a cave we can't climb out of.

"Brooke, this is a serious situation. We need to make a plan," I tell her.

She is gazing at the fire and looking at the dragon bones, happy in her calm way, like a kid in a candy store.

"I am just relieved you are alive, Kayla. Everything else is gravy. We can face it together." She smiles reassuringly at me and says, "It's going to be fine, Kayla, don't stress."

"That's easier said than done." I moan in irritation.

"I have a lighter. We will have to use it for as long as possible and get out tomorrow. For now, I need a bit of sleep," Brooke says.

"I probably should try to stay awake after I hit my head, but I think I'll risk it and sleep for a bit, too," I say softly.

My headache is worse with the smell of the smoke. I can't

resist lying down to snuggle my egg any longer, so I turn to roll over and spoon it.

I feel a wave of energy come back to me. It feels like love and is soothing my head. *How odd,* I think and move even closer to embrace my egg.

"Kayla, you need a snack, and try not to sleep with your concussion. Tell you what, why don't you take the watch first? I feel depleted and need a few hours of sleep," Brooke says while handing me food. "Here's a pack of nuts and dried fruit. Eat it and drink the water too." She sets a water bottle down near my hand.

I reluctantly sit up to eat and drink, knowing Brooke will insist. I watch the flames while I finish the snack and water Brooke gave me, then resume my spooning position. The cold marble-like stone surface of my egg is oddly comforting.

It appears my body heat quickly warms up my egg. *I claim this egg now. It's a treasure to me,* I tell myself secretly. Feeling content, I quickly drift off to a comfortable sleep despite Brooke warning me to stay up.

I woke up disoriented and unable to see. I roll over and see the red dying embers of the fire that burnt out while we slept. I hear a crackling sound that is loud and ominous. I frantically search for something to rekindle the fire so I can see because I worry the ceiling is about to cave in and fall on us, and a sense of dread fills me. The sound of rocks breaking fills the room, and I think we are about to be crushed. Noise begins to fill the dark cave room, setting off alarms for me.

"Brooke!" I cry out in fear.

The sound is as loud as concrete breaking under a jackhammer. I have an immediate rush of adrenaline, and anxiety hits me hard. I hear that humming and feel someone needing me, reaching for me. I feel helpless to find them, but I desperately need them too. The communication is just out of reach.

While I panic that we are in danger, the humming is drowned out by the sounds of rock crumbling. On my hands and knees, I feel around in the dark. I find a rib bone and toss it into the embers of the dying fire. I am stunned when the heat touches the rib bone and firelight flares.

A swirling mass of red, blue, and purple light and magic consumes the room. Brooke awakes with a start, and I cry, reaching for her. Magic colors fill the cave, and the loud sounds of the walls around us breaking apart make this moment terrifying.

"Brooke!"

I am relieved when Brooke runs into my arms. We hug each other as power and magic saturate us in a wave we have never known before. I feel an awakening of something that has been hidden. Something foreign and unknown to me.

Something inside me changes, absorbing more than someone's emotions this time—something dominant. I know, instinctively, life will never be the same. I am suffocating under this invasion of power.

We collapse in a pile together on the floor. I fall against my egg, grabbing hold by instinct, with Brooke at my back, holding on to me. Her grip is so tight it hurts. Her head is buried into my shoulders. I wait for the cave to collapse and kill us both as darkness engulfs us.

Silence wraps around us. I wonder if this is death. It feels like we are frozen in place and swallowed by emptiness.

The blackness I am in is unlike any sleep I have ever experienced. I am in a void with Brooke at my back and my egg in my arms. I feel like I'm moving in slow motion and somehow frozen simultaneously. My thoughts are in slow motion too. Maybe I'm stretching like a ball of slime being pulled apart.

I try to evaluate if I'm okay or not, and I can't describe or understand my feelings now. I feel no sense of time. I am not uncomfortable; I am in nothingness. That humming in my head starts again, and instead of a whisper, I hear a beautiful, ethereal-sounding woman in my head. *"Have faith in me, Kayla. I will bless you. I need . . .*

The voice stops mid-sentence in my head. What the hell is happening? The humming starts again.

*"I am heartbroken, but you will be the start of restoring balance and harmony to the magic of my planet. My father, the great creator, is offering me the true mates my world needs. Kayla, do not fear. You . . .* The voice fades to silence as abruptly as it appeared.

*What the hell is going on?* I ask mentally to the stratosphere.

I can see a bright room through a doorway appear out of the blackness, but I am still frozen, hugging my egg. Somehow, I am moving, stretching from the darkness through this doorway. I am placed in the exact position I was on the cave floor onto the floor of this new room.

As the door slams shut, we unfreeze, and Brooke yells, "Kayla!"

I feel her terror as she squeezes me tightly, burying her face into my back. My senses come to me before Brooke gets hers back. She's latched onto me like a scared baby monkey.

I'm so glad her touch and fear don't affect me like others, or I would be a wreck from her fear. I try to get Brooke's attention so I can get out of being sandwiched between her and my egg. It feels like a long moment.

"Brooke! You are okay! Brooke, breathe."

Brooke finally realizes we aren't in the cave anymore. She lets go of me and sits up. I sit up, trying to figure out where we are and how we got here. I stand on wobbly legs. I feel like I am suffering a fit of vertigo as I put my hands on my knees to try to settle my dizziness.

Brooke is stunned. She frantically checks around before getting my attention by locking her fearful eyes onto mine.

# CHAPTER 6

## Brooke

I pinched my arm and squeak. "Ow! That hurt."

I face Kayla and then examine my hands. "Kayla, do I seem any different?" I ask.

"Uh . . . no, Brooke, you are the same to me. Why would you be different?"

"I just thought when I died, I would be reincarnated and look completely different," I say with disappointment.

Kayla laughs at me. I feel frayed, and nothing makes any sense now.

"What's so funny?" I demand while standing with my hands on my hips, glaring at her.

"You are pouty like an angry Tinkerbell." Kayla snickers, but she sobers when she sees my face. "It's nothing, Brooke." She looks at me, concerned. "I'm just glad you're here with me. I doubt we died," Kayla says confidently as she glances around.

"Kayla! How else do you explain being crushed in a cave

and waking up in a strange place? We died!" I say, trying to make sense of this whole ordeal.

I slowly turn around to see we are in a massive grand hall full of stuff. Rows of neatly arranged crates and other stuff remind me of a medieval storage building with ornate wooden trunks with carvings that give the trunks a sense of luxurious beauty. This enormous grand hall is full of these trunks.

"This is not what I expected the afterlife to be." I am so confused about what all this stuff is.

"We are not dead, Brooke," Kayla insists, worry in her tone.

I see all the light coming from the ceiling high off the ground. It is out of this world. The entirety of the ceiling is made of crystals and is arranged in various pointed and rough-cut clusters.

The crystals light up everything perfectly. It is like a natural chandelier. Because of them, I can see this place is massive.

"Amazing!" Kayla says, stunned.

"Kayla, nothing makes sense." I feel out of place and scared. How am I supposed to be calm about this? "Well, if we didn't die, how do you explain all this?" I snap in a huff, not relieved that a strange hall is my afterlife.

That shakes Kayla out of her wonderment. She turns towards me.

"Your face is paler than normal, even stained with dirt." Kayla reaches for me and pulls me in for a hug.

I am scared. I'm rarely scared, and this is bothering me. I can see Kayla's worry for me. Kayla leans back, cupping her hands on my face. I start to cry. Kayla loves me, but she is never this affectionate. I really must be a wreck for her to switch roles with me. I feel like Kayla is breaking into that bathroom to save me all over again. I need her to reassure me.

"Brooke, you're safe. I am here, honey. I am here. We got this. I promise you we're not dead. Even if we were, we'd be here dead together. I got you, girl." Kayla makes eye contact and shows confidence I rarely see in her.

"I heard a goddess in my head. She tried to tell me something about why she brought us here," Kayla explains. I started to relax a bit because of my trust in Kayla.

"A goddess?" I ask, confused. I stop crying to get myself together. "Kayla, I have no clue what you are talking about. All I know is something magical hit us. The cave sounded like it was cracking and about to collapse. I felt so weak after that magic hit us. I just wanted to hold onto you as we died. I thought we were about to die." I take a deep breath, still unsure if we are actually alive.

"Brooke, don't you remember the nothingness in the dark? It was a portal the goddess sent us through. I understand that much, but not much else," Kayla explains, concern for me in her eyes.

"No, I don't." I wonder if Kayla hit her head so hard she is imagining gods and goddesses. I need to calm myself down, for Kayla's sake. I am just struggling so hard with everything that's happening.

I am so confused. Kayla seems unusually calm being in this strange place. I feel like I am about to crack from the inside out. Kayla takes a breath as if to explain. I hear the crackling sound again, and I jump. My heart pounds, anticipating another collapse.

"I am hit with an undeniable desire to check on my egg," Kayla says, distracted, as she steps closer to examine the egg that traveled with us. She is acting so strange. What do I do if Kayla is losing it?

The egg has a few spider-webbing cracks on the top. Her egg? Undeniable desire? My poor friend hit her head so hard.

I'm sad that her treasure was damaged somehow, traveling from the cave to this odd place. But I am still trying to figure out how we got here.

Kayla mentioned a portal before, but I am still so clueless. Kayla has an irrational attachment to this egg, and I watch as Kayla seems strangely reluctant to walk away from the egg.

"A voice in my head said she was a goddess and needed my help," Kayla says, encouraging me to trust this.

I need to get my bearings and figure out what this place is and how we got here. I need Kayla to be okay and help me figure this out.

"Come on, Kayla. I need to walk. Tell me what this goddess said."

I haven't ever heard Kayla embrace religion or talk about gods or goddesses. We got here somehow, and we were both drawn to the cave. I can't wrap my mind around it, and I am waiting to wake up from this odd dream.

Kayla must have hit her head dangerously hard because I watch her stare at the egg and see her force herself to turn away from it and start walking with me. I need to get my shit together, for Kayla's sake.

I decided the strange blue door in front of me was an excellent place to start.

"Brooke, we came here through some sort of void, a blackness, right through that door, and we were placed on the floor," Kayla insists with awe as she points back at the egg.

"A portal from a goddess. Wild, huh?" Kayla seems excited.

I walk up to it. Kayla starts explaining her recollection of what happened as she tries to open the door. It is solid, with a crystal knob that doesn't even give a jiggle.

"Well, this isn't going to budge," she says with a grunt.

I watch her wide-eyed, like a deer in headlights. I can't believe she tried to open that door. What if we got sucked into another dimension? I made a mistake going into that cave. We need to be more cautious now. I reach out and make three circles with my fingers on the door, trying to feel for any dangers. I feel nothing at all.

I see a wall with bottles, jars, and bags full of dried herbs. Candles and crystals are placed neatly on the shelves. I wonder if these herbs are medicinal.

"Maybe it's for magic spells." Kayla points it out to me.

She knows I love that kind of stuff. It could be an apothecary of herbs and elixirs. I think she is trying to distract me so I can calm down.

I need to be stronger than this.

"Okay then, we need to walk around and see what's what," I say, giving in to this new place.

Kayla grabs my hand and deliberately walks away from the egg and the blue door. I follow silently, still scared as hell, even more so, with Kayla seeming to accept this strange place so quickly.

Kayla's attempt to comfort me with the magic ingredient wall didn't even elicit a giggle. I am apprehensive and scared.

In my shock, my focus falls to the floor. It is beautiful with white-and-blue marbling that is seamless and ongoing. Like the beautiful crystal lighting, it seems too glamorous for a storage building. This place is so weird, and it doesn't make sense.

I walk up to the row of stored trunks and wooden crates on the shelving closest to us. The shelves are made of sturdy, intricately carved, dark-stained wood. It is ten shelves high, and the crates remind me of pirate chests. They are boxy, elaborately designed, and stacked perfectly. The crates have black metal hinges and latches. Each crate has a metal design of a dragon on it, and they are beautiful. Is this some sort of hoard of treasure?

"Kayla, what's the deal with the goddess? None of this makes sense."

Kayla reaches for another door, and I grab her hand, stepping in front of her.

"What, Brooke?" Kayla asks, shocked that I would prevent her from opening this door.

"Kayla, what if it sucks us through to some other strange place?" I say, exasperated that my fears aren't apparent to her.

Kayla gently encourages me to step out of the way.

"Brooke, you know we have gifts. I have mentioned a humming over the years, and while I can't hear the voice, I somehow get the indication of what it means. I'm following it as my intuitive guide."

"Of course, I know," I say. I practice building my magical connections daily.

"Well, while we were in the void, I finally could hear her. She didn't get to explain much or anything that made sense to me. I know she brought us here, and we are meant to help her. So, if a goddess has picked us and brought you and me here, I am at ease. My intuition says it will soon become clear that she has special intentions for us."

"Kayla, you hit your head. This is totally out of character for you. Don't open doors because you think you and a goddess will make everything okay. The fact is we are in a strange place. The energy I usually tap into is gone. Humor me, and let me check things before going to unknown places. If a door brought us here, who knows if one will take us somewhere else."

"What if it's a way outside of this place?" Kayla counters. "We need to figure things out, and we can't do that without exploring. Besides, I don't sense any dangers, do you?"

I sigh. "No, I don't sense any warning feelings, but we followed our intuition into the cave and ended up here, didn't we? Maybe we broke our abilities," I say.

"Touché!"

"Only one way to find out," Kayla announces as she turns the diamond doorknob, and the door swings inward into another room.

"Wow!" we both say as we walk through the door. This room has the same elegant design and high-end style with the medieval flair that the warehouse has.

This is an odd place for a bedroom suite attached to the back of a warehouse. The cozy bedroom has ceilings that are probably twelve feet high. The room is set up like a hotel, with two king-sized beds with beautifully carved wooden canopy frames. The bedding is white and gray, with a patchwork of fur blankets. The bedding does seem soft, fluffy, and inviting.

There is a dresser and armoire that match the bed frames. The flooring is white-and-blue marble, and the walls have beautiful stonework. The ceiling is tile, made of quartz, with a cluster of crystal chandeliers for lighting.

There are fur throw rugs and a fireplace in the corner, with purple flames flowing from a pile of diamonds where wood would normally be. I feel guilty about my dirty shoes leaving a trail on the floor wherever I step. Kayla walks across the bedroom to another door. This wooden door slides open like a barn door, revealing a vast bathroom.

"You might be right, after all, Brooke. I think I just discovered heaven." Kayla says as I enter the most incredible bathroom, I have ever seen.

It is tiled with a crystal mosaic, and a clear glass shower door is on the left. The shower is enormous, with enough room to lie down in. The shower handles are made of crystal, as are the shower heads on the shower walls and ceiling.

There is a sink made from cut white crystal. A waterfall seems to flow nonstop into the basin. I reach out to touch the water, and the temperature is perfect. I see dirt flow down the drain and pull my hand back. I smell lavender and chamomile defused in the air. My body immediately starts to relax.

The mirror is strange. It reflects my image, but I don't think it is made from regular glass. I register my reflection and see how filthy I am compared to this glamorous bathroom.

Kayla walks up to the tub that's shaped like an open rose.

"I think this is rose quartz," I say as Kayla admires the pink stone bathtub.

"It is a work of art," Kayla says.

I feel myself finally perking up and getting back to my usual self.

I gasp when I look up at the wall and see a massive mosaic of the beautifully detailed crest of a fire-breathing dragon. It is stunning and sends a warmth into my soul, like a gentle hug of reassurance.

"Jackpot!" Kayla yells as she slides open another barn

door to reveal a closet. We both rush in and see one side filled with red outfits and dresses. The other side is filled with blue outfits and dresses. I take the red dress closest to me.

I hold it up and say, "I think this will fit." I see Kayla walk to the blue clothing closest to her, which seems like it will also fit her.

"Odd, it's almost like these clothes were tailor-made to fit us. I guess I'm blue, and you're red," Kayla says.

"A blue dress? Seriously?" Kayla pouts at whoever in the universe thought this was a nifty idea.

"What? Not your usual Hot Topic black attire?" I ask, knowing Kayla hates wearing dresses.

"I don't care. I want to get clean," Kayla says as she grabs towels, a natural-looking sponge, and a glass bottle of soap from a linen shelf inside the oversized walk-in closet and goes to the shower.

"Oh my God, this is heavenly!" Kayla shouts over the spray of water in the shower.

I stand in the closet, admiring the clothing, which has a Renaissance style to it. I like it. The fabric feels so nice, better than anything I have ever worn.

Maybe blue will work for Kayla. We will see. The pink towels match the pink color of the rose quartz bathtub . . .

"It smells better than my favorite scent from Bath and Body Works," Kayla muses from the shower.

"I'm all done. Your turn," she calls out.

I try to bring my shield up and go with it for now. No sense bringing Kayla down to wallow with me in my unease here. I leave my dirt-covered clothes in a pile next to the shower.

"I don't want to clean that pretty tub after all this dirt," I say as I step in.

Kayla chooses blue pants and a top outfit, and I go for the red renaissance dress.

"I feel so much better now. I don't care if we die," I say, feeling bubbly as I walk into the next room, towel-drying my long, wet blonde hair.

"We did not die," Kayla says firmly, rolling her eyes at me. "You must be feeling better." Kayla eyes me up and down.

"You're right, though. I feel amazing now," I say in agreement.

# CHAPTER 7

## Kayla

Once we are cleaned up, we return to explore the hall. We make our way back to the blue door and my egg.

"Did it crack even worse?" I say with worry. I force myself to walk past it and resist the crazy urge to hug it again. Brooke thinks I whacked my head too hard, but I feel almost healed, and I know the goddess had something to do with that.

Something about this place is different. The energy that flows around me typically feels suffocating. Here, things feel natural, and there is an ease in me that I have never known before. I try to keep my cool around Brooke because my egg is the one thing that has me twisted here. I know it's crazy, but I am worried about it.

"Maybe. I am sorry the egg got damaged, Kayla," Brooke soothes me, interrupting my thoughts.

Brooke shrugs and starts to explore. I follow her, making myself move farther away from my egg. We make it to the other end of the room and find another door.

"The house of three doors. I hope it's not a Hotel California deal," I joke.

"Not funny." Brooke is not amused. She does her finger thing three times, trying to feel for danger.

I give Brooke my no-nonsense eyebrow lift. She submits, knowing I will open the door myself, even if she disapproves. We both have to push hard for it to open, and a cloud of dirt hits us. When the dust settles, I see this door has opened to the outside.

Brooke whines, "I knew opening this door would be trouble."

Brooke is annoyed as she tries to shake the dirt off her new clean dress. I can smell the pine and the wet moss of the forest. I step outside, cringing at the dirt my foot sinks into.

So much for clean shoes. I step past a mound of shrubs and dirt that fell from the hill behind me. It seems the door was concealed inside the hillside, and when we opened the door, the hillside fell away so we could exit outside. There must be magic. There's no way Brooke and I could have moved a hillside.

I walk into the forest, reminding me of the Washington State rainforest. I turn to see Brooke hesitating inside the doorway. The grand hall is inside a mountain, making the door a strange image on the side of the mountain wall. Brooke hesitantly steps outside the doorway.

*Unusual for her. She is typically gung-ho about taking on new adventures,* I voice inside my head, a bit concerned for my friend.

I wave Brooke out to join me. "It's safe, Brooke. Come on out."

We walk a path through the trees that open to a meadow. A stream of water is snaking its way across the meadow toward another tree line. I stare at the sky and see an array of purples, reds, and pinks. It's either a sunset or sunrise.

"What is that?" I ask Brooke, pointing to a giant crystal cloud hovering like a floating pillar in the sky. It's a sparkling prism of rainbow colors above us. Beyond that, a moon with rings like Saturn or Jupiter hovers, viewable above the sky, filled with the sunset colors of clouds.

"What in all the universe?" Brooke says in awe, staring up at it too.

"I don't think we're in Kansas anymore, Toto," I say to lighten the mood.

"You think?" Brooke agrees.

I shiver as goosebumps trail my skin. We walk across the meadow into the forest beyond. We are on an alien planet. I don't know what to expect.

I come across a magical shield, and I see a translucent barrier. Brooke seems as fascinated as I am. We feel the magic and are in wonder at this new planet.

I reach out, touch the shield, and feel warm tingles on my arm as my fingers skim the barrier. Naturally, I step through it, but the accessible energy I feel on the other side of this barrier changes.

Somehow, I know I am connected to everything around me, the trees, the air itself. Something tells me I am exposed, and there are dangers here.

I scream when I turn around to tell Brooke it is not safe to come through. I see a cliff at my feet. I fear I'm about to fall off, and, scrambling backward, I fall and land hard on my ass. Dead pine needles stabbed into my legs and the palm of my hands.

My heart is pounding, and I can hear my ears ring as I gaze back to where Brooke should be. I wonder if she was right, and I went to another dimension. I had nearly fallen off the cliff, and I wouldn't say I like heights.

"Shit!" I roar while standing up and dusting pine needles off my hands. I should have listened to Brooke. I step closer to the cliff's edge to see whatever I can. I gaze up and see the same great sky again, the moons and crystals floating around in the sky. Fear sets in that I may have lost Brooke.

At least I am on the same planet. Maybe I was sent to

another area. I start to panic, having no idea how to find Brooke.

Brooke's hand reaches out of thin air and yanks me backwards. I think I am going off the cliff for sure. Instead, I end up back next to Brooke, inside the shield.

"Why are you being so weird, Kayla?" Brooke asks as she picks a pine needle out of my hair.

"One minute, I'm here, and after I went through that barrier, I was somewhere else. I almost fell off a cliff," I explain, grateful to have Brooke close to me again.

"You didn't go anywhere, Kayla. I saw you go through, turn around, and stare at me like I am a rattlesnake or something. Then you fell on your ass trying to get away. Watch, I'll show you," Brooke says.

Before I can stop her, she walks through the magic barrier, turns around, and stops. Looking back at me with unseeing eyes, she looks around to find me.

"Oh, I see now," Brooke says as she shoves her hand inside the translucent wall to me.

I grab her hand as Brooke closes her eyes and takes a deep breath. She leaps at me, knocking me back on my ass.

"That's the Brooke I know! Welcome back!" I say with a laugh.

Brooke laughs. "That was wild.

"Must be an illusion of some kind," she says breathlessly. "I felt a buzz of energy on the other side of this thing," Brooke explains.

"Maybe some sort of magical security system," I guess aloud. "I felt like it was dangerous over there, Brooke."

I start to turn away from the barrier when we both hear a distant growl and the pounding of feet running through the forest in front of us. Something is coming straight for us on the other side of the barrier. I instinctively hit the ground, hiding behind a fern and pulling Brooke close. I notice tiny flowers budding on the leaves of the fern.

An enormous, mutated bear-like creature stampedes its

way through the dense trees in front of us. It skids to a stop and howls a snarling, menacing growl of frustration. Drooling black snot oozes off its fangs.

*It must have rabies or something.* I think as I try to hold my breath.

The stench from it makes me gag. I try not to puke and do my best to stay still. This alien monster scares the hell out of me. Brooke covers her mouth. Her eyes water as she stares up at the beast in fear.

It doesn't seem to notice us and instead checks back over its shoulders. It takes off again as if it is running from something. Relief washes over me, and I can finally breathe without that awful smell in my mouth. That thing is terrifying.

My reprieve is short-lived because I hear a rustle of movement right before a giant black wolf jumps in front of us. It begins sniffing the ground where the beast just was. The wolf lingers where my ass hits the pile of dead pine needles and sniffs curiously. It turns back to the black ooze that landed on the ground in front of us.

This wolf is beautiful and fierce. Its eyes are so intelligent and dark purple. In the shadow of the trees, I can't tell if the color of its eyes is accurate. The wolf is enormous and feels unreal to me. Brooke trembles in fear, but somehow I am not as scared of this beast. The wolf quickly leaps off in the direction the beast went.

I feel sad seeing it run away, and I don't want it to leave me. I feel hurt, and most of all, I fear for the giant wolf. The beast is dangerous, and I don't want the wolf to get hurt. I feel something inside me that is similar to my urges toward my egg. I feel a pulling of something deep inside me.

This magical energy draws me to this wolf. I get up and start to go after him. Still holding onto me, Brooke stops me from taking a step toward the barrier.

"What in the universe? Kayla, are you nuts? You are not going to get yourself killed. No, ma'am, not today!" Brooke bitches at me.

I shake myself out of the strange feeling I'm in.

"What's wrong with me?" I ask, trying to fight the need to go after that wolf. "Brooke, I need my wolf," I say, begging her to let me go.

Brooke's face grows strained, and tears run down her cheeks.

"Hell no, Kayla!" Brooke uses her taller form and drags me away. "Kayla! We don't play with monsters," Brooke pleads with me.

After seeing the fear in Brooke's eyes, I relent a bit and let her drag me back to the door that leads into the mountain.

"He is not your wolf, Kayla!" Brooke snaps breathlessly.

I don't want Brooke to see how distraught I am about not chasing after the huge wolf. Hot anger rises inside me when Brooke says the wolf is not mine. I take a deep breath and try to calm down. I need to figure out why I am feeling so strange.

"Great! I need a shower all over again. I loved this dress. It made me feel like a princess." Brooke pouts as she makes a beeline to the bedroom with the bathroom.

"Don't do anything stupid, like leave this place and run off after those monsters," Brooke demands over her shoulder at me. I don't think she has ever looked at me like this before.

"Kayla, please! I need a moment. Promise me you will stay put." Brooke is concerned.

"Go get clean, princess. I'm going to check on my egg. Maybe we can move it to the bedroom."

"Promise?" Brooke asks seriously.

"I promise. I am not leaving."

Convinced, Brooke skips off to the shower.

I yell after her as she runs to the bathroom. "You look sexy when you're mad, by the way." I hear a distant giggle echo back at me.

I return to my egg and need to sit next to it and touch it— another insane urge. I'm beginning to think I've gone crazy, and this is all in my head.

# CHAPTER 8

## Kayla

I sink to my knees and reach for my cracked egg. It feels warm and seems softer than stone. I feel a radiating sensation of love and reassurance. I don't know where it is coming from. I feel scared and confused. My ears have that humming thing happening again, and I hear the female's voice again this time.

*"Kayla, I choose you. Please help me restore balance and harmony to my planet. You will need to reestablish true mates again. I took you through a god portal to my planet. I am the Goddess of Harmony. I once lived among my people and nurtured my magical planet. My perfect little Eden,"* the Goddess says with pride.

*"I am beyond the veil now, where timing is different. It is difficult for me to send messages back in time between the veil and my dimension. My goddess power is suppressed, so I am doing my best to set things right. I need you to help me by restoring true mating, and we must deal with that Vampire . . .* Her voice fades then she speaks again.

*"My male dragons are suppressed, unable to shift in the*

*aftermath. You will help to restore my Dragon kingdom. I was able to spare one of Elisa's eggs. I made you to be their mother. I made you a Dragon. You must . . .*

The humming stops, and the voice vanishes. I am more confused than ever, frustrated that a god, rather a goddess, lost signal. How can she put me here with no real explanation?

I am not really the religious type. Between being in foster care, struggling to make it in a shitty world, being cursed with abilities that make me strange and unusual, and absorbing the ugly thoughts of people, why would I be? I've never really had much faith in anything other than my friendship and sisterhood with Brooke. Now I am drawn to a wolf and a fossilized egg and feel instantly attached to them as much as I am to Brooke, which is wildly against my character. I don't trust easily, but now I'm finding myself on a new planet. What did she call herself? Harmony? I have never heard of a Goddess Harmony. Why would she want me, of all people? What am I supposed to do? I have so many questions. I am in a new alien world and still unclear on a whole lot. What in the world? Did she say I was made for motherhood? Surely she did not mean this ancient egg has a living baby inside.

Harmony's Planet? Whatever it is, it's not Earth. I feel magic inside and out. I'm on a mountain, inside a forest, and hidden under a magical protective shield. My instinct seems more animal than human, and it does not make sense to me. I don't like not understanding any of this.

I am about to wallow in my bitterness again when I hear another crack from my egg. I feel a longing to help my egg. I notice a bulge, and the realization that the egg is hatching hits me.

The bond inside my soul gravitates me to my egg, connecting me. I know I am about to be a mother. I freak out. I never want to be anything like the parents I had or most of the foster parents I experienced. Fear that I will fail, my baby takes hold of me now.

"Brooke!" I scream in a panic as I wrap myself around my

egg. Tears start to stream down my face, and another wave of magic infuses me.

I am imprinting my hatchling inside the egg. Whatever is in this egg is truly mine now. My breasts swell with milk in a painful burn.

"No freaking way!" I say out loud as I grab my breasts.

I feel heat burn as milk leaks out, staining my blue top. I sense my child. What's that . . . My children are calling to me in a clairvoyant way—not with words, but a need, a longing for comfort.

*What kind of babies are in this egg?* I wonder. I don't care about this new sensation. With an animal instinct, I accept all of this. With my human brain, I am terrified, but these babies are mine, and I am their mother.

I peel away the shell and see a little human-looking fist that has broken through the membrane. All thought of doubt leaves me as I frantically tear at the egg to get to my babies inside.

The hard shell is softer, but it still cuts my fingers as I tear it apart, piece by piece. I am able to reach into the goo and pull out a perfectly made human-looking baby girl.

I pull her close to me and wipe the messy membrane and wet goo away from her nose and mouth. Just as she starts to cry, I see another fist reaching up from inside the egg. One-handed, I grab the other slippery baby girl.

I realize that I just delivered twins out of the goo. I hear Brooke running up to us.

"Oh, my goodness!" Brooke says breathlessly. She takes the towel off her wet head and takes one of the babies I am holding. She wraps her in the towel she took off her head while I hold the other baby tight and wipe off her face.

I cry, tears flowing uncontrollably as love inside me manifests fiercely for these two baby girls. The imprinting solidifies. I am full of anxiety now, worried for their safety and whether I can ever be a worthy mother.

The twins cry. The sound makes my heart melt and

somehow reassures me they are healthy. I reach into my egg's remnants to ensure I got all my babies. Brooke stands smiling down at the bundle in her arms with tears in her eyes.

I sit on my knees in the mess of the broken egg, holding a newborn baby girl who is wailing at me. They are creamy pale hot pink babies with wet, blonde hair. My amber-colored skin highlights a difference between us. Blue scales pepper my skin as my inner dragon surfaces just enough to imprint on my babies.

This is the most beautiful, terrifying moment of my life. I am instantly in love. I look up at Brooke, and we both are in shock.

"I don't know how, but they are mine," I announce, tears falling down my face in absolute awe. "I'm a mother now!" I sob, scared out of my mind.

"This is scarier than being on another planet." The responsibility of this whole mother thing has me terrified. I would never have imagined myself with two babies. Yesterday, I was worried about finding a new job and surviving the day-to-day, barely adulting."

Now, without any notice, I am the mother of twin girls—twins from a dragon egg. The otherworldly magic of this place and my newfound strength settles my pounding heart and panic. The humming in my ears sends me a wave of reassurance. Without words, I feel the Goddess bless me.

Looking at my newly hatched babies, I feel love at this moment. I have never known love like this before. Now motherhood exists in my soul. I am wholly devoted to my children.

Whatever it takes, I will love and protect them. They will never know trauma like what Brooke and I have suffered.

"*I vow it,*" I say to the Goddess, knowing she understands my heart.

Brooke reaches for my elbow to help steady me as I stand up. I mechanically follow Brooke. This time it is my turn to be in shock. She leads us back to the cozy bedroom. I can hardly take my eyes off the girls.

The bathtub is practical as Brooke helps me bathe the babies and bundle them in towels. I dress in a clean blue robe. Then I lie on the soft, fur-covered bed, and Brooke helps me adjust the babies to latch onto my breasts to feed. I am lost in shock and wonderment when I hear Brooke speak.

"Kayla, they are clearly not your children. It's so strange you can feed them," Brooke says gently.

I must have been in my own world because I have never been so hurt by Brooke before. Anger snaps out of my blissful, motherly moment.

"They are *mine*!" I growl, sounding like an animal to my ears.

I glare at Brooke like she has lost her mind. I am so hurt and angry with her. I have never felt like this toward her, but at this moment, I am livid. I am so mad that I taste sulfur in my mouth. I don't think Brooke ever intended on hurting me, but my rational self has left the building. A haze of instinct takes over.

"Brooke, they are mine! Forever *mine!*" my voice growls, and I feel like my blood is on fire.

"Kayla! Is that smoke coming out of your nostrils?" Brooke asks with shock on her face.

As soon as she says it, I see a white mist puff out from my nose. *It is similar to vaping smoke.* The thought is funny and brings my humanity back to the surface. I calm down a bit, which takes some edge off my anger. Seeing Brooke stare at me with fear breaks something inside me.

Before I can apologize, Brooke speaks, cutting me off.

"Oh, my goodness, Kayla, your arms."

I see my babies in my arms. I also see blue scales fading away, returning to my natural amber-hued skin.

Shock hits me hard as I realize I have mutated into something more than human.

"I don't know what's happened to me, Brooke," I cry. "I am so sorry. I didn't mean to scare you. I feel hormonal, and I feel changed."

I hear the little grunts of contentment from my girls as they eat, and my heart melts as I bond more. They send me waves of contentment that calm me more. The crystal lighting seems to dim and chime in a soothing tone. The magic in this place, on this planet, somehow knows what I need and does its thing to aid me.

On Earth, this is the furthest from reality for me. Here, I know instinctively and deep in my heart that I can do this. These babies are mine. The Goddess is on my side, and she blesses me.

I feel genuine happiness and genuine love. I know I haven't ever felt anything as magical and wonderful as this moment. Nothing will harm my babies, and no one will ever take them from me. Before now, Brooke was the center of my life.

Having Brooke suggest that my daughters weren't really mine hurt as badly as it did when people claimed that Brooke and I weren't sisters. I am so hurt that Brooke, of all people, cannot grasp how amazing this is for me.

"They are mine. Brooke, please understand," I say, calmer now that I have more control and don't want to get mad again.

"Kayla!" Brooke says sharply. "The devil I know is on Earth. It's one thing for me to find my Zen and center with the universe when I understand the part of my universe, but I just saw my best friend turn into something not human, with dragon scales, and you puffed smoke at me." Tears stream down Brooke's cheeks. She sinks onto the bed next to me, and her steam turns into a softer, more scared vulnerability.

"You know, using our skills and intuition to know to take an unusual route home, only to find out later we avoided a catastrophe, is one thing, Kayla." She takes a sobbing breath. "But it's another that we are on another planet. You're a dragon mother with dragon babies, Kayla!" Brooke glances down at the girls, softness lighting her features.

"They are adorable," she mumbles. "But still! I don't think I can take much more of this, Kayla." Brooke lets out a silent sob.

"I can't tell if this is a dream or some kind of movie in my head, like some twisted version of *The Lord of the Rings*. Either way, it's too paranormal to feel safe. Not to mention that we have a zombie bear and a giant wolf running around outside that shield thing," Brooke cries.

I feel like a complete ass for being so wrapped up in myself and my daughters that I forget Brooke is having her own experience too.

"Oh, Brooke, honey, this whole thing has me more terrified than anything Earth ever threw at me." I lay my girls down and walk around the bed to snuggle my dear sister. I squeeze her tight in a hug.

We hold each other and cry. Brooke breaks our hug first. She evaluates me, and then she gazes down at the girls.

"They are perfect, aren't they?" I can see something shift in Brooke as she maneuvers closer to the sleeping babies.

"Oh!" Brooke gasps as imprinting takes shape between her and the babies. A shadow of red scales appears on Brooke's pale skin. When she finally glances at me, I swear her eyes are briefly predator and animal-like, then they change back to their human shape, filled with tears.

# CHAPTER 9

## Kayla

"Kayla, I feel a bond. The soul-deep kind." Brooke finally understands. "True magic." Brooke sighs, holding her hand to her mouth in shock.

"I think it is called imprinting here," I say. "I think the goddess has instinctually explained things to me when she cannot speak clearly to me yet. I get impressions of meanings and words. I feel her influence. When we got hit with that power in the cave, I suspect the goddess Harmony changed us to be compatible with her planet. I have no walls stopping an invasion, much less an invasion from a goddess, but Brooke, you are always so grounded and have created boundaries for protection. You practice daily, and I have never taken to it. My theory is that when the magic hit me, and the goddess manipulated the change in me, I was more susceptible to it and adapted quickly." I roll my eyes at the irony.

"Brooke, think about it. Me, a mother? Seriously, this goddess must have had slim pickings. Not to mention the married-at-first-sight, true mates bullshit. True mates need to be restored. What in the world does that even mean?" I am ranting.

"Brooke, you are changed and chosen too. Let your protective walls down, and you will understand your instincts. Somehow, you will accept this place as quickly as I have. Usually, you are the gung-ho, go-with-the-flow-as-the-universe-dictates one. You're supposed to be the enlightened one of us." I say, trying to get Brooke to understand.

"I know this is not Earth or the devil we know, but it is Harmony's universe, and she handpicked us. You can't get more in tune than that." I try to convince Brooke to lower her invisible barriers. My instinct tells me she will accept all this change if she lowers her shields.

Something in Brooke's gaze tells me she is basking in her new bond with the girls. She accepts what I say and starts to chant. I know she is opening herself up to the goddess and this planet.

"You and I would talk so much crap about that *Married at First Sight* show." I take a calming breath myself. "The impression I got from the goddess Harmony is that we will instinctively know our true mates. I feel like a clairvoyant psychic getting impressions and translating the message from the goddess. How am I supposed to be helping a goddess fix her planet? I would have never chosen this for us, Brooke." I watch my girls, and my instincts give me courage.

"Brooke, please, I need you more than ever. Please try." I try to interrupt Brooke's chant to get her to acknowledge me.

" I need you. I have these girls now. I will do whatever it takes. You'll see, the dragon, this planet, you are one now. This is our home now. You need to embrace it." I see her stubborn stance in her expression as she chants, trying to ignore me. I will face whatever this planet throws at us to give them the best loving home. I can't do any of it without you, Brooke."

Brooke takes a deep breath as she sits up and eyes me. "You're right, Kayla. I'm here with you. We've got this."

Brooke sits cross-legged, taking calming breaths as she lowers her protection shields.

I can see Brooke allowing the magic in. As I see it happening, the changes in her are beautiful. Brooke's arms tint red with dragon scales. The red fades as she opens her eyes with a new understanding.

"I am an auntie! You don't have to convince me. I get it now. That bonding or imprinting thing is magical and overwhelming. I feel as if my life is a part of the girls now," Brooke says with acceptance as she crawls into my bed next to me to admire my babies.

"Yes, we are all family now, Brooke," I confirm, not taking my eyes off my babies. "Man, I'm so thirsty." I feel like I have a cottonmouth.

Brooke jumps off my bed and rummages through all the drawers for a cup or something to get me water. She waves a strange book at me.

"There's nothing useful in here, just this book," Brooke says, frustrated, as she tosses the book onto her bed.

"I'm going to search this warehouse and try to find us food, a cup, something." Brooke takes off on a mission.

I smile and get up from my sleeping babies. I go to the waterfall sink in the bathroom and drink by cupping my hands to gather water. I remember sneaking into the bathroom at night as a kid to get a drink of water this way. I don't recall tasting water this refreshing in my life, though. This water is infused with magic. It's beautiful and delicious. I drink until I feel sated, savoring every sip. I return to my babies and lie next to them. They smell so amazing. *This really must be heaven. I think as I drift off.* I fall asleep as a new mother, feeling happiness and love.

# CHAPTER 10

## Brooke

I wake to the babies crying, so I jump up to help Kayla arrange for them to feed. I feel the wet towels. "Duh. Diapers," I mumble to myself. I see the stuff I had gathered from my great hall hunt.

"Oh, I made these for you, Kayla." I hand her a stack of cut-up fabric.

"Thanks for helping me make cloth diapers for the babies." Kayla sends me waves of gratitude.

I wonder if she is aware she is using magical energy to do so. I am so uneasy with all this new magic.

I help diaper the babies as Kayla admires a pair of gold chalices I found. They are medieval-looking and fancy.

"Not the normal Dollar Store dishes for us, huh?" Kayla says, impressed with my haul.

After I finish with the diaper change, I grab the book from next to my bed to read. I fan through the pages with confusion.

"This book is nothing but blank pages, but it seems a bit fancy for a journal," I say.

I am drawn to the book in a strange, enchanted way, and I am not sure I like that. I finally accept that we are on another planet and this place is magic, but my mind wants to organize and make sense of everything. I am still trying to understand and make this wild new life feel normal.

I give Kayla fresh towels, and she swaddles the babies again.

"Thanks, Brooke. These furs are not ideal for cloth diapers. We need to figure out a better system," Kayla says as I throw a fur comforter off the bed, disgusted by its wetness from the babies soiling the towels.

"I told you, Kayla, we need creature comforts."

"Like Luv's diapers and Huggies wipes. How does someone so small make such a huge mess?" I laugh.

"Maybe we will get lucky, and this planet will have a Walmart up the way," Kayla jokes, wishing it was that easy.

"Ten toes and ten fingers. Everything is just like a human baby, except that there is no belly button. Their eyes are so beautifully unique," I say in wonderment. I fall in love with Kayla's two babies. "I promise, no matter what, I will help you. Kayla, you will never be alone." I also devote myself to the girls, even if it means being in this strange world.

I love Kayla's newfound confidence. She seems stronger here like she was always meant to be here and to be these girls' mother. I feel lost but do not want to be away from Kayla or miss out on these magical babies. On Earth, I felt so in tune with my intuition and gifts. Here, the magic is genuine. I feel so overwhelmed by it and kind of scared to tap into it.

I feel like Kayla has swapped roles with me. Here, she is not struggling, and she is accepting. I love seeing her vibrant and strong. Seeing Kayla as a mother is astonishing to me. I know our trauma and past, and I know her babies won't ever have to worry about those things because Kayla is fierce, loyal, and determined. She will give these girls love and protection with every breath she takes for the rest of her life.

Maybe not having the emotional invasions she's used to on

Earth has allowed her to bloom like I always knew she could. I have changed too. I feel an animal humming inside me. I am scared of all the new and unknowns—the real magic infused inside me and all around.

I meditate to connect with the universe, chanting and focusing my spirit, tapping into its energy, and reaching enlightenment. On Earth, it was more of a grounding, self-soothing technique, a ritual.

# CHAPTER 11

## Kayla

"Brooke! Wake up! I have a surprise for you," I announce as I hold coffee from Starbucks. I know she likes it. I wave a McGriddle in front of her nose; it's lacking the packaging, but it is still exactly the same breakfast sandwich we got on Earth.

"Coffee!" Brooke mumbles as she opens her eyes in shock. Brooke sits up, rubs her eyes, and smiles at me, reaching for her favorite breakfast.

I tell her about the instant Harmony delivery door, the blue door we arrived through.

"Brooke, I had a vision of the goddess. She is wonderful. The goddess came to me and explained that she needed us to bring true mates to her beings here. She showed me how to get some of our creature comforts too. She said her Hecat made a food replicator and a clothing dispensary. He has beings in his universe that have this technology. So, he used Harmony's magic to give us this gift. He is trying to smooth things over between him and Harmony.

The blue door is a god portal, a one-way trip. I am supposed to bring true mates, but she faded out again, and I don't know how to get true mates here or even how to manage that when they do come." I shrug, just happy to be able to treat Brooke to a familiar breakfast.

"Harmony is letting us order things from her delivery door as a thank you to us. Can you believe a goddess thanking us? She is in a space beyond the veil where the gods exist. Time doesn't work there as it does here. She is moving much slower than we are. A minute there is equal to a thousand years here. This is beyond anything I could have ever imagined." I say in excitement.

"The connection is still not great. I felt a great despair from the goddess about this planet. Details aren't clear because her voice fades in and out, but I sensed that the Goddess would use her portal to provide true mates. She showed me the book of blank pages. Creature comforts came to mind. I made a list. I knocked three times after I wrote my list, and bam! Like magic, the blue Harmony delivery door shot my goods out. The god Hecat's replicator and clothing dispensary is the bomb in my book." I explain, unsure if I am making any sense.

"I would doubt you if you hadn't just handed me my favorite breakfast," Brooke says through a mouthful.

I dress my girls in matching sleepers I got from the magic blue door.

"Cloth diapers and wipes are pretty handy to have," I mention, totally excited now. They have an alien fabric that seals them together so I can mold them to the babies, and they are leakproof.

Brooke and I explore the hall and open some crates out of curiosity. There is an armory with uniforms that remind me of medieval knights with a mix of modern and old.

"There is so much jewelry. Gold, silver, diamonds, and gems," I say with a sexy whistle.

"On Earth, we would be rich beyond our dreams," Brooke says with awe, pulling out a long strand of a beaded necklace—the crystal ceiling chimes in beat with a happy tone and subtle music above us.

"Well, we're certainly not on Earth anymore," I respond while looking at the purple catlike eyes of Hope and Faith, who give me gummy smiles. I have them snuggled next to each other in a durable basket I found in the hall.

"We should go for a walk outside. I think a little sun will be just right for the babies. I say as I walk toward the exit door.

Brooke places a pearly beaded necklace on her neck to add to her collection. She is ridiculous wearing so many. Who am I to judge? Brooke is happy, like a kid in a candy shop. As we walk, I hear the beads bounce and clatter together with every step Brooke takes.

"I need to organize and inventory this place," Brooke says as we make our way outside.

I don't expect anything less from my sister. It's always been her personality to organize and make sense of her surroundings.

"I will help you, Brooke, but let's take a walk first."

The fresh air smells of pine, and I love it. The scent is fresh and clean, intensely so, unlike Earth. We make our way to the meadow. Brooke helps me lift the basket over some brushes that we have no pathway around. We enjoy the colorful sky and stare at the clouds and the alien-ringed moons that stay ever present in the sky. We have noticed the sky is a sunrise or sunset shade all hours of the day, from dusk to dawn.

We watch the crystal platforms that float, with their spray of rainbow colors. We decide that holding the babies is more convenient than the basket, so we grab our bundles and continue to walk farther into the woods, past the meadow. Being outside feels energizing.

We are careful to stay on our side of the barrier shield.

"This is a magic shield that is keeping us safe. Wild, right?" I say as I skim the shimmering barrier with a finger.

I feel Faith stir in my arms as Faith and Hope cry together

in unison. I sit down on some wet moss to feed them. Brooke helps me adjust as she hands me Hope.

The babies' translucent shading of hot pink scales disappears as they content themselves with momma's milk. I am about to discuss how beautiful I find that physical trait in them when the giant black wolf with dark-purple eyes breaks through the ferns, sniffing the air.

Brooke and I freeze in fear. The suckling, cooing sounds of Faith and Hope seem intensely loud. The forest sounds turn quiet around us.

I feel incredibly vulnerable and exposed, sitting crossed-legged on wet moss, both my arms holding my breast-feeding babies. My face feels hot with blood, and my ears are ringing. I'm getting dizzy from holding my breath.

My anxiety is affecting my babies. Their scales return, and they cry out, worrying for me. Brooke is quickly on her knees, trying to whisper to the girls to hush.

"Shh! Shh! Shh!" Brooke is desperate and scared too.

The wolf frantically sniffs the air in front of me, with the sound of the girls crying. He howls and lunges but hits the shield. Thankfully, he bounces right back off the barrier and falls on his side, skidding into a tree trunk.

He swiftly gets up to run back toward me. Again, he bounces off the shield. I feel relieved. Brooke helps me stand, and she takes Hope from me.

"Thank you, Harmony!" I say in gratitude to the goddess for the shield protecting us.

The wolf stops and stands still. He turns his head. His ears perked as if he heard me. He sniffs the air again and catches my scent. I make eye contact, even though I know he cannot see me. I feel a zap, and I know it instantly.

I feel drawn to the wolf and have to stop myself from stepping toward him. One second, he is fur. The next, a man is standing where the wolf is, a nearly naked man standing with a pouch tied to his hip.

The man is tall and muscled, with long black hair just

past his shoulders. He is dark with an imposing presence. He resembles a movie star or maybe a wrestler. I know my mind is trying to make sense of the wolf that transformed into a massive, sexy man before my eyes. My eyes travel over his body. *Damn, he is hung.* My pulse begins to throb throughout my body.

The man puts on a pair of black pants he takes from that pouch. He walks up to the shield and touches it as it sparks and shocks the man. He sucks on his finger, then shakes it off. I feel bad that he was shocked and want to reach for him. My rational side wants to protect the babies and Brooke. The heat pooling in my body wants to rush to him and kiss him.

The man stares straight into my soul as I stare into deep purple, catlike eyes that cannot see me through the barrier. He sniffs the air and straightens, seemingly shocked, as some recognition passes over his features.

He knows. I can tell he's also feeling the twining of our souls binding together, calling for each other. We are tethering together.

The man's face grows menacing, and I am amazed at how his gorgeousness transformed into something frightening.

"Great! Of course, he's a werewolf," Brooke says with a new annoyance, breaking my focus.

"Let's take the babies for a walk, she said. Let's get them some sun. She said," Brooke gripes as she tries to get my attention and snaps her fingers in front of my face.

I can feel her unease. I can feel my babies reaching for me in that unseen way, but I am transfixed on my wolf-man. I can tell he is more than a wolf-man. I can feel his dragon stir, rising just enough to reach for me. I am about to step through the shield.

A giant zombie-like bear jumps from the trees to attack the wolf-man from behind.

The man and mutated bear-beast fight. The man turns wolf just as the beast bites down on his shoulder. Blood sprays the trees.

I hand Faith and Hope to Brooke and yell, "Run!"

Brooke hesitates a moment, not wanting to leave me.

"No! Kayla, come with us!" She begs.

My own scales pepper my arms blue.

Brooke sees my arms and stops in her tracks. Something about me scares her. She turns to run with my daughters back to the safety of the hall inside the mountain.

I refocus my attention on the fighting on the other side of the barrier. The wolf is in trouble, and everything inside me demands that I save him. The beast tosses the wolf into a tree, where he yelps in pain and falls on a fern, unconscious.

I feel a significant change transforming me as I step through the barrier. The energy that saturated me the last time I crossed this barrier feeds into my frenzy.

Animal rage flows like lava through my veins as I allow my transformation to happen. I let the dragon deep inside me surface. My breath tastes of sulfur and flame, and my eyes are fixed and zeroed in on my prey.

I want to roar angrily at seeing the wolf so injured—fire shoots from my mouth, setting the treetops on fire. I use my tail as a whip to fling that beast away from my wolf.

My soul screams *MINE!* The beast lets out a sound of terror as I stalk him, determined to avenge the injured wolf that my instinct knows is mine—time to destroy this creature. The beast runs, but I'm faster.

The beast sees his fate as I approach. He sends a statement, mind to mind, toward me. I blow dragon fire at him, incinerating him instantly. The ash statue of the beast falls apart. I understand the words the beast sent out just before his demise.

*"A dragon! It cannot be! I am doomed."*

The statement settles in my head as I turn to rush to my unconscious, injured wolf; Worry for the male fuels my reaction. I reach him and see my blue scales and claws. I grab the wolf as gently as I can. I take him back through the barrier shield to my home on the hillside.

I make it to the door but am too large to enter. I lay the

injured, unconscious wolf down and feel myself change. The robust animal inside me recedes as I stand naked, covered with ash from fire and smoke. The soot smudges on my skin.

I open the door and call out, "Brooke, I need help!"

I was looking down at the giant wolf. *True mates* flutter through my mind. The show *Married at First Sight* flashes into my head. My soul is trying to tell me something—a memory of Harmony explaining something to me.

True mates are essential, but I cannot clarify why just yet. *"I don't want a mate."* I send the thought to Harmony, unable to deny the pull I feel for the male. I feel Harmony giggle.

I roll my eyes with sass up to the rainbow skies with the daytime moons, hoping the goddess Harmony feels my response.

"You think this is amusing?" I say, frustrated. The goddess giggles over my situation. This wolf's injuries have become all-consuming. The giant wolf lays still, and I force myself to leave him.

He's bleeding badly from torn fur and skin. He is too huge for me to move alone. Fear and worry drive out any apprehension of the true mate stuff. I yell with a magic push for urgency.

"BBBRRROOOKE!"

# CHAPTER 12

## Kayla

I run to the bedroom, looking for Brooke, but the door is locked. I hear my girls crying as I beat on the door.

"Brooke! Open the door. I need your help." I hear Brooke crying too. "Brooke! What the hell is wrong with you? It's me! Open the door!"

*I don't need this shit right now. What the hell is wrong with Brooke?* I have way too many emotions going on at once. I feel fear for my injured wolf, the need to calm my girls, and the hurt that Brooke has locked me out of my bedroom, keeping me away from my babies and helping my wolf. Betrayal is raw on my nerves as I yell again and again.

"Brooke! Open this goddamn door NOW!" Anger gives way to sadness as I sink to the floor, sobbing.

My inner dragon mixes with my humanity, and I can't seem to be rational while having my volatile emotions. Animal instinct moves to the forefront, and I'm lashing out at Brooke. This is unlike me. In despair and feeling helpless, I weep. Snot-nosed as I cry, I hear Brooke.

"Kayla?" she asks from the other side of the door. Her voice cracks with her tears. She finally opens the door.

"I'm sorry, Kayla." Brooke reaches to hug me. I cry harder.

"I just need your help," I mumbled through tears.

Brooke's wide eyes stare into mine.

"I've never seen you this upset, Kayla. I am so sorry. That scared the hell out of me," Brooke explains.

"I saw you change, I mean, changing and growing into a dragon. Not just a dusting of scales. I saw you transform, and, more than that, I felt a deadly intent of rage from you, Kayla." Brooke brings me both girls.

"I am scared the dragon side of you won't recognize the babies or me," Brooke said.

I stand up and take deep breaths until I feel calm enough to stop crying. My girls are fully scaled. Their pink scales are angry, outlined with red, and smoke comes from their human features. I feel guilty for causing their little hearts trauma.

"Oh, I know, sweethearts, I know," I coo.

I send them warmth and reassurance as I grab them and hug them. I am already failing as a mother by letting them get this upset.

Faith and Hope soon calm down. Their scales vanish, and they fall asleep. I lay them down on the furs in the basket atop the bed. Now that they are safe and settled, I grab a fur comforter from Brooke's bed and speak.

"Come, I need your help." I take a deep breath, trying to assuage my guilt.

"Brooke, I am sorry I scared you and the babies. Dragon or not, I know who you are and would never harm you or my girls." I tried to think of the best way to describe my need when I turned dragon.

"This place has magic and magical creatures. Do you recall the feeling that took place when you imprinted with the babies?" I try to help Brooke understand how vulnerable and emotional I am amid my mating.

"Yes, I do. It was unbelievable in a spiritual, soul-entangling way," Brooke says in awe.

"Okay, great. Maybe this will make sense to you, then." I try to focus beyond my need and urgency to get to my injured wolf.

"Something inside me recognizes that wolf-man as my husband, my true soulmate." I reach for Brooke's hand, so my feelings and core energy can radiate to her.

"He is mine, Brooke, like the girls, but on a new level. Now that I know for sure who he is to me, I want to do everything I can to heal and keep him safe. I need to complete my imprinting. He is like the air I breathe."

Brooke lets go of my hand, and I know she understands the magnitude of my need. "Okay, Kayla, if you need this wolf-man, I will help you. Whatever you need." Brooke's features are tight from worry. This is hard for her, but she feels my magic and knows I need her help.

I've left my injured wolf so long that my worry for him has me running when I feel Brooke's agreement. Brooke struggles to keep up. I hear her beads bouncing rapidly as she runs behind me. Brooke gasps in fear as she sees the wolf lying in the doorway. She steps backward as if to turn and run to the bedroom.

"Stop right there, Brooke! Don't you dare!" I demand, and Brooke freezes in her tracks.

This is our first hands-on encounter with the people on this alien planet, other than the babies. Brooke's humanity is warring for self-preservation. I feel her fighting her fear to help me.

I drop the fur comforter next to my wolf and tentatively make my way to Brooke. She stands there, scared, like a rabbit about to bolt, and I try to calm my internal panic. I show Brooke my hands as if to calm her.

I say as evenly as possible, "It's okay, it's okay, Brooke."

I stare into her teary eyes. "I need you to trust me, Brooke."

I can tell she is struggling to be there for me when she wants to run far away from the bloody wolf.

I reach for her and gently take her hands. I send her warmth and reassurance. Brooke softens her features, and she noticeably relaxes. I take a deep breath.

"I need you to understand. This wolf is mine, just like the girls are mine."

Brooke watches my wolf.

"I tentatively understand, Kayla." Brooke sees the massive bloody wolf. "That zombie rabid bear thing bit him. How do you know he won't turn into a zombie wolf next?" Brooke says, clearly hesitant.

I squeeze her hand in reassurance and then let go of her. I go to my injured wolf and kneel to pet his fur. Feeling his breath makes me feel relieved. I want to curl up around him on the doorway's threshold.

"I need you to trust me, Brooke. I know he's mine," I say as my breath blows his silky fur near my mouth.

My fingers trail his fur and feel the warm stickiness of his bloody injury. A soft whine comes from him as he lies in a coma-like state.

"He is not going to turn into a zombie?" Brooke worries out loud.

"Trust me, Brooke. He needs our help to heal," I state as my emotions scramble from not having my mating bond completed.

The urgency for imprinting has me on the verge of turning feral. His pain tears into my soul, and I jump up in worry.

"Please, Brooke, he is hurt badly. Help me get him to our bathroom," I beg.

Brooke is determined to work past her fear and takes a deep breath. Resolve replaces the fear on her face. I instantly feel relief as she helps me roll his bulky, furry body onto the comforter. It takes the two of us a great effort to drag his sleeping wolf body to the bathroom.

I try my best to wash his wound, and he is sleeping like he

is under anesthesia. My concern for him mixes with my need for my babies. I go to the bedroom to feed my crying babies.

*Please, save him,* I beg Harmony with a prayer in my heart.

Brooke uses her ingenuity and makes a wrap out of a dress and towels to compress his wound to stop the bleeding. Then she enters the room and sits on her bed, looking at the bathroom door as if it will burst open any minute. I follow her and try to explain.

"I have an animal instinct. My new magic is in limbo, and I need to finish my imprinting. I will know the second he wakes."

"Stop!" Brooke says. "My head hurts, Kayla. I get there is a soulmate bond. I feel the magic and can sense you're imprinting. I also can feel your stress. The babies even understand and sense it. All I want to do is help you feel better. I can't stand my fear, but that huge werewolf scares me. I am trying my best to accept that he is family now. I haven't imprinted with him. To me, he is a dangerous stranger."

Brooke petulantly sits crossed-legged and starts to chant in her meditation.

I take a deep breath. "Auntie Brooke is taking it better than I thought," I say in a baby voice as I coo to the girls, kissing each one on the nose. The melodic sound of Brooke's chanting in rhythm with the universe gives me a sense of normalcy. Will I be able to be a wife now? Married at first sight. Craziness!

"I understand this is scary for you, Brooke. I love that you are trying to fight your instinct for my sake."

I settle my girls to sleep next to their chanting aunt. Then I return to the bathroom and my injured mate.

# CHAPTER 13

## Brooke

I begin chanting—my go-to, especially when I am overwhelmed. I'm just getting used to the magical babies and the general concept of being here. I envy Kayla for her easy acceptance. I never minded embracing the universe and following my intuition back on Earth.

This life is something that I could never have imagined. On Earth, I would have never been the one struggling when faced with actual magic. At least, I thought I would have been the one to embrace it.

Monsters here are real, not just the humankind ones I know all too well. I want to hide in this bubble the goddess gave us and stay safe with Kayla and the girls. Kayla is a freaking dragon shape-shifter. She brought a werewolf here to our new home, and now she is marrying the creature. He isn't even awake yet!

I understand the imprinting. I have a bond with the babies. It is a soul-piercing bond that will be a part of my being forever now. I recognize these girls both magically and spiritually.

The word *family* doesn't seem to express this connection adequately. This imprinting business is more profound than that.

I felt the goddess—actually felt her—touch my soul and connect me to the girls. That goes beyond my generic "keep in tune with the universe" chants. I thought I was enlightened, but this place ripped open my enlightenment and introduced a paranormal reality.

I can't get a grasp on reality here. I focus on my chants, trying to keep strong and be the support my family needs. Kayla doesn't need to see how scared I am. I have already snapped at her enough.

Guilt eats away at me for not being stronger than this. I need to be calm, and I need to support her. She is getting married to a stranger, for the universe's sake. Surely the goddess would give Kayla a decent man—uh, wolf-man—to be married to, right?

I'm allowing my fear to drown out Kayla's feelings, but she needs me, and the girls need me. Regardless of this strange addition to our family. I will watch over them and protect them. One thing at a time. *I got this. I can do this. No need to panic.*

I mentally coach myself as I feel my nerves settle. *Breathe in and out, slow and deep. Just try to be calm. Breathe in, breathe out. Steady my heart, calm.* I can hear the hum of my chants as my ears ring, and I press hard to build my shield to shut down the relentless whisper. *Breathe in, breathe out. My walls are up. I am okay. I can do this. I can be there for my sister and her new family.*

"Kayla," I softly say. "I am here for you. If you say the wolf is safe, I trust you." I take a deep breath and stand up.

I walk to the bathroom door to check on Kayla and see the relief in her eyes. She accepts my support.

"I will take care of them while you care for the injured wolf." I need the comfort of holding the girls more than Kayla knows for my nerves.

Kayla seems relieved that I got the reins on my anxiety.

I slide the bathroom door closed and let out a soft sob. The girls' skin is shadowed in pale scales, and I feel waves of love. A true calmness envelops me.

"Aww! Thank you, sweet girls," I coo.
you bowing again?"

# CHAPTER 14

## Kayla

After feeding my babies, I must be near my wolf again. Feeling my wolf stir awake, I give Brooke my girls as I enter the bathroom. I am startled to see a man kneeling on the floor. Head bowed in prayer toward the mosaic tile image on the wall.

I feel awkward, and I need him awake and well. For so long, I have been running on intuition. Now that he is up, I have to engage this stranger, who is now aware of me. I don't know how to navigate human contact and conversation over instinct.

So, I resort to my goofy self when trying to engage him. With my fingers splayed, I hold my hand up. I am trying for a gesture of peace. Isn't that protocol when greeting aliens?

"Hello, I am Kayla. I come in peace," I say, announcing I am in the room now.

Heat flushes my cheeks in embarrassment. He looks up when he hears me, giving me a clear view of his smoldering, dark-purple eyes. Caught for the first time in the mesmerizing beam of his eyes, I stand there like a fool with butterflies fluttering in my stomach. *Freaking butterflies!*

I have never felt this before. I feel our imprinting engage again. It's happening. Our souls are merging. It is an intense swarm of magic. I've had the experience of maternal imprinting with my girls. However, this is entirely different. He manages to move stealthily and fast, and suddenly he stands before me, towering over my more petite frame.

I suck in the air and taste the man's scent in front of me. My arms turn blue with scales. I know my whole body shows my dragon. She rises inside me just enough to announce her presence to the beast inside the male in front of me. *Mate!* hums in my ears.

A wild expression of lust hazes over this man's eyes. Our imprinted souls are bonded as I stand breathlessly with my back to the door. My body reacts with a need for this sexy man to touch me. He sniffs the air.

Now, he has turned primal, more animal than man. I sense his dragon, his wolf, and the man. His whole being brings heat to my core. My desire drifts to his senses. My scent drives his instinct to mate with me, and his scent is turning me primal too.

Before I can even process my animalistic need, he moves and pins me up against the closed door. He gently grips my face, with me caged firmly between his chest and the door.

*Wow! I love his touch.* This stray thought melts away any lingering worry. My need for him to touch me creates a craving I have never known.

He stares into my eyes, and I can see how beautiful his purple eyes are, much like my daughters'. The vertical slit-shaped pupils dilate, and I feel heat envelop me. My humanity is gone. Rational thought is gone. This soul binding has me wanting to mate, to consummate and entwine my soul with his.

A needful lust rushes through me like liquid heat. My body

quivers, and my clit throbs in tune with my heartbeat, fast and hard.

He sniffs the air deeply, finally breaking eye contact. He drops to his knees and buries his face into the apex of my legs, inhaling deeply.

"MINE!" One animalistic, growly word, low and commanding, escapes his lips.

*I understood that, so at least he speaks English.* The goofy thought is quickly redirected to the huge male on his knees in front of me. I try to fight the animal, my wildness, inside and regain my rational humanity.

"Hey, there, big guy, let's just take a step back and relax for a minute."

I try to push the guy to move back a step slowly. A howling growl is his response.

"MINE!" he yells.

Feral purple eyes catch mine. His grip is rugged on my hips, forcing me to stare down into his pleading eyes. I am caught up in his eyes again, and my feral need for him ignites. Any awkward human feelings evaporate, leaving a sexual nature that drives us to complete our mating and imprinting.

I moan, reach down to grab his head, and pull him up to kiss his lips.

I latch onto his mouth with mine. This first taste of male and pine has me lost. Our fates are sealed with this kiss. As I taste ambrosia, my heart seizes on his lips.

Fast and furious, I set the pace. His hands and my hands roam everywhere. Coherent thoughts are gone. The primal need is all I feel. His blissful touch is heaven. Something dominant inside me takes charge.

I make him walk backward as we kiss and touch. I eagerly push downward, and he lands on the fur pallet I had made earlier. As he lies on his back looking up at me, I flip my hair back and tear my shirt off, revealing my full breasts.

He follows my hands with his eyes as I squeeze my dark nipples, then trail my fingers from my nipples to the heat of my pussy. Seductively, I take off my panties, baring myself fully to him like an offering. I stalk toward him and step over him to straddle him. My need to claim what is mine has me wild.

Slowly lowering myself onto him, teasing my wetness over his shaft, I place my finger on his lips, coated with my desire. He is lost as he tastes my finger. I capture his mouth, mingling my essence with our kiss. My breasts press up against his chest, and my hardened nipples demand his attention. He breaks the kiss to suck on my nipples.

The sensation sends a surge straight to my clit and drives me crazy. Without thought, I grab his huge, thickly engorged cock and slam myself to the hilt. I slide down hard on him. The sting of his cock being sheathed by my wet, hot core is so brief I barely notice it in the throes and haze of my lust and mating desire.

He releases my breast with a wet pop. He howls as he feels his shaft break through my maiden barrier. This moment makes him mine. I willingly give myself wholly to him.

I do not feel real pain, just blissfulness. My lust drives me to ride him, wanting to give fulfillment to us both. I sit up on him and anchor my hands to his chest. I push myself up and down, grinding into him. His smoldering eyes take me in. I feel like an enchantress as I take him. He grips my hips and arches himself up into me, keeping my pace.

My face feels hot, and I light up in a euphoric rush—blue scales pulse, highlighting my body. I crest and squeeze his shaft hard in the tightness of my core. He has his release, unable to last any longer.

I fall on him, and on instinct, the next thing I do is bite his neck. The sharp inhale of his breath, and the rhythm of our panting together have me completing our bond. I taste the copper of his blood. I feel our souls combine as my humanity sends out a stray thought and a surge of power zaps through us. *Why did I bite him?* Feeling fabulous in the aftermath of my first sexual experience, I stare into his eyes and see an expression of pure delight and euphoria. *Love,* I think. *This is what love is like.*

Then the darkness takes us both. We collapse together in a heap on the bathroom floor. Our mate bonding unites us forever as mates and locks our life force together.

I come awake tangled in a sweaty heap on top of the handsome man I have lost myself to. Not knowing how long I have been out, I peel myself away from him, only to have him snap his eyes open and grab me. He sits up, gripping my arm lightly.

"Don't leave," he says softly with pleading eyes.

"How is it that you speak English? I am just curious. I never thought an alien world would ever have a language close to English or any Earth languages?" I mumble as I try to adjust to this new reality.

I feel exposed now that my animal instinct has subsided. Grabbing a fur blanket, I hold it to cover myself and sit up to face him. I gently pat the hand that grips me.

"I'm not leaving," I reassure him.

He lets go reluctantly, looking at his hand. I see he feels a bit awkward too.

I laugh, unsure of what to do. "We need to talk."

I gaze into his mesmerizing purple eyes. *Get a grip,* I think to myself, trying to shake off a budding need that is building again.

"I am Kayla." I introduce myself.

"Kayla," he softly says, testing my name with his voice.

Hearing my name on his lips for the first time makes those butterflies go wild inside me again.

"Beautiful," he says as he gazes at me.

He lifts his hand to his shoulder, feeling my claim, my bite mark, on him. I see the movement of his hand to feel the wound I gave him with my bite. Gasping with shock, I place my hand to my mouth.

"I can't believe I bit you like that. I'm so sorry." I feel significantly terrible since he just healed from that beast's attack.

"Do not try to take back your claim. I bear your mark with pride. A true gift of the goddess," he says proudly.

"Yes, the goddess and our arranged marriage thing. True mates," I say.

Looking at him, I ask, "So, what do I call you besides mate? You got a name, big guy?"

He must still be shocked as my question is left unanswered for a few moments.

"Talen. I am Talen Drake, Dragon King of the North. But if you prefer to call me mate, I will gladly take the title. As far as speaking English, my world is magical and balanced. We all speak the same language, or how would we be able to communicate otherwise? I cannot fathom a world that would have other languages," he says.

I laugh. "Well, we both have a lot to discover about one another. Welcome to my world, Talen. It's time for me to explain a few things to you." He watches me eagerly. I sweep my hand in a motion to display the bathroom.

"This is my family's home. Well, this is the bathroom, but my family lives here. Maybe we should take a shower and get clean. Before we figure things out, it's better if we get dressed first."

"My Dragon Queen," he worships reverently. Talen hits his knee and bows to me.

*What in the world is this man doing?* I am perplexed again.

"Listen! Talen, we need to establish a couple of things. First off, get up. I am not cool with you bowing at my feet. I mean, maybe if we decide that's a kink we want, but that's beside the point. Absolutely no bowing to me. Have you got that? Get up, please," I ramble.

Talen slowly rises off the floor. *Great! Now he is an intimidating giant of a man.* I gaze up at him. "Secondly, you must understand that my priority is my daughters and my sister. We are family. Harmony, the goddess, hasn't explained . . . Whawhat?" I stuttered as the muscle man hit the floor again. "Not that again. Talen, get up. Why are you bowing again?"

# CHAPTER 15

## Kayla

"You have spoken directly with the goddess?" Talen asks as he stands once more, looking stunned.

"I know, I sound nuts. But in a way, yes, kind of. The goddess Harmony sent my sister and me here. She blessed us. She gave me my daughters. The Goddess Harmony has spoken to me in my head, but to be honest, she keeps getting cut off. I guess there is a lousy reception between here and the god realm. I don't understand a lot of her messages, either. But I am getting the gist of it, here and there."

I can see Talen is as confused as I am, but I give him credit because he is trying to understand. He seems to revere me, hanging on every word I say. I'm not sure how this is making me feel.

"I know we have a bond, that whole true mate thing. I'm going for it, which is huge for me. But, Talen, we must get to know each other. My number-one thing that I need you to understand is if you are going to be a part of my family . . . Talen, my number-one rule is family comes first. My daughters and my sister are my priority. You will have to accept them and protect them. Oh, and I don't want you to worship me like some god. You need to be my partner."

"We are mates. We are family, Kayla. Mine is yours, and yours is mine," Talen interrupts with an easy pledge.

"I need you to understand I don't have a traditional family. I never really had one. I did not give birth to my girls, but they are mine. I delivered them myself, right out of their egg." I give Talen my most badass expression to drive my point home.

"Talen, you do right by my family, then you will be a part of it. Otherwise, I don't care if the goddess arranged our marriage. True mate or not, you better do right by my family, or I am out." My chest burns in pain as I say it. I don't care, though. I will have a healthy, loving family, or I will raise my babies alone on my own!

*"Come on, Harmony, don't make me live with an evil man,"* I pray.

Talen melts my heart when he grabs my cheeks and gently kisses my forehead, whispering, "Kayla, your family is my family. I am beyond blessed to have you, my dragon queen, and three more females to add to my family. This is rare and unheard of. The goddess Harmony must find me truly worthy. I will devote my life, and all that is mine to you, Kayla, and our family." The feeling of pride and honor rolls off Talen in waves, hitting me full force.

"Just don't bow to me anymore. That will be a great start," I say in a goofy response. I feel so much for this man. I kiss his chin. His whiskers scratch my lips in the most delicious way. Then I kiss my way to his lips. I break apart from him before my lust takes over again. I'm eager to get to my girls and see how Talen takes to this whole instant family thing.

"Get cleaned up," I say, pointing to the shower and putting a robe on. "I'll be back with some clothing. Then you can meet the rest of the family."

I feel butterflies as I go to the Harmony delivery door to scribble a big and tall clothing order. We need food too. This is the most girlish way I have ever felt before. *Butterflies,* I think, feeling all giddy.

I hear Brooke and my babies, along with the movement of metal clattering on the floor. I walk up, offering Brooke food. She seems relieved to see me.

"What's all this?" I wave my hand at all the jewelry and gold and silver things scattered across the floor. Brooke must have ten beaded necklaces on, and is that a tiara? I give Brooke a raised eyebrow as I take a sip of coffee.

"Don't judge me with those eyes, Kayla. The babies like the sparkles." Brooke blames them, laughing as she reaches for another trinket.

I decide to join the fun, and I reach in elbow-deep and grab whatever my fingers can find as I grip my treasure.

We collectively gasp as our upper left arms burn briefly with a warm, tingling sensation. I check on my babies, who yawn two little gummy smiles at me before falling back asleep in their stroller. I see a dainty armband on one of my baby's upper left arms. It is a dragon wrapped around the arm. I examine it, worried it will hurt them, but it seems attached to them, unmovable. Now a part of them, the arm cuff, seems alive somehow.

"I have it too, Kayla," Brooke says as I stare at her trying to grab hold of hers.

I let my robe fall down off my left shoulder enough to see that I have one too. It's beautiful and feels . . . comforting. I feel a bridge of magic connecting us even more through the amplifier of the armbands that are now a part of us.

"Just another weird thing to add to the list of weird things," I say.

"I like it. It's pretty." Brooke goes to dig through the chest some more. Of course, she's fascinated with weird, magical jewelry.

"So, how'd it go with the werewolf guy?" Brooke asks, not looking at me as she digs for more trinkets.

"Well, I can kiss him without getting disgusted," I say

happily. "And I have butterflies!" I smile at Brooke, who finally smiles at me.

"If you're happy, I'm happy," Brooke says with easy acceptance.

"Let's go. I want to introduce you and the girls to him." I am excited as I pick up the clothes and food to head back to Talen.

"Brooke, he is genuinely sweet and pleased to be with me. He is almost worshiping me, so that's weird, but you know I will stop that nonsense," I ramble as Brooke begins to worry, showing a little bit of her anxiety.

"I think it's a culture thing. There's a lot we still need to figure out. I didn't mean to make him seem stalker-like. Please wait until you feel his energy, Brooke. You'll see."

"Kayla, you are gushing over a man. I never thought I'd see the day like this," Brooke says with genuine happiness.

I enter the bathroom and see my sexy man with a pink towel wrapped around his waist, the ends barely staying together. He is hand-drying his long black hair while staring at the mosaic tile of the dragon.

"I hope these fit," I say, clearing my throat to interrupt his deep thoughts.

I put the coffee on the counter, and the food replicated burritos that I hope he likes.

"I'm going to shower quickly while you dress and eat."

I make quick work of it and pull on another blue outfit. I feel a lingering ache between my legs. I am still in shock. I had sex, and it was amazing. Empowering. The lingering soreness I feel has my mind on Talen. I watch him put on a pair of jeans. Damn, he is sexy. He messes with the button fly as I admire how his ass looks in denim.

"They're called jeans. They fit you well. You look great!" I hand him a black T-shirt and walk him to the door.

"Ready?" I ask because I need to get out of this bathroom, or else I might jump him again. His purple eyes meet mine, and he stands tall and proud.

"After you, my dear." He gestures with his hand, and he follows me into the bedroom.

Brooke stands, holding my girls, all bundled up and sleeping. As soon as Talen sees them, he hits his knees and bows.

"We talked about this, Talen. Get up. Please." I roll my eyes. "This guy, he likes to bow a lot," I say to Brooke, feeling weird. I step around him to the girls.

"Talen, this is my sister, Brooke." I put my hand on Brooke's shoulder and glance down at my girls. Talen slowly stands up.

"I am honored," he says as he bows his head in respect toward Brooke. I grab Hope from Brooke and face Talen.

"This is Hope," I say with pride.

As Talen looks down at the baby in my arms, her purple eyes open and lock onto his. I feel the imprint between the two, and it's fantastic to see the emotions flood Talen's features as he stares down at his new daughter. I can sense the parental imprinting. I am not sure if I am quite ready to share this claim. The magic is affecting me, and my instinct is to accept this.

He is stunned, then shudders as tears brim in his eyes while he bonds with Hope. Love beams out of his eyes with fatherly affection as the imprinting completes. When he looks up to meet my eyes, he pulls Hope and me in for a hug.

"You still need to meet Faith," I say, mumbling into his chest—and, oh boy, he smells delicious. My mind is challenging my heart and the easy acceptance of my animal nature. I am lost to the imprinting and my budding need for Talen.

He chuckles and steps back.

Brooke and I swap babies. I turn to present Faith to Talen, and Faith stares up into Talen's purple eyes as they imprint too. Talen's features morph again into a fatherly love that shines from his eyes.

"Just like that, we're a family," I announce, trying to brighten the energy as Talen starts to cry full-on tears as he soaks up the moment. I want to cry but am sucking up my tears and high emotions.

"This is the best day of my life," Talen says, wiping tears from his eyes.

"Sit here," Brooke insists.

She points to the edge of the bed, and Talen does. Brooke lays Faith down in his arms.

"Welcome to the family, Talen," Brooke says, accepting Talen.

I put Hope next to her sister in his massive arms too. The sight melts my heart, and I am trusting Talen with my most precious family.

Talen stares at Brooke with fatherly pride. I feel his bond and imprinting start with Brooke, establishing a sibling bond.

"That is too sweet," Brooke says as she stands beside me, watching Talen hold the girls for the first time.

I am wrapped up in the scene myself, feeling happiness. I know Talen is committed, with no hesitation, and he is now a massive part of my life. He is bonded to each of us as a family. Brooke has imprinted, too, as she quickly accepted Talen, and her anxiety vanished.

"Um, Kayla, we need to talk about all the men outside," Brooke announces out of the blue.

"What men?" Talen asks, concerned as he stands up fast, his serious gaze staring us down.

Brooke and I are taken aback by this gentle father turned fierce. But as he holds the girls, his grip is still tender.

"What men?" I ask Brooke, concerned myself, blue scales appearing up my arms.

"Kayla, calm down. It's safe. They are on the other side of that shield." Brooke tries to soothe me.

"I went outside to check on the fire you started when you saved Talen." Brooke nervously plays with her beads.

"I saw men gathering and putting out the flames, but they didn't even know I was there." Brooke shrugs.

# CHAPTER 16

## Kayla

After feeding the babies and ensuring they were sound asleep, we showed Talen the shield. We all stand as we watch the crowd of men busy setting up a camp. The fire left an ash clearing where the trees once stood. I feel guilty for burning so much of the beautiful forest.

"I feel the trees cry. I don't understand it, but I feel it," I whisper. Brooke hands me Hope, so I hold my sleeping baby.

"I feel it too," she whispers back.

My heart hurts, and guilt eats at me because I burned the trees. The energy that flows on the other side of this barrier is almost tangible, with so many magical beings gathered so close to the border of the shield.

With our new armbands that amplify our connections, Brooke and I can feel the forest crying at the damage and loss of trees. The intensity of nature being mistreated is breaking my heart. I can sense Brooke's incredible urge to heal the nature around us. Instinctively, we know we can use our ability to heal and mend what I never should have burned so badly.

Guilt has me tearing up. Talen uses his thumb to wipe away my tears as one trails down my cheek. He leans down and kisses my forehead.

"These are my men. It's safe," he whispers.

"I'm not ready for all this," I say, taking a step backward, knowing people will swamp me with their energy.

I can already feel uneasiness and worry coming from both the men and the forest.

Brooke is on her hands and knees and has shoved one of her hands into the dirt, chanting. She is willing the trees to heal. Gratitude comes to us in waves, and it sounds like the trees are chiming.

"How are you doing that, Brooke?" I whisper as I walk near.

"I'm helping the trees," she says.

Her voice carries on the wind, and the scuffling men stop in their tracks! All the men turn toward us and sniff the air.

Brooke puts her dirty hand over her mouth, eyes wide, as a colossal man stomps his way through all the men to stand in front of us. He looks exactly like Talen.

"My twin brother, Fang," Talen whispers in my ear.

*Oh, my gods, there are two of them!* I think.

Brooke stands up fast. She sees the massive man on the other side of the shield and panics. She glares at me.

"Aw, hell no. Kayla, it's one thing that it happened to you. Nope. Not me." Dread transforms Brooke's face.

She takes a step toward the man who looks like Talen before she stops herself. I feel the jolt through my armband. Brooke understands that she has discovered her true mate.

"Too much! Too fast!" Brooke says as she takes Faith back from Talen. She gives me a pleading gaze for me to hand her Hope. I feel she needs to hold them, so I give her my bundled daughter and watch as she runs back to the hall in the hillside, her beads jangling together as she bolts.

"Seriously?" I call after Brooke as she abandons me to all these men.

I turn and see the huge guy, Fang, jump at the shield, get knocked on his ass, and thrown back to the ground.

Talen startles me as he laughs and laughs.

"You're not helping," I snap at Talen as he tries to compose himself.

"Now that we have an audience, I think the jig is up." Talen steps through the shield to confront his brother and his men.

"Great! It's about to get peoplely." I moan.

"Calm, brother. I have the best news." Talen says.

Fang dusts his ass off as he evaluates Talen. He stares at Talen's jeans and black t-shirt like they have horns or something.

"They're called jeans," Talen says with pride. "My true mate gifted them to me."

Fang sniffs at his brother. "Have you been turned?"

Laughing, Talen says, "No, brother. I have a dragoon queen as my true mate."

All the men start murmuring in disbelief.

Fang seems even more concerned for Talen.

"You've gone mad, brother. Did you hit your head?" Fang turns from Talen.

He stares at me without seeing me as he steps toward the cliff edge. He reaches out and is zapped as he touches the illusion from his side of the shield.

"What trickery is this?" Fang bellows as he turns back toward Talen.

"I need to get beyond this magic. Something is demanding me to go forward." Fang grows angry, growling and looking feral.

"That vampire has some new traps in place. He must have sent a different kind of siren, perhaps?" Fang says.

"No trick, Fang. The goddess has not forsaken us." Talen is full of joy, trying to explain to his brother.

"There is no more dragon. Our dragon beast is trapped, suppressed, and will never rise again. Certainly, there is no dragon queen. We have lost our females. Brother, the sirens have you fooled." Fang says, exasperated, tearing at his long hair in frustration.

"The sirens try to fool me right now as you distract me with nonsense." Fang eyes Talen with pity in his eyes.

"We will get you to the healer. Get the witches to disperse this trance before you turn berserker. Brother, I will save you." Fang vows as he tries to shake off the magic he feels trying to ensnare him as well.

"You are not hearing me. I have found my true mate, and she is a dragon queen. I am not ensnared. This is a blessing from the goddess herself, Fang."

I see the lost expression on Fang's face as he thinks Talen is crazy. I need to reveal myself to these men. Old fears assault me as I step through the shield to reveal myself.

Once I step through the shield, I am thoroughly blasted with the world's energy. My armband amplifies this ability. The forest is suffering from my burning of the trees, begging me to heal the nature around me.

My dragon magic sends a general greeting letting the men know I am their natural dominant and Dragon Queen. I want to end the strange encounter and try to withdraw from the connection of others when a cloud of ash puffs out of me as all the men hit the dirt and bow.

They must have got a sense of my magical energy. Fang sinks too. His eyes bulge in shock just before his forehead is pillowed in the ash on the ground like the rest of the men. I throw my hands up and step to Talen, who, thank the goddess, no longer does this bowing crap.

"Introduce me to your brother, Talen," I say as I stand next to my true mate.

None of the men move, and I feel all at once a mass imprinting binding me to these men in a new way. Fang imprints as a brother, soul-deep. Now I understand Brooke's easy acceptance of Talen.

The men were imprinted as a community dedicated to

serving me. I feel wholly uncomfortable and have no choice about this imprinting business. These men want to worship me, and I do not want any of it.

As soon as the moment passes, I feel the tether retreat and silently plead for Talen to help with my eyes. I need to escape this odd encounter. I wish Brooke were here because she typically handles weird social moments for me.

"Fang, please stand," Talen insists.

Fang stands, looking goofy with gray ash coating him.

"Fang, this is my mate, Kayla, our Dragon Queen."

Fang takes a tentative step closer, and I try not to flinch away. I'm not being ambushed with an invasion of unwanted emotions, but I still want to keep my distance. I am raw after being bonded to all these men.

Thankfully, although I do feel his astonishment, it is subtle. I take a calming breath, trying to be encouraging. Fang eyes me up and down and stares with disbelief.

When Fang makes eye contact with me, it feels like family warmth. It lets me know in my soul that Fang is my family. Fang sinks to his knees again, with his hand fisted over his heart as he vows allegiance to me. The men follow his lead and vow the same.

"Talen?" I ask him for help. "Please make it stop." I step back and feel myself panic. "I don't want to be worshiped. I am naturally introverted, so all this attention is uncomfortable."

My armband warms up, and I can sense Brook and the girls sending me love and calming energy. *Nice!* I feel my anxiety settle a bit. I glance around at all the men on their knees, giving me loyalty.

"Thanks," I say because I don't know what else to say.

Talen breaks the tension with his booming laughter.

"Time to celebrate, brother. Rise, men, rise."

The men hoot and holler in cheers. Talen gives his twin brother a bear hug.

"Come, brother, spend time with my family."

Thankfully, Talen can lead the men through the shield because I sure don't want that job. The men wash up in the stream by the meadow and gather around a fire. I keep my distance. I feel too overwhelmed by so many strangers. I move off the side, sink my hands in the soil, and connect to nature. Understanding the cries for healing, I begin to send out my magic and feel the gratitude grow and the pain ebb as the natural balance of nature mends itself.

Men gather fallen pine tree limbs and bring the "good wood" to Talen and Fang, or so one of the men informs me as he shows off his pick of the excellent wood.

"The trees give limbs for newborns. Our kind builds cradles with enchanted wood. The trees whisper ancient lullabies and give the babies peaceful dreams," Talen explains as Fang sorts through the wood to start making cradles.

"It is a tradition we rarely have the opportunity to embrace these days because births are now so rare. "We take care of nature, and she takes care to nurture us in return. When the balance was healthy, life flourished here. Newborn life was joyful. Even the trees wanted to cradle the infants, creating a bond at birth that built symmetry between the flow of energy in the element and the souls that cultivated that energy."

"This is right up Brooke's alley. She would love this tree stuff," I say, wishing my sister would get her ass outside and face all this with me. *Little Miss Goes-ith-the-low being all cowardly now.* I send my sister a mental image of me sticking my tongue out at her.

I feel her send it right back. "Brat!" I say to the sky, hoping she can feel that too. An image of Brooke rolling her eyes at me like a sassy Tinkerbell flashes into my mind.

"I have had my fill of being social for the day." I lean into Talen for a kiss.

"I will walk with you back to the hall," Talen offers.

"No, it's okay. I need to have a chat with Brooke and feed my girls. Maybe I can get her to bring you some food," I say, encouraging him to stay with his brother. I wink at Talen when he is hesitant to stay behind.

"I need a minute with her myself," I assure him.

Fang stares up from carving a piece of good wood.

"Tell your sister I look forward to meeting her."

I shrug and look at Talen. "If he only knew," I whisper.

"I am sure she will be happy to meet you too," I say louder, knowing Fang and Brooke will imprint the moment they meet.

I leave Talen with Fang and his men as they carve the magic wood. How amazing is it for the trees to give so much and become something to soothe babies? Brooke is going to love this.

# CHAPTER 17

## Brooke

I'm on my bed chanting, trying to resist my desire to find Talen's twin. I have been trying to settle into the way things are here, but everything happening is so much. Everything is moving too fast. I feel like I am losing myself. I focus on keeping a solid wall up and giving myself time. My spine stiffens when I hear Kayla enter and walk to the babies.

"Brooke, are you going to be okay?" Kayla asks, worried.

"It's one thing watching you go through it, but I am just not ready, Kayla," I plead.

"Ready or not, he's your mate. It is so weird saying mate or true mate. Why don't they say boyfriend or husband here? We both know he is yours, no matter the title. I don't know how you are able to chant. I felt ill and broken when I couldn't get to Talen."

Kayla stares at me in the bedroom.

"You think I don't feel broken? I am so sick with anxiety, but I am just not ready to be some stranger's wife." With trembling lips and tear-rimmed eyes, I stare into Kayla's eyes and acknowledge my truth.

"I wasn't expecting it. I was adjusting to Talen being a part of our path, and now that guy too?"

"Fang," Kayla says, clarifying his name for me.

My gut clenches with need, and a ringing in my ears drives a consuming desire to seek out Fang. Kayla continues speaking.

"Brooke, you have to accept that this is not Earth. We are who the goddess has handpicked. We are dragons now. You have all the magic in you, real magic. I know you are fighting, keeping your walls up." Kayla is ever concerned for me.

"Please, I need you. We need you. Tonight was the first time I got anxious, and you bailed on me. This is not the Brooke I know. You are hiding when you need to trust your intuition to guide you. You can't fall apart on me now. I know once you accept things, you will be happier than you ever could have imagined, and I want that for you."

"You make it seem so easy," I snap a little too harshly. "I felt your struggle tonight, but I cannot help even myself right now, Kayla. I am not able to help you. All I want to do is find that Fang man. But that need is not my own. My mind says getting married to that man is stupid. I don't know him. Married at first sight is stupid, Kayla!" Fear escalates my anger toward Kayla. I'm taking out my roiling emotions on my friend. Kayla rushes to me and gives me a bear hug.

"Brooke, sweetie, you're changing. See?"

Kayla points to my red scales. I taste sulfur. I see myself in the mirror and I have grown. I realize I need to calm down.

"It's okay. I am here, Brooke. I'm here." Kayla soothes me.

I hug my leathery scales and feel her send me a wave of comfort and love.

"I got you. You are not alone." Kayla tries to comfort me.

"I know you are so scared. I know you felt nature take over, but you can adjust, and you will be happy if you just let it." Kayla holds me as I become my human self again.

Deep down, I know she's right. But what if nature made a mistake and this Fang guy is awful?

"Kayla, what if Fang is a terrible husband?" Kayla squeezes me tighter in her hug.

"Then I will roast him with my new dragon flame," she says. Kayla pulls back to make eye contact with me. "Brooke, try, and if you hate him and this whole true mate thing, I will find a way to save you from it. I don't care if the gods demand a marriage. I will figure it out and fight for what you need." Kayla's eyes tell me she means it too.

"Seriously?" I ask.

"I pinky promise." Kayla holds her hand up, extending her pinky to me.

"I will always be here for you, Brooke. I am here for you now. I feel like you are in for a surprise. You will love this new chapter as a wife or true mate as they say here, and you are a badass dragon queen now too."

I feel reassured that Kayla will have my back if I don't dig this Fang guy. I got a glimpse of him, and even though he looked like Talen, I felt attraction so fast and deep that I ran. I wonder if having a moment to prepare for meeting Fang will give me a rational ground to stand on so I can see if he is worthy of having me.

Kayla and I gather pitchers of water to offer the men. We haul them with ladle spoons so they can drink. We approach them, and instantly a man takes our burden from us. He carries the water to offer to the men around the fire.

"We thought you might be thirsty," I offer as the men take turns drinking. I smile, looking radiant in my red dress with my blonde locks. Kayla convinced me only to wear one string of pearls for tonight.

"This is my sister, Brooke," Kayla announces.

Surprise, surprise! The men fall to their knees.

"I don't think they can help themselves," Kayla says as she waves her hands in the air in aggravation.

I don't notice the men or pay much attention to Kayla.

My eyes are locked onto Fang's. Talen grabs Kayla's hand and moves her back into the shadows.

Fang and I both stare at each other. Fang still stands on the other side of the firepit between us. He is staring at me while all the men bow low to the ground. Fang's eyes smolder. The fire gives him a sexy glow as shadows flicker in tune with the flame.

A breeze picks up, and I feel my red dress blow around my legs. I want to speak, but I am not sure if I can concentrate on words when my body and soul feel the threads of my core connect to Fang and twist together.

"Hi, Fang," is about all I can muster.

Fang stalks around the fire, heading straight to me. I see his eyes, and he holds me captive with his hungry gaze. Talen and Fang are twins. But I only have lustful eyes for Fang.

Fang slowly reaches for my face. I snuggle my cheek into his palm, and he leans in to kiss me. I grab Fang's face and kiss him hard. A primal need to have Fang replaces all my anxiety from earlier.

I feel like the world around me has disappeared. Any worry I have melts away, and I am consumed with need. Fang smells smoky and all man. His lips start a frenzy in me, a whirlwind of lust. I wrap my legs around his waist, and Fang runs off into the dark with me.

I feel the heat of Fang and smell his wild scent of mountain and pine and ash. I lick his neck because I have to taste him. Fang jolts in his steady run and slows. He growls a sexy sound as he holds me up and places me against a giant tree.

The world fades away around us, and the roughness of the tree bark only spikes my desire. I rub my core against his stiff shaft, hating the material barrier between us.

"Please!" I beg with relentless kisses, peppering him wherever my mouth can land on skin.

Intoxicated, I can't describe this need in me. Fang peels my legs from around his waist, and I feel shaky and unsteady as

I stand in front of him. Fang takes a few steps back, shaking his head.

As he comes out of his haze, I feel a need inside me to dominate. I shove off the tree and walk a seductive circle around Fang. He turns, watching me as I close an invisible lasso around him three times. I make a sacred circle and step inside it to take my soulmate.

"You belong to me now." I use my finger to point to the ground, a silent demand he lay down on his back for me.

Fang's whole body reacts to my need. I feel so seductive and strong. My body grows hot, and my nipples pebble against my dress, creating a delicious ache.

"My mate." Fang nods his head slightly, not breaking eye contact. "Do with me as you please." He holds his arms out in total surrender.

"As I please," I state with a sultry voice. I take his face in my hands, lean down, and kiss him.

Fang stands with my kiss, and I take his shirt off. I grip his hair and kiss him deeply, letting my tongue absorb his taste and essence.

Fang tears his pants off, not breaking his kiss with me. I reach down to grab his engorged length. I gasp at the feel of his girth and size. He growls in pleasure and hisses as he maneuvers my hand to his shoulder instead. He sinks to his knees, pulling my legs up and over his shoulders.

He holds me up by my ass. I moan in bliss as he devours my core, sucking on my clit and rolling his tongue, teasing and exploring my pussy.

"Oh God, you feel so fucking good." I moan as I grip his long braided hair.

He holds me up with one arm and uses his fingers to enter me, stretching and working until I crash over the edge with a crescendo of bliss.

"That's it, my Queen, come for me just like that." He demands in a deep smoldering voice.

He allows me to sink to the ground with him. He lies back and moves me to straddle him.

"You feel too damn good," I say as I slowly kiss him from his mouth to his chest and sink onto his giant, stiff shaft. I feel him stretch me even more than I thought possible when I have him fully sheathed inside me.

"Fuck!" He moans.

I lose any sense of the world around me as thoughts of slow lovemaking vanish. I move hard and frantically. Fang keeps pace and is wild in passion when he takes over, flipping me to lie with my back on the ground.

The pine needles, leaves, and dirt at my back make the moment raw and intense. I come again as he roars my name while he spills his seed inside me.

"Mine!" I declare as I bite down on his shoulder. The copper taste of blood fills my mouth as I claim Fang, making him mine.

"Mine!" Fang growls as he takes my bite.

I sense his wolf and his dormant dragon stirs enough to show me he is there.

We break away from each other just enough so he can stare down at me with love in his eyes. We pant together, and I lick his chest to bask in the aftermath with a delighted smile. This is the best moment of my life.

Fang kisses me passionately, the taste of us mingles in my mouth. I feel a spear stab my thigh and see the pain in Fang's expression when he breaks away from my lips. He tries to roll off of me, and I scream in pain, rage replacing the beautiful moment with terror.

# CHAPTER 10

## Kayla

I face Talen. "You didn't even warn him, did you?"

Talen laughs. "Where's the fun in that?" he says.

Talen sits me next to him to show me the cradle he and Fang are making from the magic pine.

"Oh, how beautiful," I say as I admire the work and carvings in the small cradle. Running my hands over it, I feel soothed by the trees.

"Amazing," I say in awe.

"It's a tradition, an ancient one. I am honored to bring it back," Talen says, proud of his work. He shows me a carved wolf that is howling.

"I made this, too, for the girls."

"This is stunning." I admire the craftiness and am shocked at how fast these guys work and that Talen has created these gifts for the babies. Something inside melts. I grab Talen's hand and take him back to my room.

"I think we need a long shower together," I suggest.

"A long one," Talen agrees with hungry eyes.

I have the urge to try something a little more aggressive. Maybe I can encourage Talen to explore that with me. As Talen and I enter the bedroom, he blows off all the sawdust from his wolf carving and lays the good wood next to the sleeping babies on the basket. They are safely sleeping in the center of my bed.

Talen leans down and kisses the babies as they sleep.

"Sweet dreams, little ones." The wolf hums a sweet lullaby, and the crystal lights chime in tune with a low blue pulsing glow.

"This does feel soothing," I say in amazement at the magic on this planet.

I take Talen's hands, and we go into the shower. I am just about to chat about discovering a kinky side to lovemaking when my armband lights up in a burning fire of pain. I hear my babies cry out in pain too.

My knees hit the floor as my blue scales appear, and smoke streams out of my nose and mouth. Sulfur fills the small space.

"It's Brooke!" I growl, sounding animalistic as I force myself to breathe and stand up.

I walk into the bedroom toward my crying babies. I barely notice their pink scales and the steam coming from them before Talen grabs them both and holds them close to trying to soothe them. I trust Talen with my girls and take off running toward the exit to save Brooke.

I hear Talen's howl of warning to his men as I run through the forest, past the shield, wholly focused on Brooke. The moment I clear the shield, I transform into my dragon. This time I take flight, searching for my sister.

Above the thick canopy of trees, the night sky is starry, and the crystal platforms glow with soft colors. I have to dodge one to avoid crashing into it. I fly in circles, trying to find Brooke. I swoop down when I sense Brooke through some trees below, crashing hard into the dense trees.

Brooke stands defensively over Fang as he lies up against a tree trunk, naked and unconscious. Brooke is naked too.

Her red scales are prominent, and her thigh is bleeding badly. Steam steadily rolls out from Brooke's nostrils.

The sight of her like this has me furious. I blow a puff of fire and light up the dark in front of Brooke and Fang.

A group of things stands there, holding spears. There is a female that screams like a banshee at us. Black ooze spills out of her mouth, and her eyes are black orbs. The males stand with their spears ready for an attack.

I step in front of my sister and her new mate. I roar and blow my flame at the evil creatures in front of me. The ones that do not disintegrate scatter, and the battle is on.

The males are just as foul as the screaming female here. Blackness stains their mouths. They have skeletal-looking features and a smell of rot. Evil energy tries to suffocate me. My anger has the dragon in me let loose my fire in a steady stream. These fools think they are mean with their zombie bears trying to attack me. I think I'm meaner.

A monster zombie bear runs at me, storming through the evil people. He knocks the screaming evil female on her ass. He jumps at me, and while I blow fire at him. As he's in midair, the beast disintegrates.

Another zombie bear comes at me from the side. I flick it with my tail and blow more fire. He becomes a firebomb, taking out more black-oozing males like a blazing bowling ball striking down my prey.

These mutated monster bears resemble the ones that attacked Talen. I have a special hate reserved for them. I have wanted to destroy them all. In the light of my fire, I see fear enter the faces of the evil people in front of me. If my dragon could smile wickedly at them, I would. Instead, I show my teeth, and they turn away in defeated retreat.

Brooke's red dragon joins me. We blow fire, disintegrating the trees, with the evil things running away. Brooke grabs Fang in her talons and flies off, leaving me to the rest of the fight.

*"The men from home are almost there to join you,"* Brooke tells me through our mental bond.

*"Take care of Fang. I got this,"* I respond as I whip my tail out to throw a berserker zombie bear into a tree.

I bite down on that screaming siren bitch to cut her in half. I blow fire to get the black acid rot out of my mouth.

As the evil female is eliminated, Talen's men come to battle. Whatever threats are left breathing, manage to run away scared at this point.

I have already eliminated most of those gross bastards. Once I feel Brooke is safely back home, I transform into my feminine skin form. I am still blue, but my temper is calming.

I stand naked in the ember of my fire and ash. I feel the trees cry at my burning them again. I kneel and put my hands on the ground to send healing energy. I hate that my fire hurt them. My magic puts the fire out, and the trees send me a thank you. I want to hug them and say I am sorry for causing them harm.

A man offers me his shirt. I gratefully take it and put it on. The shirt hangs to my knees. *Are all of these men made big and tall?* I try to understand what I just did as a dragon. I have a stray thought about being in front of strangers, and am not upset about it. I am not sensing anything lustful coming from these men. I only feel a need to fight and protect myself.

The men send scouts to follow the retreating attackers. Most of them gallantly surround me to protect me. I laugh internally, thinking it's sweet of them, but I am feeling invincible and know I will protect them if a battle begins again.

I am not the same as I was on Earth. As men surround me, trying to protect me from further threats, I feel like a genuine badass.

We march our way back to the hall, where Talen makes his way through his men to get to my side. I feel relieved to see him. Then I feel an instant worry.

"Where are the girls?"

Talen inspects me for any sign of injury. He pulls me in for a tight hug when he is assured that I am well.

"The girls?" I ask again.

"I left them with a worthy warrior to be their guardian."

I feel uneasy that my daughters were left with someone other than Talen or Brooke. My blue scales appear as I try to calm my nerves. I send my girl soothing love through our armbands.

We safely return to the hall, and two men guard the door. They bow their heads silently and step aside so Talen and I can enter.

I sprint to the bedroom, where I see a giant man pacing back and forth, rocking Hope and Faith. My girls seem content with the huge warrior. I feel pride and honor coming from the man. He is dedicated to his duty to guard my babies.

"This is Barron." Talen introduces me to the warrior.

"Thank you for keeping my girls safe. It is nice to meet you, Barron," I say as my anxiety melts a bit after meeting Barron.

I feel his energy and accept that he would give his life for my children.

"Can you stay a bit longer?" I ask.

"I am at your command. Whatever you need, my Queen," Barron offers proudly.

"Thank you, Barron. I need to help my sister and her boyfr- . . . mate," I say as I go into the bathroom.

I grab Talen's hand and take him with me.

"Oh, Brooke! Honey, how can I help?" I say, letting go of Talen and rushing into the shower, where Brooke is leaning over Fang.

Brooke is crying and trying to clean a wound on Fang's head. Blood falls from a significant stab wound on Brooke's red-scaled thigh.

"You're bleeding too!" I grab a towel and try to put pressure on Brooke's thigh.

"I don't care, Kayla. Save him!" Brooke snaps at me through her sobs.

"Get Balthazar!" Talen yells out the door.

Talen joins us in the shower and inspects his brother's head.

Another hulking of a man steps into the bathroom. "My king, I am here."

I gaze out of the shower at the huge man. Something is different about him. He doesn't have the same energy I feel from most of the men I have encountered. Balthazar has different eyes, too—dark brown, no slit. I sense his eagerness to help.

"We need to give Balthazar room to examine Fang. Balthazar is a shiften. He is a healer," Talen says as he urges Brooke and me to move out of the shower.

I grab Brooke's hand and send support, trying to get Brooke to follow me out of the spray of water. The man Balthazar steps into the shower, leans down, picks Fang up, and lays him on the bathroom floor.

Balthazar kneels next to Fang's unconscious body. He rubs his hands together, then places his hands on Fang's head, and a warm light glows outward from his hands as he chants softly.

Brooke cries as she picks up on Balthazar's chanting and adds her chanting to the healing process. Fang snaps his eyes open and sits up straight.

"Brooke!" he roars, looking around frantically. At that moment, Brooke faints from her blood loss.

"Shit!" I cry out as I catch my sister before she falls.

Fang is there in an instant, taking her from my arms.

"Healer!" he roars, turning toward Balthazar.

Fang is angry and scared as he holds Brooke out to Balthazar. The huge shifter man's eyes are wide with shock.

"I did not know she was injured, or I would have healed her first," he states as he repeats his healing magic over the stab wound in Brooke's thigh. He stops his chanting.

"She needs blood." He eyes me.

"Take mine!" I offer, holding out my arm.

The giant man grabs my wrist. He has one glowing hand on my wrist and the other over Brooke's wound. I feel dizzy as my blood magically leaves me.

The healer uses his magic to take my blood and put it into Brooke's body. I sway with relief when Brooke opens her eyes and locks her gaze with her mate. Fang is still bleeding from the bite mark on his shoulder. Brooke leans in and kisses Fang tenderly.

I become aware of my wet shirt as I notice Brooke and Fang's nakedness. Why does all this seem normal? Talen thanks Balthazar as a blush creeps into my face, and my ears burn with embarrassment.

On wobbly legs, I grab a robe when Talen picks me up and takes me to my bed. The men leave, shutting Brooke and Fang in the bathroom together to collect themselves.

# The Vampire

"A blue and a red dragon?" I ask with deceptive calm. My temper is about to explode beneath the surface.

"Yes, Sire. She easily killed the sirens and all the beasts," my minion replies. I caress the mutated face of my creation lovingly.

"You're excused," I say with a wave of my hand.

"Yes, sir, as you wish."

I turn my back on my minion, so he will not see the rage in my eyes.

"Wake the warlock!" I command as my creature leaves my space.

I will venture down to the caves to taunt the warlock and discover how a dragon queen exists again.

I am powerful, a god on this planet. This world is mine. These gullible creatures are ripe for the picking, and I will not lose my reign to the dragon kingdom. Dragons are supposed to be extinct.

My thoughts go back to a time when I was a mere human.

My mother was a skank. She fell out of a tree and hit her

head as a teenager. She hit her head so badly that she was never right again.

She managed to marry a cop and had six kids in the fifties. That woman should have died in that fall, never birthing any of us. We would have all been better off never born, crazy bitch!

Then she cheated on the cop and got pregnant with me. The cop hated me, a boy that was never his, and he knew it. He died on the job. Shot dead. Good riddance!

My mother was schizophrenic and always saw demons or thought she was a holy healer like Jesus, laying hands on people with her delusions. She always swore I was a demon, throwing holy water at me and waving her Bible like a shield against me.

After his death, the government took us kids and placed us at an orphanage in the city run by nuns. My brothers all got adopted, but I was left behind. The nuns beat me with rulers and made me eat expired canned spinach as punishment.

They had me kneel with bare knees on raw rice while holding bricks out straight in front of me, and they would lash me when my arms fell. Those holy bitches tried to impose their will over me. If I had my god power, I would have enslaved them all and made them my minions.

I ran away at thirteen and ran the sidewalks of the windy city. One day I got a job with a mob boss running packages through the alleyways. I worked my way up, and this is what I thrived at.

I was a hitman, on call as needed. My first kill order had me take out the family of a man that stole a load of money from my boss. Good riddance. The man's utter terror as I killed his wife and kids in front of him was thrilling.

My euphoric moment was interrupted when a god took me away and zapped me right off Earth into a between dimension.

"You have an evil soul," the god said as he evaluated me.

I felt like a fly stuck on a sticky strip. That arrogant ass of a god judged me disdainfully.

"I would normally smite the likes of you. However, I have need of a villain like yourself to correct a wrong," the god said.

With a wave of his hand, he made me the vampire I am today.

"I made you what you are now, and you are the only creature that can kill Lilith. I need you to assassinate her swiftly so I can rid this place of Lucifer."

Power enveloped me, and I had the compulsion to hunt. Acid burned my throat. All I wanted was this Lilith's blood.

"I made you in the likeness of a creature that was made long ago. Know this: you are only a tool to me. You are not deserving to be a vampire; you are a mutated version." The god held me in an invisible sphere.

I was like a bug under a microscope, burning for blood.

"I am Hecat. My power is grand. The great creator cannot see how grand I am when he focuses so much on this insignificant Earth and Lucifer. I will have this small intervention and rid the world of that demanding brat Lucifer once and for all." The angry god declared.

"Unfortunately, Lilith is the key to my plan. She is his true mate and only vulnerability." A sad expression crossed the mighty God's eyes, just a glimmer before he glared at me.

The god Hecat ranted out loud, not caring if I understood. He waved his hand, and I was zapped to hell to devour Lilith. My programming had me zero in on my prey. The moment I caught her scent, the scariest son of bitch I ever saw appeared in front of me.

An angry Lucifer evaluated me with disgust. I could tell he fought his desire to destroy me. I was feral, hissing and trying to break free of the invisible hole he kept me captive in.

"A declaration of war, Hecat." The devil seethed through clenched teeth as he smoldered in rage.

"Let me return the favor and see how you like it," the devil said to Hecat through the veil as he waved his hand and sent me here to Harmony's planet.

I was a pawn in the antics of those heavenly gods. I've been a pawn my whole human life. They made a mistake sending me here. I am a pawn no more. Here, I am a god. These beings and their magic and goodness were too quickly conquered. Here, I am immortal and have my way in everything I desire.

Whatever the devil has planned, I do not care. I should thank him because I am god here and will also conquer these dragon queens. I will harvest their powerful blood and continue my reign.

Shaking off ancient memories, I reach for my pet inside the dirt wall. The warlock, encased in mud forever, stands before me now. I love taunting him.

# CHAPTER 19

## Kayla

The next night, Brooke and I walk to the fire in the meadow to meet up with our men.

"We need to send a messenger and scouts to the kingdom," Talen suggests as Fang finishes his mead by the fire.

"Yes. We need to get the queens to the safety of their thrones," Fang agrees.

"It will be dangerous to travel with the young ones." Talen voices his fear. He wants to protect his daughters and the precious female dragons.

"The vampire will come. It's better to be in the fortress of the kingdom than out here in the remote borders of our land," Fang insists.

"He's a superior strategist, always using the best maneuvers to defend our kingdom," Talon says to a male next to him.

"We have hundreds of men, and we have two full-grown dragons," Talen reminds Fang, trying to rationalize standing our ground here in the hall.

"Every instinct I have tells me to move them to the kingdom, Talen," Fang says firmly.

"I feel it too, brother," Talen agrees reluctantly. He feels in his core that we need to move, but he second-guesses it, wanting to protect his family.

"We need to convince our mates," he says.

"Convince us of what?" I ask, overhearing their conversation.

I am getting a sense of their feelings. I walk up to them with food in hand.

"We need to talk to you and Brooke," Talen says. He stares up into my suspicious gaze.

We hand each man an offering of food. They both stand, graciously taking the treat. Talen urges us toward the grand hall.

"Time for a family meeting," Talen says through a mouthful.

Brooke watches me, and we hear the men tell us their plan to move us to the kingdom's palace. Hope and Faith are fussy and need to be fed. I have them swaddled in blankets of animated Disney characters. Clothing dispensary magic is my favorite magic here.

I giggle as I explain Disney princesses to Fang and Talen while they admire the finned, redheaded Ariel. They insist the cartoon girl does not accurately resemble a water dweller. Brooke and I enjoy our appreciation for something from Earth.

We redirect ourselves back to the issue at hand. Should we attempt to travel with the girls to the castle?

Brooke holds my hand, circling her fingers three times. She uses our armbands to amplify our ability to seek direction.

"We feel our intuition urging us to move as well," I say, speaking for Brooke.

"Let us talk strategy. We need to prepare." Fang explains his plan and the safety measures he wants to take for our family.

I stare down at my girls as they feed and are simply enjoying this moment of happiness. I sit there with my family. A true family. The foster kid I used to be was stuck in the system of hell. Those days seem worlds away.

I see the twinkling crystal lights and send the goddess Harmony my prayer of thanks. *Please keep us safe as we travel,* I send a silent thought to Harmony.

Brooke pulls out a chest full of extravagant medallions hung on thick gold chains. The pendant is a dragon crest depicting the same symbol on the mosaic tile in the bathroom. Brooke is so proud of her find.

"Kayla. We can give the men these as special thanks for protecting us." Brooke bounces with excitement, making her beads clash in tune with her movements.

"I agree. It is the least we can do." I love how childlike Brooke can sometimes be.

We are sending five men ahead with a message sealed with the dragon crest. The orders were to ready the kingdom and gather more soldiers.

Talen turns to me. "Are you ready to give this grand gift to the men?"

I smile. "This is all, Brooke. She will have a blast issuing these."

As I step back, Brooke stands next to Fang. I am rocking Hope while Talen holds Faith. Brooke is stunning with her beads and red dress. Fang places the oversized chest in front of her. All the men stand at attention, waiting to discover why we rallied them here.

"All of you men are worthy warriors. My sister and I want to ask if you will become our special service warriors," Brooke asks.

Fang then announces, "You are being offered the position of the elite royal guard of the dragon queens."

Brooke's beads bounce as she bends to open the chest of medallions. The men fall to their knees at once. I laugh.

"Of course, they start kneeling again," I say sarcastically to Talen.

Fang directs the men to line up as Brooke places a sacred dragon-crested medallion over each of their heads. Brooke thanks them for their service.

I feel the warriors' morale soar as their energy grows with their honor and pride. I am so glad Brooke thrives in this area. I like taking to the sidelines and being a spectator instead of an announcer.

After the ceremony, the men get ready to leave. Brooke and I stand in the meadow, trying to transform at will into our dragon form. The most I can conjure up is my blue scales and a little steam.

"Aww, come on, Harmony," I say moodily as I can't get my body to change.

"Stop! Kayla, you might make her angry."

"So what?" I say. "She did this to us with no clear explanation. Now we are supposed to travel with babies while that evil vampire is out there." I sigh.

"I only want to keep them safe. We should be able to change at will." I know my irritation is because I am worried about leaving the protective shield.

Brooke sits cross-legged and starts her chant, hoping the universe will help her figure out how to unlock the dragon.

"Ignore my rant. Fine, I give up for the day," I say. I stomp off, leaving her to the universe and her ritual. I go to find Talen and the girls.

Most of the men have changed into their beast form, and many of them are wolves. Fang is securing the cradle they made to the back of a giant bear. It turned out beautifully, and it's my new favorite possession.

The song it hums is a constant soothing lullaby from nature. Talen is rocking both girls in his arms, cooing at them. The sight of him fathering our babies melts away my current frazzled feelings.

I take a moment to absorb how surreal the scene is in front of me. It is unlike Earth; with werewolves, werebears, and shifters, the magic of this planet is just amazing. I walk up to Barron, the girls' guard—the giant bear with the cradle saddled to his back.

"Thank you for carrying my girls, Barron," I say as I scratch his neck, feeling new freedom, not getting ambushed by crazy emotions like I was on Earth.

I feel a knocking for a mental push and realize the energy is Barron. I accept the tether mentally.

"*It is my honor, my queen,*" Barron says inside my head. I feel his genuine happiness to be guarding my daughters and serving me.

I am grateful Barron has linked with my mind so I can check on my girls at will. I am grateful for so much now that my life is here in Harmony.

Talen hands me Faith as we walk back to the hall together. I want to get whatever I can from my Harmony delivery door since Talen says my door is the only one on the planet. I am going to miss my instant Starbucks and In-N-Out animal-style cheeseburgers.

"We are going on an adventure," I softly say to my sleeping girls as I kiss their foreheads, tucking them securely in the cradle to sleep while Barron carries them on his back.

A giant moose with majestic antlers walks next to Barron's right side. It is the healer shiften Balthazar who is carrying my packed goods on his giant back. He winks at me with his moose eye.

It's a funny thing to see. I feel a familiar nudging knocking in my mind. I know it is Balthazar.

"*My queen, I will walk near your girls. They will be protected.*"

He's reassuring me that he is devoted to my family's safety. I don't know why the goddess chose me, but this new world feels much better than Earth. People here don't suck. The only horror I have felt here so far has been with the vampire creatures.

There is purity in the essential core of the people here. Maybe it's the ability to communicate with both words and energy magically. There's an honor code in life here, a need for nurturing and love. Life has respect, a balance of give and take that's lacking on Earth.

Talen kisses the girls and places the wolf carving he made in the cradle, adding even more soothing songs from the enchanted wood.

I look into his gorgeous purple predator eyes, and he pulls me close for a deep kiss. Oh, how I needed this kiss. My face turns hot when we break apart to come up for air. A warrior was patiently waiting on us to finish.

"Kayla, my love, this is Hudson. He's a wolf of the Dragon line. I have asked him to join our daughter's guardian squad. He is one of my best men and my friend."

"Nice to meet you, Hudson. Thank you for protecting my babies," I say with a blush.

"I will give my life to protect them and you, my queen. You have my allegiance."

I feel his loyalty to my bones. Talen nods his head in acknowledgment to Hudson, dismissing him to his duties. Hudson seems to be high-ranking as he turns to give out orders, organizing the march and positioning specific warriors around us.

The "royal family." Funny, I don't feel royal. I feel a bit overwhelmed by all this. I don't like the attention and title, but I like being here around these pure people.

"We will need to camp soon. There is a mountain pass that will be the most dangerous terrain for us to travel through on our way to the kingdom. It's icy, and we have to navigate a narrow rock trail to get to the other side," Talen explains to me and Brooke, who at this point really hates that we can't change into dragons whenever we want to. Traveling like pioneers is not as cool as *The Lord of the Rings* made it out to be in the movies.

# CHAPTER 20

## Kayla

I'm sore from walking and sore from riding Talen's wolf form. He is the size of a horse when in that form. But it's not at all like horseback riding. Now I'm cold as we travel higher up the mountain. These men have stamina and want to go, go, go. I'm just irritated, sore, and cold.

*"It's best if Fang and I hold the girls when we get to that point,"* Talen suggests in his wolf form.

*"We will not let harm come to them."* Fang assures me.

Brooke and I glance over at my sleeping babies cocooned in the cradle on Barron's back.

"At least they are safe and comfortably warm," I say through chattering teeth, thankful for the good wood and its magic, as it helps to keep my daughters warm and sleepy.

We make it to the base of a towering snow-capped mountain where we finally set up camp. I cuddle up with my twin babies. Talen has made us a tent with a pallet inside. This is another magically infused thing, alien material, lightweight but completely blocking most of the cold. The pallet is made with thick faux furs blocking the cold and wind.

The giant warriors assigned to be guarding the girls take their job seriously. They lie alongside the outside of the tent in fur form. Their bodies help heat the inside. Brooke lies on the other side of my girls. We snuggle up, warm and exhausted, and fall fast asleep.

Fang wakes us up with hot coffee in hand.

"You know exactly how to wake a lady." Brooke rewards him with a tender kiss.

"Good morning, handsome." She smiles at him as she brings the mug up to her lips.

"Good morning, my queen," he growls soft and sweetly.

I feed, change, and re-dress the babies in little purple baby jacket suits, mittens, and hats. They give me gummy grins. I am just so pleased they are safe and genuinely happy. I drink my coffee, even though it has cooled down by the time I get the babies settled.

Talen gives me a kiss that sets off butterflies in me. I only want to get somewhere safe and warm to show him how much he affects me. Talen holds my hand as the wind picks up and snow begins to fall.

Within the snowstorm, we trudge our way along a path that gets smaller and more uncomfortably cold. I thought of a trail to walk on. I know he said ledge, but I am thinking of Washington and the nice walking trails there.

This is insane! Talen abruptly stops and turns to me, reaching to take the baby and giving me a view of the cliff ledge we are about to climb. It is an even smaller ledge. A foothold is more accurate.

"You have to be out of your minds!" I snap as Brooke holds the other baby tight.

Luckily, we can burrow our way into a small cave there right before we step on an icy ledge. The men expect us to rock climb our way across this mountain with infants.

"I thought you meant there would be a passable trail. This is like cliff climbing. You are *nuts*!" I yell.

I give Brooke Hope, too, so I can stand in front of Brooke and my girls. Steam bellows out of my nose and mouth. I know I am turning blue.

Talen stands at the mouth of the cave's opening. Ice and snow whipped around his head. Blizzard winds cover him in a layer of white.

"I promise safe passage," he hollers over the raging winds.

He reaches out, waiting for me to hand him one of my babies. Brooke and I just glare at him angrily. I don't move an inch to deliver my girls to him or Fang.

"Like hell!" Brooke yells.

Her smoke clouds the air, red scales starting to tint her face as she turns around, using her back to block the men from my girls.

I reach back with one hand to grab ahold of Brooke, focusing on using our bond and the added influence of the babies' powers. I reach for a sense of direction. I'm trying to call my dragon, begging her to come fully forth.

Brooke does her finger-circle thing three times on the back of the cave wall.

I feel energy wash over us. The frozen rock wall Brooke is touching transforms into a door that swings inward to open. I catch Brooke as she loses balance at the unexpected movement. She stumbles, gripping the girls in her arms securely.

We step through the archway of the magic door. I move deeper inside and see unique bridges and pathways carved into the hollowed mountain. Crystal spheres of light softly light everything up.

"If Gandalf pops out and screams, 'You shall not pass,' I swear I will shit my pants right here," I say.

Brooke laughs at me.

"You're so silly, Kayla."

The magic crystals light up the walkway in a warm invitation.

It's a beautiful moonlight glow. A six-foot wide, three-foot-thick rock bridge seems to be carved out. Pathways weave throughout. The hollowed mountain is breathtaking. I go to the pathway that leads up.

"Yeah, I can see the elven flair to this place. But I think we shall pass," Brooke says, making fun of me as she taps a glowing crystal placed on a carved-out handrail.

Everything has an elven style woven into its design. Brooke giggles.

"I don't feel a threat," I say as the men shake off the snow, entering the doorway behind us.

Talen steps up behind me and wraps me in a hug. He leans into my ear.

"You are truly amazing, my fierce dragon."

Fang takes Hope from Brooke and hands her to me. My anxiety calms down now that we aren't going to rock climb with babies.

"I am still upset with you two," I say.

The two men are somber when Talen speaks.

"My heart, I promise, Fang and I would never let harm come to you or our children."

"I don't care about your promises. Don't ever take our kids on some dangerous path like that again," I snap back.

Talen grabs my cheeks and gives me a soft, gentle kiss, whispering, "Whatever makes my mate happy."

"Why am I not surprised?" Talen says to Fang as he turns away from me and laughs. He slaps his brother's shoulder.

Barron, Hudson, and Balthazar take their skin form. They carry packs full of gear and position themselves behind Brooke and me while we hold the babies.

"This is going to take some getting used to," I say to Brooke, feeling my inner demons at the closeness of others. The men are respectful, and I sense they are sending me soothing vibes. But still, this is just a lot.

"I think it's adorable," Brooke says as she shakes her beads to entertain Faith in her arms.

"Of course, you do." I roll my eyes.

We follow Talen and Fang. Eventually, coming to a large enough platform to set up a camp. Hope and Faith looked up at the beautiful crystals hanging in rows above the platform. Lighting up with a prism of colors, it feels like a magical chandelier.

I lie down on the bed pallet to snuggle up with my babies. We gaze up in wonder, looking at the crystals.

"What is this place?" Brooke asks.

"It must be an ancient passageway from one side of the mountain to the other," Fang surmises.

"It's stunning," Brooke breathes out.

"You are stunning," Fang tells her as he kisses her romantically under the light show.

"This will open up a world of opportunity for our people to migrate to the remote side of this mountain in the future," Talen says as he thinks through plans.

"Well, it sure beats the suicide path you planned on taking my babies through." I say bitterly.

"I would never cause them harm, Kayla. I would have brought them safely across," Talen replies. "But I am thrilled you discovered this path instead." He seems proud of me for this discovery.

"There's no way I would have ever let you or Fang take them on that ledge. You'll never convince me it's safe," I say as I lay my sleeping girls down.

"I promise I will never attempt to travel that route with them again." Talen tries to appease me.

"Come here." He pulls me onto his lap.

"I might forgive you," I say, teasing him. He kisses me.

"What can I do to make it up to you?" he asks with a peppering of kisses.

Brooke and Fang take off to a secret passage to be alone. I unravel myself, getting up from Talen's lap, and I pull his hand. He stands and calls for Barron to watch over our sleeping girls.

I find a small crystal room. The feeling of magic encompassing this small room feels perfect. I take my mate and kiss him eagerly. I have discovered that my sweet Talen has a dominant side. We tend to trade off our dominant roles sexually, and I love how he takes over when I want him to.

"I have to have you, Talen. Right now."

Talen hisses out a breath as I grab his engorged cock, rubbing over his pants in invitation. He grabs me and kisses me with a fever as hot as mine. My whole body enlivens at his touch.

Those butterflies turn molten heat inside of me. He grabs a handful of my hair by the base of my head, which is the hottest, most dominant thing ever happening to me.

"Give me the alpha tonight, Talen. I need you. I need it a bit rough tonight." I kiss him with need, sending him my magic energy to trigger his dominant side.

Talen pushes me away from him and gives me an order in a low, seductive growl. "Turn around and grab the crystal wall." He stands behind me.

"Be as quiet as possible. Obey me, my queen," he leans into my ear and whispers.

*Oh yeah, this is what I need.* He nips my ear, and I suck in a breath with a gasp of need.

"Yes, sir," I reply in a whimpering moan.

"Face the wall and undress."

I obey. I can't get undressed fast enough. Standing back and looking at the softly lit array of colors highlighting the wall in front of me, I feel like a goddess—naked in front of magical crystals.

Talen undresses, watching me like I am the most beautiful woman in the world to him.

"You are stunning, my queen," he says in his low, sexy tone.

He moves my hair over my shoulder so he can kiss my neck. He grabs my face and makes me stare back at him so he can kiss me, his tongue diving between my plump lips, tasting me, tasting us together. My mouth has never known ambrosia like this before.

He breaks away from my lips to kiss my neck and nibble my ear. His sexy growl of pleasure shoots goosebumps across my arms as he trails kisses down my back. It builds my fire hotter and hotter.

"Stand still until I tell you to move." He reaches around me and feels my breasts, pinching my nipples, rolling them between his fingers with just the right amount of pressure coaxing my arousal to a peak.

I reach down behind me to grab him.

"Not yet, love. Hold the crystal until I tell you to let go." He places my hands on the glowing wall again.

I grip the protruding crystals like a handle. Their magic sends a jolt of desire, adding to my arousal as the colors start to pulse. The lights match the tune of my excited heartbeat. I moan in need.

"Good girl, just like that," he praises as he kisses his way down my back. He grabs my ass and stands.

"Mine!" He growls in my ear. He makes his way leisurely back down my body, driving me mad.

He reaches around and finds my folds, finally touching me where I need him most. He plays circles around my wet clit.

I moan. "There, yes, please! More, there."

He dips his fingers inside my hot channel. I am wet and so ready. He builds me up and up to my peak. When I am close, he pulls back.

"You will come when I tell you to."

I writhe, moving my ass against him, begging him to release me.

"You like my touch, and you respond so well. But I am just getting started, babe." He grabs my tits and gently squeezes them, his palms full of my breasts.

"Yes, anything you want. Please, Talen." I am so hot and ready. My need is burning me up. He is so fucking perfect.

I grip my crystal handles hard, and another magic jolt of

heat shoots through me. I move my ass back, arching into him to feel his hard cock press against me. He backs me away from the wall, moving me down on my knees. I kneel in front of him, still facing the wall.

"Bend over and spread yourself wide for me."

I obey, presenting myself to him. He lies down behind me and feasts on me, eating my pussy from underneath me.

I obediently keep my hand in front of me as he uses his fingers and tongue. I almost fall over the edge in a crescendo of ecstasy. His enchanted mouth is truly my favorite magic here.

"Talen, please," I beg, asking permission.

"Come for me now, Kayla," he demands, finally permitting me.

When his mouth sucks on my clit, I shatter, adding wetness to his face.

"That's my girl. Now you are ready for me." He grabs my hips and slides his huge, hard cock inside my wet, throbbing pussy.

"Perfect!" he growls as he pounds fast and hard. When he feels me crash again, squeezing him in a vise of liquid heat, he pulses, pumping his seed into me in waves of bliss.

The magic from the crystals and our combined orgasms makes us fall asleep, still entwined and in love.

# CHAPTER 21

## Brooke

The magic crystals are humming this morning, giving a soft melody throughout the camp, the universe sending affirmation that we are on the right path. The lighting all around us brightens.

Our souls feel the embrace of the mountain's womb, welcoming us with all the magical crystals. The chimes sound like chants, and I know the universe understands. As we pack up to continue our journey, everyone is happy.

"I think those crystals have healing qualities or something that fed into my magic," I mention as Kayla hands me a cup of coffee.

"I feel the same. It feels amazing," Kayla agrees. She glows this morning, and my heart is happy to see her genuinely in good spirits.

We travel at a leisurely pace, and eventually, we find another door that opens to a safe trail leading down toward the kingdom's stronghold, the castle on the mystic mountain.

Rounding a bend in the mountain, I get my first view of a

beautiful white castle nestled securely against a vast mountain. Fortified by sheer cliffs, waterfalls pour over the cliffs' sides, making mist billow up around the base of the castle's gated walls.

I see Kayla stiffen the moment she sees it. She would prefer the quiet in the woods over a castle with its little city feel. She glances my way, and I pretend not to notice her slight tell.

Looking down, it seems like a giant river cuts the two mountains, separating them as the river splashes into the ocean beyond the two mountains.

We travel toward a classic castle with rock walls and a lifted bridge at its gates, which is being lowered to allow passage from one mountain to the other. The castle gives off an aura of power.

"It's a fortress," I whisper in awe as I see how it sits, protected as part of the mountain and unreachable without passing over the drawbridge.

Fang reaches for my hand. He seems happy to be bringing me home. Sentinels stand watch as the group of us make our way to the entrance. Talen and Fang present themselves tall and dominant. My insides go molten seeing Fang in his element.

The ocean waves crash, singing an endless tune of rushing water ebbing to and from the shore. The waterfalls create a spray of mist. The smell of pine and ocean spray is soothing.

A village reveals itself beyond the wall; cobblestones paving a roadway throughout the village. The gates close behind us as we are greeted by warriors who resemble medieval knights dressed in shiny armor.

The village men lined the streets in greeting as they had heard of the queen's arrival. The shiny soldiers keep the villagers out of our way as we quietly travel to the castle. I don't notice any women—I only see men. The odd sensation of no females takes a back seat when all the men fall to the ground, bowing reverently. Our armbands start to glow.

The bowing men seem like they are kissing the ground.

Silence greets us now, broken by the babies' giggles as they are delighted by their glowing armbands.

"It tickles," Kayla says, feeling the same sensation from our bands. Then Kayla rolls her eyes. "Seriously?" She eyes me and points toward Talen and Fang.

Fang and Talen are also bowing, along with all the men we traveled with. I try to pull Fang up. "This is silly, Fang. Get up."

"Talen, what do you think you are doing?" Kayla snaps, feeling uncomfortable.

"This is like a little city," I say as we see all the buildings in the village.

"It's huge," Kayla agrees.

Remembering how much she hates people; I can tell she's overwhelmed.

"It didn't seem this massive, looking at it from the other side of the drawbridge," I say as Kayla finally gives up on Talen and the trance these fools seem to be in.

Kayla holds Hope while I grab Faith, trying to understand what's happening.

The girls' armbands glow too. The babies seem interested, and we watch all the bowing men as we hold them up.

Kayla grows more uncomfortable. Her blue scales shadow her face and arms. Smoke puffs out of her nostrils.

"Talen, I swear. Get up and stop this, now," she growls in a tight whisper.

"No luck," I say as everyone stays low on the ground, bowing. It's like *Sleeping Beauty*. These fools are frozen. My mind starts to calm down when I feel it. They are all imprinting on us as dragon royalty.

I hold hands with Kayla as we hold her daughters. I close my eyes to focus, trying to understand the craziness.

"Kayla, it is another form of imprinting." I try to reassure my sister.

Harmony's ethereal voice enters our minds.

*"All is well. The men are imprinting to their dragon queens. Accept their allegiance, and the trance will dissipate."*

The four of us, as dragon queens, naturally accept, and just like that, the spell breaks. Talen and Fang rise first.

I call out, "Rise, men. We are happy to be here," knowing Kayla needs me to take the initiative.

"There's no need for all the bowing. Please get up, and relax," Kayla says, retreating behind me a bit.

Talen holds Kayla's hand and walks again, guiding us toward the castle.

I try to take in the kingdom's beauty, but reverent eyes watch us, and I worry for Kàyla. The attention here is much harder for Kayla, so I try to send her waves of encouragement. I smile as Fang holds my hand, and we follow Talen and Kayla.

We come to another set of gates that lead to the main castle grounds. More shiny guards hold the gates open in invitation as we pass through. We continue through a beautiful garden path that has water fountains with stunning statues.

Dragons, bears, and wolves are depicted in sculpted stones. They even have a giant one with a statue of a gorgeous woman. She stands centered, crowning a water fountain. The elaborate fountain rests in front of the entrance to the castle.

"It represents the goddess, Harmony, "Fang says as he notices my curiosity.

As we walk up marble steps to the castle's entrance, two more shiny armored men hold open two giant wooden doors.

"Here we go." I take Kayla's hand to lend her support. Holding the girls, we follow our mates through the doors.

Inside is a massive hall with bright marble flooring and the grand luxury one would expect of a castle. Men in white robes resembling ancient Greeks stand in greeting, offering a welcome to the kings and us as their queens. Kayla grips my hand harder.

"We've prepared your royal wings and have scheduled a feast for you, sires. Relax and ready yourselves in your royal wing," the lead man says.

"This is our head housekeeper of the castle, Richmond. He also happens to be our father and staff manager," Fang explains.

Talen motions for his guard to part, revealing a better view of the queens to the men in front of them.

"Let me introduce you to—" He is interrupted by the men dropping to their knees, bowing to the floor in front of us, their four queens.

"My queens," Richmond says with his head firmly sealed to the ground.

Kayla rolls her eyes and rocks her baby to distract herself from getting overwhelmed.

"Rise, Richmond," Talen begins again. "As I was saying, let me introduce you to our true mates. This is Kayla Dragon, my true mate. These are our daughters, Hope and Faith Dragon."

Fang steps forward. "This is my true mate, Brooke Dragon," he says with pride.

"It is very nice to meet you, Richmond," I said kindly to the older man.

"You must be busy managing this whole castle. Everything is so beautiful," I say in greeting.

"Thank you, my queens. Anything you need I am at your service," Richmond vows.

"How are you and Dad these days?" Fang asks Richmond.

"He is great, sir. Excited to prepare a feast in your honor. He's preparing your favorite for tonight, sir." Richmond sounds proud, with genuine love shining in his eyes.

"I love his cooking. I can't wait to dig in. Tell Dad I love him when you see him," Fang says casually as he pulls Richmond in for a bear hug.

"We are tired from our travels. If you could show us to the bedrooms?" I ask eagerly once the sweet moment passed and they pulled apart, wanting to get Kayla a reprieve from so many new people.

"We got this, Richmond. Thank you," Talen says to his father and takes us to the royal wing to settle in.

"I thought you said there hasn't been a true mating in a long time. Richmond is clearly in love," I say, curious.

"Richmond and Stan have been together for years. I have no doubt they love each other deeply. Unfortunately, the bond of true mating hasn't happened for them, but I don't think they will let it stop their love."

I feel joy that men can love men without it being taboo or shameful in any way. I never understood that kind of judgment on Earth anyway.

# The Vampire

"What do you mean, the goddess is not destroyed?" I bellow at the warlock encased as mud whose silhouette stands there looking bored in his dirt.

In the monotone voice of the golem warlock, he replies, *"I told you then, you cannot destroy a goddess. Why do you bother me still?"*

I knew this warlock wouldn't help me. I take every opportunity to torment the warlock in retribution for casting a spell that denied me his powerful blood. He turned himself into muddy dirt so I would never have his blood. He is a pet for me to toy with now.

"Well, why is it that a blue dragon destroyed some of my minions and my precious sirens just days ago?" I question.

*"If a true dragon has reemerged in this realm, the goddess has found a way to rebuild her strength here."* The warlock says the obvious without concern.

"Well, fix it, warlock!" I demand.

*"I am just a husk, cursed to linger without end. I will never aid you, vampire,"* the warlock drones in his mud form from the wall of my cave. *"Leave me to my desecration, vampire. I have no answers for you."*

I laugh, taunting the warlock. "You've doomed yourself to dirt to deny me your blood. After all this time, I finally have dragons to hunt. You will see from your dirt jail that I will triumph over these Dragon queens too. I will be more powerful with the blood of dragons than your blood ever could have powered me." I mock him as I storm away.

Harmony is getting her power back, but no matter. I will find a way to defeat her and that arrogant god who created me. I am power itself now—a god in my own right—nothing will take that away, not even the gods.

# CHAPTER 22

## Kayla

I sit at a fancy banquet table, feeling incredibly out of my element. Picking up a golden spoon, I examine the design carved intricately on the spoon.

"This is too beautiful to use for eating," I whisper to Brooke.

I see the table setting, which is too fancy for my comfort. The table is long, and men take seats all the way down on both sides of the giant rectangle table while a line of servers pour drinks and attend to everyone's needs.

The head chef, Stan, comes out with some of his staff and walks right up to us. Talen stops to greet Stan, his other dad. He had told me how Stan and his partner raised him and Fang after his real father was killed in a battle with the vampire. His shiften mother had been turned into a siren. She was hunted and put out of her misery by her royal guards.

Fang and Talon were barely two, so the castle stepped up to raise them. They bonded with Stan and Richman who imprinted themselves as their parents and the twins always looked to them as fathers. Talon says he could never convince them to cease with the formalities.

"Sire, I wanted to hand deliver your favorite dish tonight. I needed the excuse to come meet our new queens." Stan smiles sweetly at Brooke and me.

"You know I am eager for you to meet our mates. When will you let these silly formalities go? You are family, Stan. You will always be my father."

"I loved your father. He was a fair and just king, and we were friends. I love you boys like my own sons. I feel wrong making such a bold claim in the kingdom I serve." Stan says softly and sweetly. His eyes were beaming with love. "But you know you are my sons and always will be."

"Stan, you have outdone yourself. Everything is amazing," Talen praises, letting the old argument go. My heart aches a bit for all of them.

I smell the delicious food, and my hunger kicks in. My mouth waters and I'm drooling at the food. Stan places a dish in front of me and then Brooke.

"Ladies first," he says.

"Thank you so much," Brooke says, trying to get Stan's attention on her so I can have a moment to gather my social ability.

Stan eagerly waits for Brooke to take her first bite. Holding the gold spoon, I bite and almost moan loudly at the best food I've ever eaten.

"That's it. You are hosting the holidays, Stan. I love your food. All family events need delicious food." Brooke insists.

"I am usually in charge of all the castle events' catering and dining," Stan says seemingly pleased.

"That's wonderful Stan, but I am referring to our private family celebrations."

I notice another server placing a dish in front of Talen too. The meal is beautifully displayed, looking like art. I hesitate to eat something so extravagant, but that reluctance washes away with the flavors exploding in my mouth.

Feeling Stan's eyes on me, I explain. "Stan, this is the best thing I have ever eaten."

Brooke agrees with her moan of deliciousness. Stan claps his hands together in glee.

"Wonderful, wonderful. That's music to my ears. Enjoy the rest of your evening." Stan retreats to the kitchen with pride shining in his eyes.

The food is so yummy that I forget how awkward I'm feeling and enjoy my meal.

"He does understand that I meant our private family holidays? Stan and Richmond are essentially our fathers-in-law." Brooke says through a mouth full.

"We will work on that. I think you two will be able to sway them, especially with grandbabies." Fang says.

After dinner, I stand in the shadows in a hallway with Talen as we watch the ballroom full of people. I love seeing Brooke swirl in her red dress as Fang dances with her around the ballroom floor. Beads bounce with every step she takes. She is so happy, and I am so happy to see her this way.

Talen stands next to me as silent support as I observe the partygoers. Stan enters the ballroom. He scans the faces until his gaze connects with Richmond. Stan smiles, and the two men step toward each other.

They freeze. Richmond falls to his knees with his eyes locked on Stan. The whole ballroom stops in its tracks. I feel it from where I stand.

The magic imprinting of a true mate bond radiates throughout the room. Stan and Richmond begin imprinting, their souls binding together. The music is in tune with the crystal light strobing colors over the dance floor, the only motion and sound filling the air. Everyone is watching the couple.

When the imprinting completes, Stan rushes to Richmond and falls to his knees as the two embrace each other. They kiss so intimately that I feel like watching them was intruding on something private.

Stan takes Richmond's hand, and they run off together as

the men in the room call out in cheers. Brooke jumps in place, clapping and cheering, her beads bouncing.

I am swamped with a rush of energy.—a wave of radiating hope. I gaze up at Talen, who has tears brimming in his shiny purple eyes.

"My parents finally have the true mate bond," Talon says, a bit choked up.

"I think this is wonderful. I am so happy for them." I take his hand, and we go to our celebration.

The following day I walk around in our grand royal wing with one of my babies in my arms. She keeps me company for a bit.

"I'm going to go see Stan and the kitchen staff," Brooke says, excited to congratulate Stan and get to know him better.

"I can't believe we have a kitchen staff. Our fathers-in-law work for us as servants in the castle. This is all so extremely odd." I say.

Brooke shrugs. I am glad she is going with the flow in her usual ways again.

"I want to see if Stan has ingredients for some of our favorite Earth dishes," Brooke says.

"This is all so crazy. It's hard to get used to all these men," I mutter. "I'm staying right here with the girls. I preferred our magic blue Harmony delivery door," I say, feeling a bit homesick for our protective, secluded hall. "You go have fun exploring, Brooke."

Brooke hugs me. "You'll change your tune when Stan figures out how to make animal-style cheeseburgers," she says, wagging her eyebrows at me.

"I doubt he can pull that off but be my guest and try. If he makes every dish as delicious as last night, I am okay with that." I say as Brooke turns to leave.

Brooke winks at me. "I am so proud of you, Kayla. You're handling all this well." She blows me a kiss and shuts the door on her way out.

I feed, change, and lay my girls down to sleep in a round

and fancy crib. The Disney blanket I swaddled them in for this fancy princess bed seems out of place.

I seem out of place being in this grand castle. Seeing something familiar and from home helps me calm my nerves. I place the carved wolf Talen made next to them, and I feel the wood give off its magic.

Barron knocks gently on the door and asks if I need him to watch over the babies while they sleep. I can tell he wants to be close to them, so I agree and explore the rest of the royal wing.

I'm not sure I'm cut out to be a queen. I examine the intricately tiled ceiling for a moment before I go to a corner of the room and sink against the wall to process.

When I lean back against the wall, a panel behind me pops open and reveals a hidden passage. *What the hell?* I pull the panel door open. I follow the spiral steps down, crystals lighting up as I walk.

I exit another door and find myself in the basement of the castle. I wonder if I'm going to a dungeon; instead, it's well-lit and clean. The hallway is almost clinical—a clean white.

A shiny knight guards a doorway in front of me. I approach him curiously.

"What are you guarding behind the door?"

The man bows his head and stays standing. I'm relieved he didn't kiss the floor in his bow.

"My queen—" the man explains, but I interrupt him.

"Please, sir, just call me Kayla." I need a break from all the royalty for a minute.

Shocked, he tries again. "Your Highness, Kayla, I am guarding the women's wing."

Heat washes up my face at his *Highness's* remark. And then a flash of anger hits me. My blue scales surface. The guard sees evidence of my dragon and hits the floor awkwardly, clanging metal in his shiny get-up.

"My dragon Queen." He bows reverently.

"Never mind that," I snap, stepping over him to enter the doorway behind him.

Brooke was the only woman in the ballroom last night, so the revelation of women being here is shocking. I want to see this women's wing to ensure they aren't being held against their will.

I've lived in many foster homes and a few group homes. The guard blocking a doorway from the women is so triggering to me. The warrior behind me struggles to get up off the floor in his shiny armor.

I enter another hallway and see several doors on either side. It reminds me of an office hallway—lain and white. The door closest to me is the first door I try to open. Besides the oozy siren things in battle, the first adult females I have seen on this planet appear in front of me.

The woman standing near me is tall and strikingly beautiful. She has glowing, bright turquoise/aquamarine-colored eyes that stand out in contrast to her dark ebony skin. Her hair is styled with crochet braids that fall to a bob, framing her face.

"Hello, I am Kayla," I announce myself, stepping into the room, my blue scales fading.

# CHAPTER 23

## Kayla

The woman recovers from her momentary shock to smile warmly with kindness in her eyes as she greets me.

"My queen, we are pleased to meet you. I am Star, and this is Gemma." She waves her hand to indicate a tiny pixie-looking woman with an unnaturally bright-white skin tone.

Gemma walks to stand next to Star. I notice the pixy girl is shimmering with sparkles. I stare at her glittery skin for a moment too long before I catch myself and take in all of her features.

Gemma has dark hair with streaks of color ranging in blues and purples, styled in a more extended, shortish, messy cut with bangs in a pixie style to match her tiny ethereal features.

Her deep emerald green eyes lock onto mine with cheeriness as she says "Hi" in a melodic bubbly voice. I feel kindness coming from her.

"This is Kit," Star continues as the woman, Kit, takes her place on the other side of Star.

I am reminded of the legend of the Amazonian warrior

women I've read about in my life on Earth. I stare into the vast but beautifully fierce eyes of Kit. She has a predator gaze. The tall woman is toned and firm. She has bright blue eyes and red hair that lies in unruly thickness down her back. She is bronze in skin tone, something more orange than humans see on Earth.

Kit's smile removes the edge of her fierceness with a transformation of warmth. "Hello. Welcome." She bows her head slightly. I felt joy and hope from her.

I'm grateful the women don't kiss the floor like the men.

I take a deep breath to calm myself and assess the situation. This all feels a lot like the group home institution where Brooke and I used to live. Only worse, with the guards. This feels like a gilded prison. My instant emotion is anger.

I reach out to sense the energy in the room and feel warmth and comfort. I need to understand first because I wouldn't say I like discovering women in the castle's bowels this way.

"Forgive me." I try my best to smile warmly back at the women. "I'm new to this castle. Well, this planet, in general. I'm meeting people in this area for the first time. I still find myself a bit confused. Would you be willing to show me around and explain how you live here?" Star's brilliant, bright, straight-toothed smile lights up her face.

"Of course, dear. We were working on a schedule. Gemma and Kit can finish, and I will give you a tour."

I follow Star to a giant library, and then we walk through the dining area to the bedroom area set up like a dorm. The infirmary is well-stocked. It all seems exceptionally clean and cozy for a group home setting.

"We are not prisoners," Star insists.

"The guard is to protect us, not to keep us locked in. We can leave when we like. For safety, we schedule our outings, and most of us are just more comfortable inside. Some of us enjoy the gardens, but that is as far as we usually like to venture out."

"We can sense all the men and their sorrow, and most of us

prefer to hide away from them. We feel guilty that there are so few of us women and that the men have minimal opportunity to have a love match." Star tries to soothe me as she explains.

"That vampire has done a number on us as a society. I heard rumors the goddess restored our dragons, but to my shame, I did not dare to believe it. All of the female dragons are extinct. leaving males of the dragon line to live without access to their dragon counterparts as the beast within slumbers with no hope. However, I see you now with my own eyes and feel your alpha dragon inside. This makes me hopeful for our future."

I try not to cringe at the adoration on Star's face. I smile and encourage her to continue as I sink into a seat as she continues.

"Our beloved Dragon Queen Elisa died when the vampire entered our world. He attacked Elisa in her nesting cave. He took her dragon blood and fed off her. This fueled his power. No one on this planet had ever encountered true evil before that moment. Our Goddess Harmony lived among us and blessed us with her love." Tears fill Star's eyes.

"Harmony tried to get that vampire when she felt evil in our world. Unfortunately, another god reached into our planet. We think he intended to capture the vampire creature. When that god sensed our Harmony, he stole her from us instead. The vampire was left to run free, spreading his evil."

"I am so sorry this has happened here to your world. I really can't stand evil assholes." I say.

"He killed Elisa with that first attack, but with her being the Dragon Queen, her life-lock wasn't severed before her death. Her true mate died, and all the females of the dragon line also perished because we often vow our life to our family and close friends. Binding us in a life lock is magic and an imprint that comes naturally to us." Star says.

"How can you sever a life lock?" I ask.

"We live long lifetimes and work together to have balance and experience a beautiful life here in this world. Some of us grow weary, and when we want to travel to the afterlife, to spend time with our ancestor's energy, we allow ourselves to age, slowly letting our magic back into the circle of life on this planet. until we pass and transform to our next phase in the afterlife. We call our ancestors our guardians of the skies. It's usually a sacred passing. We can sever our life lock shortly before we choose to pass. In an emergency or unexpected accident, it can be tricky, but we all hope to be able to sever the life lock to allow our loved ones more time to live. True mates are the only exception—one cannot live without the other."

Star takes a somber breath and continues. "This evil vampire was never expected, so when our beloved queen died, she couldn't sever her life-lock imprint with her female kin. All the mated pairs died. All of them at once, the loss has never been healed."

I feel a deep sorrow that envelops Star as she tells her history.

"I am so sorry that happened to your dragon bloodlines," I say, tears brimming in my eyes.

"The few females that remained were of the fey, shiften, and water dwellers," Star says.

"The ancients were struck with the grief of losing so much and experiencing the taint of evil for the first time that many of our originals could not adapt and chose to give themselves up to the lands, sacrificing their bodies. They became energy to feed the magic in the land and seas, to find peace with their ancestors, and be with our lost loved ones."

I feel so much sadness for the loss of so many on a planet. It had been a genocide.

"The male dragons haven't shifted into dragons since because of the imbalance of the missing female dragons. The loss of so many of our females has the men-to-women ratio at an extinct level." Star says sadly.

"That is why we females shelter ourselves away. And we are offered the opportunity to breed. Volunteer females can become surrogates when their heat occurs. Some females feel the calling to accept the sacred duty of rebuilding our population."

"Some have hope enough to try, but most know extinction is inevitable. Plus, fathers and mothers now do not have a love match. Most pregnancies are conceived through our medical insemination process." Star shows me the infirmary.

"The parents create an arrangement to raise the child. The young typically stay with the mom, with the father occasionally visiting. The males usually move to the father's home upon puberty. The mother visits her son, and everything is amicable. But it's not natural, not having true mating. Female offspring are not being born. Our balance is off." Star says.

I take a silent moment to contemplate. I feel guilty that I can't possibly save these people.

"I am stunned at how small the population is," I say.

"The city is so large." Star nods in agreement.

"I would like to offer a way for you females to have the chance to meet your true mate. Would you consider a grand ball, a true mating event—for females to meet men and have the chance to get their love match? It seems shameful that you hide away and do not have your happiness. If the men have a structured event to attend, then maybe a hopefulness will outshine all the loneliness," I offer as a start.

"Yes. I will go to Gemma and Kit and start making plans to rally the women together. Having the dragon line restored will make everyone eager to celebrate." Star smiles with excitement.

"My sister Brooke is going to love meeting you ladies, and I am sure she will take the reins on event planning with you and your female friends," I say, feeling my heart grow heavy from hearing the history of the vampire.

# CHAPTER 24

## Kayla

Later that night, I lie in a luxurious bed in the fanciest room I have ever been in. I notice Talen as he crosses the room toward me.

"I tucked the girls into bed. Are you feeling any better?" Talen asks. He leans down to kiss me.

"I don't know. I feel a bit off." I look a bit pale, too, in the mirror. I settle next to Talen as he lies on our royal bed.

"I'm worried about Brooke. She went to the kitchens and has been gone all day. But I reached out to check on her and felt she was calm and unharmed." I snuggle into Talen.

And then I sit up fast with wide eyes and cover my mouth. Saliva starts that dreaded pooling in the back of my throat, telling me I am about to puke.

I bolt out of bed and flee to the bathroom. Talen hurries after me with worry when he sees me heaving over the toilet to vomit. He rushes to me, holds my hair, and rubs my back.

I groan. "Gross! You shouldn't see me paying homage to

the porcelain . . . uh, golden god like this." I sit back on my knees.

"I can't believe I puked in front of you." Embarrassing heat creeps up my face.

"Please, Talen, let me do this alone."

Talen kisses the top of my head as he holds my hair back.

"Don't be embarrassed. I will be here by your side until you feel better." Worry etches over his features.

I stand to brush my teeth, using the jar full of alien paste that refreshes and whitens my teeth with a natural wooden alien toothbrush. Then I take a shower, trying to ease my sick tummy.

I roll my eyes at Talon, shadowing me everywhere I go.

"You're lucky I'm too sick to fight you," I mumble.

Too sick to insist I am fine on my own, somehow. In the shower, he stands behind me, calmly washing my back and whispering sweet, soothing words. It feels nice.

"Let's get some fresh air," I insist as I dry myself.

Talen's eyebrow raises in concern.

"I am about to call a healer," Talen declares.

"No. Talen, there is no need for that." I dress and pull my towel-dried, damp hair back in a messy bun. "Please, Talen, humor me. The fresh air is all I need. I need to tell you something."

We head outside and walk in the romantically lit garden under the night sky.

"I think I might be pregnant," I reveal as Talen squeezes my hand.

We stroll under the stars and the fantastic night moons.

"I am sorry you are feeling so ill. I feel nothing but happiness when I think of you having our child. You already make the best mother. I am truly the most blessed male." Talen's smile spreads wide with pride.

I smile and feel love in my whole heart. "I love you, Talen," I say for the first time.

"I love you too, Kayla. I have from the moment I saw you." Talen seals his words with a lingering kiss.

Feeling loved and happy, I explain, "I never thought I'd have happiness like this. I could never have imagined this life, growing up the way I did." I stare up at the unfamiliar stars.

"I know we have a fight ahead of us, but this world is amazing!" I need to express to Talen how much I value him and our home.

"I love the beauty of this place, the trees, and the sky. The magic I feel flows so beautifully through everything. In my world, we have sunsets in the evening and sunrises in the morning. During the whole day on clear weather days, our sky is blue. It took Brooke and me by surprise to discover this sky has a wave of colors painting it all day long. This planet has the most beautiful skies, day or night, and I love it here. I want to fly up to those crystal platforms so badly. I hate that I can't figure out how to change at will." I'm rambling, but I can't stop.

"Do you have constellations? I don't recognize the stars here. I love how the moons have rings around them, like Saturn or Jupiter in our solar system. Beautiful. Breathtaking. I would love to learn about your constellations."

"Constellations?" Talen asks with confusion.

"Yes. On Earth, we have constellations—astronomy to learn and map the stars. The Big Dipper was my favorite because it was easy to spot."

Talen is confused. "The Big Dipper?" he asks. I am mesmerized by him.

"My home planet's name is Earth, the third planet from our sun. The Big Dipper is the placement of stars in the skyline up to outline the shape of a spoon," I reply.

"Why would you name your planet Earth?" Talen inquires, curious.

"I don't know who named the planets or the stars. It was taught to us in school. That reminds me. What is the name of this planet?"

Talen laughs. "I wouldn't presume to name this world. This world belongs to the goddess Harmony. It is hers to name. I call it home."

I smile. "There's acceptance here. I've never experienced how welcoming and full of acceptance everything seems to be in this world. I am so blessed to be raising my children in this place. I'm glad to call it home, too, Talen. I know I will be fine if I can figure out this vampire problem."

Talen takes me to the fountain of the goddess. I sit, running my hand through the water of the pool.

"This should be a wishing well," I suggest.

"Woman, you say the oddest things. I think you are adorable. What is a wishing well?" Talen asks as he kisses the top of my head.

"I'll show you adorable." I splash water at him, but he laughs.

"Do you have a coin?" I ask.

Talen passes me a golden coin with a dragon on both sides.

"Beautiful," I say, admiring it.

"There was a wishing well at the zoo I went to once on a field trip. My favorite part was the wishing well. I would take a penny, a coin used on my planet, and would make a wish with all my heart and toss it into the wishing well."

I take his gold dragon coin, stand and face the statue of the goddess, and wish for my family's safety. I seal it with a kiss and toss it in the pool of water.

"That's it. I declare this the official wishing well of the castle," Talen says joyfully.

"Your turn," I say, urging him to make a wish.

"How much is this coin worth?"

"What do you mean?" Talen says.

"You know, money. You buy things with money, right?" I wonder why there is so much gold and treasure if they don't have money. Talen gazes at me as he explains this planet's culture a bit.

"We are all connected to our planet. We cultivate and

nurture our lands and seas. In return, nature takes care of us. From birth, we are naturally drawn to our talents. My brother and I are warriors, while my dad Stan is a chef. Our people are driven by their connections to our planet."

"We work together, making our lives comfortable as a unit of people. Some of us are extremely talented with our callings and able to craft things like this coin and the jewelry Brooke loves so much." He gives me a genal kiss before he continues.

"We all support each other, so we value the beauty of these trinkets. We choose them for ourselves in support of the people who make them. We can touch them and feel the nature of our planet. We don't buy with money. We naturally work for the whole of us as we do what we are called to do." Talen takes another coin out to make a wish himself.

A loud siren blares through the calm night. Soldiers scatter, trying to get to their posts. The attack came too fast to anticipate, coming out of nowhere as a tentacle grabbed me.

It sandwiches me between two slimy suction cups. I feel a swoop as the giant sea creature that grabbed me takes a dive falling back into the ocean from the mountainside, leaving the kingdom behind.

I'm dizzy with vertigo and overwhelmed by the energy of the creature's terror. Sea water slushes around in my bubble as I try not to puke. I might be in trouble here. I feel my armband burning, and I sense my mate in despair.

I'm trapped. I'm disoriented and moving so fast. I keep bouncing in the circle of two tentacles suctioned together at the seams to cocoon me, creating a wet, sticky circle that cages me.

I jostle around, feeling nauseated. I need to get my bearings and think. I am also absorbing the emotions of the creature that holds me captive. Chaos and fear have me struggling to concentrate.

# CHAPTER 25

## Brooke

The waterfalls roar and the river runs steadily into the sea as a paralyzing moment passes before an eruption of chaos fuels the devastating reactions of the men.

Talen howls in despair and rage. He roars louder than the waters. Every person in the castle wakes to a stunned realization that one of the queens was stolen. Men are in shock. My beast rages inside me, my armband burns, and I see red.

I make it outside as I feel Talen's rage tangible in the air. I see him transform into an angry wolf and lunge toward the beastly sea creature, but the thing is fast and vanishes with its prize—his stolen mate and my sister.

Soon the giant creature appears tiny, and then the sight is gone. Fang tries to calm me and hugs me tight, as if not to lose me too. Fang yells to his brother. "She lives, brother, she lives, or you would not."

But Talen is too far gone with grief and rage. He can't be calmed.

Smoke whirls out of his black wolf nostrils. Talen transforms from a howling, angry wolf into a raging, black dragon. The dragon leaps into the air and blasts off to the sea, diving deep, searching for his mate.

My armband sears fear into my soul, and I know the girls need me to help them deal with this too. I am stunned and can't get my body to move. Shock has me frozen in fear.

Talen rages and searches aimlessly, seeking Kayla—diving in and flying out of the sea, blowing flames of his dragon fire, and steaming the ocean's surface. He dives back into the sea.

The ocean begins to mist, creating a fog, sauna steamed up in a cloud from his dragon boiling the water's surface. He's pushing his newly released dragon to its limits. Talen unexpectedly transforms back into his skin form, and he falls to the ocean, unconscious. I am paralyzed with despair, watching through numb eyes.

Men around me mumble things like, "Under the protection of the strongest fortress, our castle, one of our queens was stolen."

Fear and dread filled me at how easily this was accomplished. I need to get my shit together and focus. I see all the stunned men, who all stand hopelessly facing the sea. Fang is the only one who seems to have his shit together, standing next to Jag, a shiften warrior, who recovers before the rest.

"Fang, we must send out ships in search," Jag suggests.

Fang shakes his head and stares at me. "Brooke, lock the girls in the dorms of the mountain."

I break out of my spell, feeding off Fang's strength, and I rush to get to the girls. A few guards follow me. By the time I can calm the babies and settle them in the dorms with Star and her friends, I have to fight my way past the guards Fang sent to keep me stowed away too.

The moment I make it outside I transform and fly to the sky, bellowing my dragon's fire in rage. This can't be happening. I panic.

I swoop down to land near Fang and fall naked into his arms, burying my face into his chest, sobbing.

"I feel her fear," I cry. "I want to go after her, but I can't leave you or the girls."

Jag evaluates me. "Beautiful Dragon Queen." Jag cannot believe his eyes.

"Two dragons," Jag says in awe.

"The prophecy." Jag hits his knees.

"I vow to fight, come what may." Jag's energy draws my attention as he pledges his allegiance to me as a dragon queen.

" Sire!" one of the men calls back as he stares out to sea with a line of spectators searching the ocean for answers.

Fang removes his shirt and dresses me before he steps with me to scope out the sea. There's no time to acknowledge Jag as we all move to the man who called to us.

Sea dwellers in a mass swim along the surface, following one who carries a body toward us. I take off my shirt, and in my fear, I turn into a dragon. I grab Fang and fly down to the docks to wait.

I transform and am again a naked woman, yet I stand as regally as possible. I watch a water dweller deliver Talen's unconscious, limp body. Fang reaches to retrieve his brother from the water dweller king.

*I return one of your kings.* The voice vibrates in our thoughts as the man in the water gazes up at us. *As we rule the waters, we usually leave the land matters for you to handle.* The water dweller pushes the words into our minds in greeting. I notice the water dweller, my curiosity apparent, but my worry over my sister is more significant. For now, the mermaids will have to wait for my inevitable questions.

"Your octopus took my sister!" I growl.

I notice the strong water dweller with long, dreaded hair braided back. I can make out his fin whipping in the water to keep him waist-high above the water. He has gills that flare open along his ribs.

When he smiles at us reassuringly, he has pointed fangs for teeth.

"You remind me of a shark. I didn't expect that of a

merman," I blurt out. My nerves are too frayed to hold my tongue respectfully. The heat coming off the water's surface and the taste of cooked, salty seaweed permeates the air around us as the water dweller king is amused in his battle form.

"Thank you for bringing my brother home," Fang says in acceptance. He holds his limp brother, still in shock and defeat.

*"I am known as Trent, alpha king of the water dwellers. We respect the land and are rejoicing to discover the dragon has returned. However, we cannot have you boil our water."* He sends his voice to our thoughts again, giving us a stern gaze.

Fang knows who the water dweller is, so his introduction was for my sake and not anyone else's.

"My brother's true mate was stolen. He was unable to control his fires," Fang says to King Trent.

*"We have a mutual enemy, an evil creature who captured a cluster of eggs. Our grand octopus has recently laid her eggs. Many lifetimes have gone by, and this is her first and only breeding. She is desperate for her eggs, so she sets out to retrieve the ransom the vampire requires—a dragon queen. We will ally with you and fight this vampire together."*

*"We heard the cry of our revered grand octopus, guardian of our seas. We knew the violation. We sent a sonic sound in the waters, and we tried convincing her that we would fight to recover her young, tried to stop her from stealing your queen. Sadly, she was blinded by her desperation and could not be reasoned with. We were on our way to the castle to defend your queen, even if it meant putting down our great revered octopus. But she is fast, and we were not successful."*

Trent pulls himself out of the waters and transforms into a man. His eyes fade to green, and his skin takes on the tones of blue. When he smiles, his teeth are flat, regular, and handsome. Trent speaks with a strong, deep voice. "We will aid you in your fight with this evil, as he has violated our waters. We cannot stand by and let the vampire take our precious young."

Trent offers his alliance with a respectful bow.

I acknowledge the water dweller's pledge. "I understand a mother protecting her young. Kayla would, too," I say softly.

I feel deflated and sit on the pier's edge, putting my legs in the warm water. I start chanting in my way, knowing I must send a healing energy to cool the water to its average temperature.

Fang tries not to concern himself with my nakedness, but I sense his discomfort.

"My dragon destroyed my clothes, and everyone has seen what they have seen. They also know I am only yours," I say to Fang as I stare out at the other water guests waiting in groups out in the sea. The clear blue ocean magically lit up from the seabed below.

"Can you help us determine where the grand octopus took Kayla?" I ask my new water dweller friend.

Jag and other guards make their way down to the docks. Jag offers me a robe for covering. Fang gives Jag a thankful nod, and his features relax a tad. Two guards offer to carry a sleeping Talen back up the cliffs to the castle. Fang reluctantly gives his brother over and sits next to me to engage in the alliance between water dwellers and our people.

# CHAPTER 26

## Kayla

Trapped in the sphere cage of the giant's tentacles, I close my eyes and send out feelers to gauge what kind of trouble I am in. I receive a swarm of panic from the creature that has me—a communication in feeling and images, not so much a language of words.

I see the giant sea creature deliver her strands of eggs. The cluster flows gently, like a chandelier in the sea. I sense her feeling of pride and joy in creating new life. Then comes an image of her eggs being sucked into a magical sphere, a circle containing them, and watching them leave the safety of their nest in the sea. Her eggs are taken to the land. On the shore, the ball of seawater cocoons the eggs.

In desperation to retrieve her eggs, the octopus leaves the water to the sting of the air and cutting of the sand, only to be blocked by a magical barrier with the feeling of evilness flavoring the invisible wall.

An evil creature lurks there and sends a command to

retrieve a queen. An exchange is promised: a queen for her eggs.

I understand the fierce sea creature and send her calming energy, letting her know I would willingly help her retrieve her young. The creature inwardly cries as it swims on to its destination.

Just as quickly as I was taken, I was released and deposited in the sand under the night sky. Cold and wet, I focus, looking at my surroundings.

An ominous feeling taints the air. I see the moons high with rings and hear the waves crash behind me. The feeling of evil in the air drowns out the beauty.

A fire illuminates an area of the beach ahead of me. Beyond the beach is a dark tree line. I can make out shadows of beings lurking and moving, seemingly avoiding the lights.

An orb of eggs hangs perilously close to the fire in threat. The giant octopus desperately tries to get to her eggs but is blocked by a shielding barrier. She tries to break the barrier to get to her eggs, and I'm furious with her.

I want to change to my dragon, but no matter how much I try, I only turn blue with scales and hear my inner beast say, "*Young ones*" in my head as if that explains everything.

I hold myself tall and robust as the giant limbs urge me closer to the barrier.

"Allow us in and give the mom her eggs!" I call out.

The giant sea creature is digging, flinging sand and smooth rocks like shrapnel, trying to dig under the barrier, seeking entrance.

Limbs and suction surround me. Somehow the octopus, in her frantic attempt to retrieve her eggs, is still mindful of me as I am trapped, unharmed, between the giant and the transparent wall. I can sense pain. The octopus is damaging herself and burning her flesh, and sacrificing herself slowly with agony to save her eggs.

I am swamped with the negative energy that envelops the area, and I want it to stop. Helplessly, I watch as the vampire enters the light, revealing himself. His glamour illusion flickers, showing a handsome, alluring man—tall, with lean muscles and dark hair. But then his true nature reveals itself, and he is skeletal and decayed.

He seems to be drooling, savoring the moment as if the trauma somehow feeds him. I feel disgusted. I only want to be away from him and the agony in the air.

The vampire motions toward the shadows, and two males and three sirens push a heavy cage through the sand. It is like something I once saw in an old movie where a circus held a tiger in a giant metal kennel.

The deranged creatures resemble zombies, with dark black veins creeping prominently up their arms and faces. They obediently maneuver the cage directly in front of me, with only the barrier blocking me from the open gate.

The vampire walks to the sphere of eggs. He casually reaches into the watery sack and plucks out one watermelon-sized egg. He holds it mockingly, like a baby. He rocks it in his arms, and with an evil sneer, he glares directly at me and holds the egg to the flame.

The octopus snaps her beak at the barrier in desperation. I try to enter the cage, but the nasty barrier burns me. The vampire removes the singed egg from the flame and moves to the cage. He taps the barrier in front of me with his nasty finger, pointing me to go inside. I step through, crawling into the cage.

The vampire closes the gate and the barrier. The barrier slices off a part of the octopus's limb. She tries to follow me through the brief opening in the barrier to reach her eggs. The octopus lets loose a black ooze that splashes against the shield of the barrier and the sand.

I retch at the taste of death and decay that is even stronger inside the barrier. The vampire laughs and tosses the egg into the flame. It sizzles and pops with a disturbing hiss.

I look at the sphere and see it hanging from a contraption. I can't quite place what it is. I try to focus and stop dry heaving.

I plead with him. "Please give the eggs back." The vampire's features light up with the victory.

"You females are all so predictable. Your young make you weak."

Appalled, I promise, "You mess with children, you will pay. Momma Bear doesn't play. You are a fool to think you will come out of this unscathed. Children give us females strength. Anything that threatens them will have hell to pay."

Ignoring me, he casually walks to a rope attached to the sphere. He moves the sphere and locks it into place on the gadget.

He points to a spot in the sky and sets loose a lever so fast that the primitive device snaps and catapults the eggs through the roof of the barrier, the sphere of eggs flying fast and far out to sea. The vampire seems pleased with the horror he inflicts.

The giant sea mother quickly bolts to the sea to save her eggs. I say a silent prayer. *"Please save the eggs."* I'm hoping the goddess will help. I watch the vampire reseal his evil barrier.

He walks to his minions that delivered the cage. They are still waiting obediently off to the side of the fire. Lovingly, the vampire caresses one female.

He bites his wrist and offers her a drop or two of his blood. He gives all five of his followers their rewards. They greedily suck at the drops and moan with need. They begin writhing with lust. Soon an orgy is taking place openly in front of my cage.

The smell of rot and the sick sound of demonic sex suffocates me. In the shadow of the tree, evil lust spreads. Hidden things make hideous sounds of sex. I turn my back to them and watch the ocean. This shit is seriously disgusting.

I'm trying to center myself and put up a shield as Brooke tried hard to teach me. The nastiness around me makes it impossible for me to focus. The vampire reaches into my cage, pulls my hair, and slams my head against the bars.

"Soon, it will be your turn to join the fun, so watch and learn." He sniffs and inhales deeply.

"You are mine now. I will drink you slowly and savor your dragon."

My eyes sting with tears I refuse to shed in front of this piece of shit, still looking at the ocean, disobeying his orders.

I see silhouettes of people crawling onto shore. I try to focus. I see fins shed by people standing on the sandy shore, a group of women carrying spears made from the coral reef.

They move like sharks, pacing in circles when they reach the barrier's shield. They move steadily and smoothly. They are fierce, with long dreadlocks for hair.

Wildness and primal energy come off them in waves. They are under the night sky, but from what I can tell, they have varying skin colors and features, some similar to the cultures I am used to on Earth, but also alien colors, purple, green, and blue. They have more of a deadly shark feature in their faces, not resembling anything human there.

They form a pack and mean business. They are scary with their battle formation. They do not yell. They do not speak. They silently prepare to battle.

I feel a nudge in my mind. A strong lady steps out of the pacing circle and makes eye contact with me. Her black eyes would have frightened me on Earth. I feel her probing me, assessing me. Protective energy is sent to me from the water dweller, who scans me with her shark eyes.

*"You are young,"* a voice in my head acknowledges. Talen has told me about clairvoyance. Telepathy is the way of communication for the water dwellers in their sea animal forms and battle forms.

I am still getting used to the mental push as well as the first encounter with a water dweller. The intimidating presence of these strong females here, willing to fight for me, makes me feel a bit of hope. Encountering them is indescribable.

I nod slightly in confirmation. The woman's face turns vengeful. Her angry eyes lift to the vampire. They are the most enthralling women I have ever met. I feel so much power emanating from them. I almost feel sorry for the vampire. Almost.

I can't bring myself to care about his consequences. He needs to be dealt with. I am team badass warrior woman. The minions still having demon sex are lost in the stupor of the vampire's blood. They're oblivious to their annihilation lurking just outside the barrier.

The female that stares down the vampire in challenge silently scans him up and down. Sharp teeth smile wickedly at him in a confident challenge.

Kayla

*"You can't hide in your bubble forever."* The voice booms in everyone's head inside this barrier, finally catching the minions' attention. I shake my head to clear out the threat that laces the words. That promise wasn't meant for me.

The vampire and his cockiness show no sign of fear.

"When I am ready for you, you will be my next treat," he says, licking his lips with hunger in his eyes toward the females ready to battle him. "You're irrelevant, all of you. I am god here. The only purpose anything on this planet has is to satisfy me whenever I choose to play with it," the vampire declares.

"I think you messed with the wrong momma's eggs and are clearly delusional. A god? Laughable," I say with an attitude.

"That female and her friends will kick your ass before you die a slow death." I mock him, giving him my best sneer.

The minions in the light stop having their orgy and move to cower in the shadows, feeling fear in the threat that radiates through the putrid air like an unseen wave crashing over them.

The vampire returns his attention to me. Damn, when will I learn to keep my mouth shut? In response, he pulls my arm through the bars with a slimy grin. He bites his fangs hard into my arm and drinks.

"You seem human for a dragon, like a broad that would show me nothing but disrespect back on Earth." The vampire laughs, gripping my arm painfully as he gently kisses my arm. I want to puke in disgust at his touch.

"I am God here! You have entered my world, bitch," he says with twisted anticipation.

"I don't care if you have become a dragon. You are my pawn, a source to tap into and feed."

I scream at the burn of his bite. I feel his power charging at the intake of my blood. My armband lights up in a heated glow to repel the harm. I yank and pull my arm, fighting to free myself. I am ambushed with his energy, flashes of his slimy past both on Earth and here. His evil, vile soul consumes me more than his venom. I want this torture to end.

"Get off me, you Dracula freak!" I yell and beat at him with rage.

Finally, he pulls away and releases me. "It's been a while since I heard that name, Earthling." He laughs at me. "Your dragon blood is so invigorating." He moans in satisfaction.

"I think I've found my new favorite pet."

He closes his eyes. In Hannibal Lecter style, he sucks at his lips in the thralls of orgasm after drinking my blood.

"Nasty." I hold my wrist, glaring at him.

"You're already dead, demon. You're just too stupid to realize it yet." I cry as a painful fire invades my veins.

The vampire laughs even harder, his beautiful glamour in full effect, strong and not flickering. The vampire rubs his groin suggestively to the warrior women, taunting them. "You're next." He points at the lead female.

"*I will sever it and use it as chum to feed our sea lions.*" Her voice echoes in our heads, a promise.

The vampire, unaffected, blows her a kiss.

"I will bend you over and take you in front of your cunt, Earth friend here. Teach you both a bit of respect, for I am your god. Know your place, bitch!"

The vampire turns and carelessly goes into the shadows to join the slapping of bodies and gross tangle of decay and evil.

I hold my arm, and it feels like viper venom is spreading from the bite. I try to calm my racing heart as I fear for my pregnancy.

The woman stands in front of me behind that stupid

barrier. She's trying to send me healing energy to help ease my pain and reassure me that they will get me to safety.

*"Take what I offer freely, sister of the land—use my magic to help you heal."* The water dwellers chant in my head, adding their essence to help me.

Fire spreads throughout my body, and my inner dragon tries to fight back with its fires, burning out the poison. My armband tries to create a dam, preventing the spread as it squeezes tighter, like a tourniquet. Every part of me worries for my baby and fights to prevent the spread of the poison from reaching my womb.

I am unaware of the enormous wave making a tsunami, heading straight for me, carrying my mate and water dwellers in an army united to save me. The water dwellers hold a floating platform full of men, powerfully holding the platform back as the humongous wave crashes into the evil bubble off the east shore.

I hear Talen's dragon roar in my head. *"Stay with me, baby. I am almost there."*

I fight the dark. My body is being attacked with venom and the spiritual swamp of evil. I feel myself fading into darkness and fighting to stay awake. I barely open my eyes to see the dragon fire melt a hole through the barrier. Water rushes in, and I tumble into my cage from the force of it. I'm about to suck in water when my mate's claws pull my cage from the water and wrench open the bars. Weak and unable to fight any longer, I fall back into darkness.

# CHAPTER 27

## Brooke

I stand next to Fang and Jag on the floating platform and watch as Talen's dragon form breaks the force field and rescues Kayla. It all happens so fast. The water recedes, and the platform lands hard on the beach. Water dwellers shed their fins and join the battle.

Jag and Fang run fast ahead in search of the retreating vampire. I transform and give chase after the vampire while blowing my fire on anything in my path. I almost burn a water dweller who's hard on his tail. I encounter a female water dweller who is after the vampire too. She turns and hisses at me before my dragon form registers with her.

*"My apology, Dragon Queen."*

I watch her spear a siren and tear it in two before she gives me a slight bow.

This woman warrior is super scary, and I am momentarily caught off guard at her sweetness and manners toward me in the middle of a bloody battle. She can present as a predator, fierce and scary, while only directing that energy to her enemy and not her allies. She amazes me.

Jag catches the attention of her feral eyes, and he seems to admire the dweller's worthiness in battle.

"Have you ever seen anything so magnificent?" Jag asks as he spears a minion.

I use my tail and tear through a minion before seeing the water dweller more closely.

She has burns on her body, probably from being too close to the dragon flame. She still bravely charges into the battle. Jag's slit cat eyes dilate at the sight of the fighting dweller. When her eyes roam over Jag, the water warrior sends Jag great energy. Jag seems paralyzed. I have to take out a minion before it gets Jag's throat.

Fang jumps between Jag and me, trying to be near me in battle.

"Get your head straight before you get us killed," Fang demands to Jag.

That reminds me to focus too. I jump into the air as the female lets go of her hypnotic energy.

*Was that the start of an imprint?* I ask, amazed at how badass these women are.

The water dweller female continues her hunt. She smells blood in the water like a shark and wants that vampire badly. Jag staggers and then regains himself, following the female and battling anything that comes at that female's back.

Another female water dweller takes a stance next to Jag, and they move, sinewy and fighting together as if they trained together. Having each other's backs, all three become one lethal machine. In the chaos, it is a surreal sight.

I am stunned, watching the instant grouping. Fang fights a siren to my left, leaving Jag to his new water dweller battle buddies to fight at his back. The lead female glances back at me but takes out another siren before letting me fight the minions in front of Fang.

I swoop down and spike my tail through a group of evil

minions, making a dragon tail shish kebab. *"Gross, I need a shower!"* I cringe as I shake the corpses off my tail.

I sense the vampire getting away, but my will won't let me leave Fang alone to fight these nasty things. He is like a dark Viking warrior, all sexy and capable, but I can't risk not being near him.

I notice the other females ruthlessly taking out the minions. Making quick work of the minion in front of us, I sense the vampire retreating into the forest as the sun rises. I pick up a trail and follow fast, trying to catch the creature, but the vampire is newly charged with dragon blood. With his new strength, he's just too fast.

I lose his scent, and the trail disappears as the sun lights the morning sky. The vampire has escaped.

Fang howls in defeat, breaking my heart that I can't help him catch that bastard. We return to the shore to let Fang evaluate the battlegrounds and thank the water dwellers for their alliance. That female water dweller crosses my path with Jag and another female at her rear. She glares past me, scanning for the vampire.

*"I will hunt that creature and kill him slowly."* Her frustrated voice chimes in our heads.

*"Coward!"* She sends out a mental wave. She wants the vampire to know she is after him.

*"You are no god. You're just fish chum!"*

I am not huge on violence, but I get it and am glad she is on our side. Realizing that a fight with the vampire will be for another time, the water dweller reluctantly returns to acknowledge me with a nod.

Jag and Fang follow the water dweller and her mate, the other female. I stand there feeling deflated. I transform to skin. Fang stares at me and comes to give me a long hug and a dirty kiss.

We break apart, and he raises his eyebrow at my nudity, but he notices I am curious about the water dweller and whatever is happening with Jag.

The water dweller eyes her mate, and they both scan Jag. Something must be igniting in them, their natures recognizing him as their true mate. I feel the energy of the three of them imprinting. Love is the energy this time.

I sigh. "Aww."

I am intrigued that true mate imprinting can happen in more than a two-person coupling.

After moments pass, a man gives me a shirt, making Fang relax. We all work together to clean up the battle and burn the bodies of the tainted.

"I am Jag." I hear the shiften introduce himself to the fierce females he is so taken with.

The tall warrior females stand in front of Jag, inspecting him once more, thoroughly circling him like prey.

*"I am Mystic Marine. You can call me Rina."* The lead female speaks in her telekinetic way so we all can hear.

The slightly smaller female leans in to sniff his neck.

*"I am Coral."* The fierce female introduces herself.

Fang whispers in my ear, "They are about to make a claim publicly, in their way, to add Jag to their mating pod."

"Fascinating," I say in excitement.

"Rina," Jag says reverently. "Coral," he purrs as his familiar recognizes his mates.

Taking a battle stance, initiating a spawning challenge in the way of the water dwellers, the two females spar with him. Coral lands the first punch on him, her energy challenging him for a battle dance—a request for his show of dominance to win her and claim her.

Jag isn't used to the mating rituals of the water dwellers. But he's a quick learner. Jag grins, and the fight for dominance is on. The intent is entirely different from that of the brutal battle earlier.

Trent nudges Fang with his elbow and grins as all the people make a circle, an arena for the blooming bond, to allow Jag to assert dominance.

"This is a grand day. We saved the eggs of the great guardian octopus and the Dragon Queen. Now we have a battle dance, a true mating. This will be the first spawning between a land dweller and water dweller in many lifetimes," Trent announces as he rubs his hands together in anticipation.

"Can you taste the change in the energy?" He is full of hope. Trent seems overly excited at the change and turns to watch the fight, rooting for the male to win the female's favor.

"Strength is honored among our kind. There needs to be an equal among them as a grouping. Jag will fight the females in our spawning tradition to prove his worthiness and ability to protect the females, and their future young," Trent explains for my benefit, happy to witness the new grouping of true mates.

"It is already a match since they scanned him and felt the true mate call. A battle dance is to proclaim their bond in public, showing off the prowess and strength of the mating claim." Fang explains.

I try to understand the strange mating ritual, my instinct railing against a man fighting a female. But the energy in the air is charged with good intentions and well wishes for the union. The females fight hard without holding back. They land blows, and Jag's nose bleeds.

I flinch, "I know that hurt," I tell Fang.

Jag is fast and wrestles the females one on top of the other, not throwing any punches or kicks. He gets the upper hand and subdues the females together on the ground.

Rina, the lead warrior female warrior, uses her legs to throw Jag off them both. He lands on his feet, and with a flirty smile, he pounces on them again.

When they realize he has them both in an unbreakable hold, Rina takes a submitting position, Coral and Rina turn their heads and expose their necks, lowering their eyes in a graceful defeat.

Jag takes Rina's face in his hands, turning her to gaze up at him. He leans down, bloody and all, and takes her lips in a hard kiss, accepting his award for the win.

Rina melts into him with her softness, the formidable warrior retreating. Her eyes turn green, and her teeth go smooth into a straight, warm smile smeared with his blood. She loses her wicked-mean, shark battle form and becomes an ethereal beauty.

Rina breaks her kisses and bites down on Jag's neck and left shoulder, marking him publicly as her mate. Jag roars like a mountain lion, and a wave of happiness emanates from him.

Rina sends out a declaration *"MINE!"* she roars to all who witness her spawning challenge.

"You are the most beautiful female," Jag says.

Rina lies beneath him, dusted with sweat, blood, and the sand—unbearably, beautifully displayed with blood and all.

"Thank the goddess for this blessing," Jag says, slowly releasing her.

Rina pulls Coral into the mix, and the three of them celebrate Rina and Jag's imprinting and public claim.

Jag leans over Coral. He kisses her just as fiercely. Coral moans and her features transform into another ethereal beauty as they kiss. When he pulls back to look at her, blue eyes shine up at him adoringly, "You are the most beautiful female too."

Coral also sends out her claim—*"MINE!"*—just as she bites down on his right shoulder with her mating mark, claiming Jag publicly.

Cheers erupt. Rina helps Jag and Coral to their feet, kissing Coral, then Jag and celebrating the mating of Jag and Coral together as hoots and hollers of well-wishes fill the battlegrounds.

Jag, Rina, and Coral take hands and retreat to their own private place, to form a bond and complete the mating.

This is the strangest wedding I've ever witnessed, but this feels spiritual like I just witnessed divine love. I am moved to tears, happy for the trio.

"Fang, they are so beautiful," I say, stunned, with a cry in my voice. I've already witnessed Trent lose his battle form before, and somehow the shark-like scary ladies seemed scarier.

Watching them transform, they turned enchantingly beautiful before my eyes. Almost angelically stunning. The moment is surreal.

"That group will make some beautiful babies in the future," I whisper to Fang.

"Yes, they make a strong pod," Fang says. "However, nothing compares to your beauty, my fiery queen." Fang kisses me hard.

I love this man. "I want to invite them over for dinner soon." I want to befriend those incredible people.

I'm glad I witnessed the triad union. Now, all I can think about is returning to the girls. I try to turn dragon and want to cry that she won't let me transform at will. I thought I was past that after transforming so quickly during this fight.

Fang has Trent escort us through the waters to get home as fast as possible, leaving behind men to help with the cleanup.

My armband constantly burns, but it sears me, amping up its fire as I reach the girls. They cry out too.

"Kayla!" I cry in pain and fall to my knees.

# CHAPTER 28

## Kayla

Heading to the closest safe place, Talen takes me to the wildwood where we met. He transforms into a man and rushes me into the empty hall.

"Talen." I weakly mutter. I fall into darkness. He takes me to the shower and strips me. I awake under the spray of water, screaming in pain.

"I am here, Kayla. Stay strong, and let me help you," Talen says, trying to soothe my pain.

I feel he is desperate to clean me and see my injuries. He sees the bite on my arm. The dark venom spreads, going up my arm. I try to stay aware of him through the pain. He desperately sucks at my bite mark, trying to get the venom out. I'm terrified he's getting infected, too, as he spits the vile stuff out and continues his efforts. I hear Talen as he prays to the Goddess.

"Save my mate, Goddess. I beg you."

My armband burns, squeezing tightly. Humming in my head has my ears straining. I feel my babies crying through their armbands, connecting to me. I feel Brooke's fear throughout the band. I feel other females chanting with Brooke, sending me healing energy.

I hear Brooke inside my head. *"Kayla, I am with you. I have females here helping me. Gemma has helped me to amplify our connection through the armband. These women are truly amazing! Focus on our healing song and take what we give you freely."*

I am washed with healing energy that eases my pain. I hear them singing a healing song and feel each woman gift me a part of her life energy. I feel a life lock sealing between us all.

I see black ooze draining from the bite on my arm, followed by my red blood. I see the fear in Talen's eyes as he cries, holding me under the spray of hot water in the shower. The women singing in my head fade as I pass out.

Harmony, the goddess, comes to me in a vision in my darkness. "My fierce little queen, I am sorry you have suffered. Only one as strong as you could fight off that bite."

I see the beauty of the goddess. Her ethereal glow almost hurts me to lay my sight on her.

"Did I die?" I ask, confused.

"No, dear, you are not dead. You and your young ones live. Time is much different here where I am. If I were able, I would have rid the world of the vampire the moment he entered it. The stronger god Hecat has me for now. He thinks to win my heart." The Goddess laughs with amusement.

"We will see if I let him after the mess he made. I want my little planet to have its Harmony and balance back. I want that evil cast out," the Goddess declares.

I feel the longing in the Goddess to restore her world.

"How can I help?" I humbly ask.

"My meddling Hecat has offered me a boon. The door, my dear Kayla. I tried to advise you before. Sending a part of my consciousness back to the right time to deliver a message is still difficult for me. I am a goddess, but my parents have suppressed my powers." She sighs. I can feel her worry.

"However, I have created my little planet Harmony, and I have lived among my people since the beginning of my creation. Now that I am in the god realm I am still figuring this time discrepancy out." The goddess Harmony glances at me affectionately.

"My father is the great creator, and he loves me. Many lesser gods want his attention, hoping to gain his favor and be granted more god power. Gods and goddesses can be quite arrogant."

I stare at the goddess, feeling serene and wrapped in her power. Her love and affection for me are divine. I try hard to focus.

"In many ways, I am like my father, only wanting to tend to my creations. My mother is the goddess of true mates. Her love design is a fundamental law among all gods and universes. My mother also has a sense of humor. She thought pairing me—my father's baby girl—with an arrogant, power-hungry, attention-seeking god-like Hecat would ruffle my father's feathers a bit and teach Hecat some humility." The Goddess before me shows irritation as she shakes her head and takes a deep breath, blowing out a raspberry.

"I know that Hecat and I are destined to mate. However, I have an infinite amount of time to decide when I am ready. I want to live among my creation and care for them, enjoying their happiness and harmony. My god attribute is the ability to create harmony and balance. I love my world." I feel the Goddess's heartache, and I sob for her.

"Excuse me, dear. I will calm my emotions, for your sake."

I'm able to calm down and continue listening.

"I knew if I shielded myself in my world outside the veil of the gods, and using the shield my father has placed on me, the arrogant Hecat would not be able to detect me as his true mate. Once he did, it triggered our true mate imprinting." Harmony stands before me, trying to explain so I can understand.

"Hecat was determined to gain favor with my father, and in his arrogance, he meddled in my father's affairs."

Harmony kneels to sit next to me as she continues. The air that swishes over me at her movement smells heavenly.

"The politics of the gods is complicated. Generally, gods and goddesses tend to stick to their own universe and creations. My father, the great creator and most powerful, doesn't have the luxury of going unnoticed by other gods because he has power over us all and can grant more power to us." Harmony explains. I lean closer to smell her heavenly scent.

"Plus, being under his gaze and having his attention feeds us like a drug. Therefore, some of the stronger gods do whatever they can to gain my father's attention, even if they risk his anger. His wrath is unmatched, so he tries not to anger easily." Harmony smiles as a daughter who loves her father as she speaks.

"My father, he loves me. I feel his love so deeply, but my father keeps it a secret, never revealing how he watches me and loves me. He loves my world and that I have a successful Eden." Harmony winks at me.

"That's a secret between you and me." She giggles, and the sound is music. Actual Harmony vibrates through the air between us. I love this Goddess with my whole being.

"My father shields me, so I am unnoticed by most gods because gods can be jealous, especially if my father shows favor to any of us. Hecat is one of those jealous gods. He is so jealous of Earth and unworthy humans. Mostly, he was jealous of Lucifer. He was jealous of Lucifer getting so much attention for being bad. My father's relationship with any of his children or creations is no one's concern. But these power-hungry gods only want my father's attention and do as they please to get it." Harmony's annoyance rolled off her in waves. Harmony reaches for my hand to examine the arm that was bitten.

"Hecat tried to attack Lilith, who is innocent and the true mate to Lucifer. He thought he was correcting a wrong in his twisted eagerness to get my father's favor. He turned that evil man into a vampire, the only creature that could kill Lilith.

The life-lock that the true mates of gods and heavenly creatures have was Lucifer's vulnerability, as he could die with Lilith." The Goddess heals my wound.

"My mother, the Goddess of true mates, already knew Hecat's intent and warned Lucifer. Lilith is one of my mother's creations, and my mother favors her. Lilith is like a little sister to me. We are friends. She is aware of me and my true mating with Hecat. I've vented to her in the past, revealing that I was enjoying my world before I let Hecat know of my existence." Harmony grows frustrated as she tells me her story. Her forehead wrinkles in stress, and I feel her remorse.

"With my mother's warning, Lucifer intercepted the vampire assassin sent to kill his Lilith. Even though Lucifer wanted to destroy the creature, in his anger, he sent the vile thing to my planet, knowing hurting me would grieve the arrogant god Hecat more than any other suffering would."

As if on cue, the Goddess flickers. Humming in my head resumes. "It has only been moments since Hecat reached into my world to retrieve the vampire after my father demanded he fix the mess he made. Once his hand reached through into my Harmony's atmosphere, he felt me. The mating call made him grab me instead of the vampire he was seeking, and he pulled me to the realm of the gods." I feel the Goddess's sadness. She is saddened at leaving her planet and creations.

"Beyond the veil, in the god realm, only seconds have passed since I was pulled from my planet. Time is different. Lifetimes have passed with every second that passes here in the god realm. So going through time to communicate is difficult as I am not as strong as other gods." Harmony flickers and I feel her fading.

"Hecat created a god portal, trying to assuage my anger. The door is for true mates, females from other worlds—unattached females with the DNA to be compatible with my world. My father has offered his Earth females as a gift to support my need to heal my world. I chose you, Kayla, you and Brooke, to lead the way for the others. Use the door. They will come one by one. You may ask for anything you may need for comfort as well. Only things compatible with this world can enter through the door. Use the blank enchanted pages."

Harmony's face turns frustrated as the connection fades in and out. I sense she wants to continue explaining.

I instantly understand but still ask, "What about the vampire?"

"It will be some years in Harmony's time before I can reach in and cast him out. Fight when needed. I will come for him. Focus on the true mates."

I'm confused, but I vow it. "I will do my best."

The Goddess moves her mouth to say more, but the words are soundless, and she fades. Her message is left incomplete again as her image vanishes.

I open my eyes to Talen staring down at me with relief. I focus on him as he leans down to kiss me. I lose myself in the feeling of home. An all-consuming love that I have for this man wraps around me.

# CHAPTER 29

## Kayla

I hold Talen's hand and focus hard, projecting my message through my armband as a direct link to Brooke and the girls. I use Talen's energy to boost my thoughts.

*"I am at the wildwood. Bring the book. I am too pregnant to leave. I need you here."* I sent the same message over our pathway until I felt a pushback.

*"I am coming, but what? Too pregnant?"* Brooke's soft energy touches me in response.

I smile up at Talen. "She heard. She's coming. I may have shocked her with the news of being pregnant." I took his hand and guided it to my unbelievably round belly.

"Is this normal?" I ask again with a tremble in my voice. "I only just discovered my pregnancy. On Earth, humans have nine months before giving birth. Overnight, my belly has grown so huge."

Talen is concerned. "The healers will know what to do."

I take a breath to center myself, standing in the open hall, looking at all the treasures. I have a longing in me to gather the gold and treasures.

"I think I am nesting, dragon style. That or I like trinkets, just like my hippie sister Brooke."

Talen laughs. "You amuse me, mate."

He starts opening and moving the crates of treasure as I point out the boxes that call to me. With his help, I save the trinkets and gold and silver around until I build a circle resembling a nest. The colossal pile is occupying a large area of the grand hall's floor. Talen watches me in wonder.

"I have never seen anything so unusual before. The circle is beautiful, Kayla."

I followed my instinct to make a pile, Talen did all the heavy lifting and moving. He wouldn't allow me to overexert myself. I stand back and appreciate my beautiful nest of treasure.

"Did I seriously do this? This is a Brooke thing to do," I say, missing my sister. I feel the energy of the people who crafted these gems' magic radiating off each piece with intent. The charms, precious stones, and metals sing a soothing, welcome tune.

He laughs. "I'd say you had me do this."

"I made a nest out of dragon treasure that was intended for me, for us, for this event. How did the people who crafted these know about me?"

"I tried to touch on this before when explaining that we work together as beings on this planet with our connection to nature and magic. Balance is cultivated by how everything one does here affects the whole of us." Talen replies.

"We are all connected and value one another, so the ground herself gives up her precious stones and metals to our jewelry craftsmen and craftswomen, who in creating, are inspired by the spirits and influence of the divine flowing around us. A spell is crafted in the creation, and the final product will pass to the hands it is meant to touch, giving the energy of the magic to who it was intended for." Talen cups my cheeks and tenderly kisses me.

"This treasure is calling to you because it is eager to embrace our young and support you through our birthing journey. Similar to the good wood the trees gave up for our daughters. The treasure gives you this magic, calling to your dragon and you. In return, the birth of our young will recharge the power being blessed to you. Then, someday, another will feel the pull to connect and receive the magic." Talen is so handsome and sweet. He enjoys teaching me the ways of this world.

"I feel how the Earth, water, everything around us connects us universally through a vibration of magical energy. Inanimate things have power, a living intent to add value and support." I am completely amazed and find it challenging to word thoughts appropriately.

Talen wraps his strong arms around me in a delicious hug.

I kiss him, thanking him for appeasing me and my crazy pregnancy urges. "Thank you, love."

I see my treasure nest and feel assured I used every piece calling to me. I am pleased and appreciate the beauty and sparkle of my nest. I grab Talen's hand and lead him to the blue door.

I tell him about the vision of the goddess Harmony. A new hope lifts our spirits as we wait for Brooke and Fang. Brooke is bringing the magic book she carries and keeps close, like one of her trinkets.

"Oww!" I buckle over in pain as a hard contraction hits me.

I glance up at Talen. His expression is just as scared as I feel another wave of pain hit me.

*"Brooke! I need you. Please hurry."*

# CHAPTER 30

## Brooke

Star pokes her ebony face into the library to check on us. Her brilliant turquoise, aquamarine eyes lock onto Hudson. The guardian assesses Star, ruling out a threat at the sight of her. He does this when anyone comes near us. Everyone is on high alert. That is why I'm down here in the library with the babies. The small group of women who live here are supportive and have been extremely helpful.

Star smiles brightly at the all-too-serious male. Breaking eye contact with Hudson, she watches the sleeping babies. Star's eyes tell of her affection for them. Star glances back up at Hudson and says, "Relax, I'm just checking on them." She rolls her eyes at his silliness. Star winks at him, and I catch a hint of flirtation in their exchange.

If I'm not mistaken, these two may have been imprinted. I feel the same energy in the two of them as if they were one. I examine Hudson as he valiantly stands guard. I notice the mating bite mark on his neck peeking through his uniform. I am truly happy for the couple.

I'm so grateful to Star and the other females, especially Gemma, the shiften healer. She is so tiny but mighty. The moment we returned from the battle, I felt Kayla's pain and her battling the venom in the bite. Gemma jumped into action and helped me connect to Kayla, and they all offered a life link to her to save her from the vampire bite.

It was like another form of imprinting. We gathered in a circle, holding hands, and Gemma said a spell of some kind, radiating magic.

Star offered herself first. "Take my life force and lock onto mine. I offer a part of my soul freely to save yours."

I felt Gemma use her magic to reach into all of us, holding hands and connecting us as a unit, managing the magic in each of us.

"Take my life force and lock onto mine. I offer a part of my soul freely to save yours," Gemma repeated.

Every other female in the circle repeated the spell, one by one, each dedication jarring as I felt their source of life inside me as they connected to Kayla.

I spoke the spell offering myself, the last female in the circle to do so. The moment I did, I felt connected to my sister deeper than ever, which was telling. I knew my life was locked to hers, and the moment Kayla died, I would follow and be with her in the afterlife if we did not sever the bond beforehand.

I would be connected with the sisterhood of ladies in this circle for the rest of my life. Our life mates would die with us—all of us together, in this life and the next.

Gemma started chanting a healing song. I learned the words and chanted, adding to her song. We all sent power through my armband to Kayla to heal her from afar.

I will be forever grateful to these ladies who chose to die with my sister when she died to save them. That kind of sacrifice and dedication is astounding to me as a human learning the purity of this world. The bond between us is formidable. I trust these people. We are now family.

Fang comes through the door, looking like a mess after the

battle. He scans the room and locks eyes with me. Something in his presence calms me. I let out a breath of relief, a tension I wasn't aware I had.

I pluck a piece of seaweed out of his messy braids.

"I am going to have to fix this hair of yours." I smile. "This is not the style I had in mind." I wave the weed in front of him, taking a sniff of him. "You smell."

Fang laughs, pulling me into him and rubbing his scent deeper. "You smell now too." He playfully tussles my hair.

"Eww!" I groan, but I am just happy to see him.

Fang hands me a pink pearl necklace. "I got this from a water dweller. I thought you'd like to add it to your collection."

I squeal with glee. I take my pearls and kiss him hard.

"We need a shower," I say after tasting the sea on his lips.

"I think I'm going to give you a Viking-style haircut." I'm eager to get my hands on him to distract myself from all this stress.

After I'm done, Fang is hot! His new hairstyle sets him apart from Talen. I am impressed with myself for styling his hair. I am hungry for him. I'm about to jump him when Kayla breaks my thought with her mind connecting to mine.

I come out of my trance, connecting to Kayla, frantic to get to my sister. "I need to bring Kayla the book," I tell Fang.

This whole magic world is exciting, and I am still getting used to telepathic calls. I wish I understood how to wield all the magic proficiently, especially my dragon on demand.

"Fang, let me see if I can fly to the wildwood." I'm standing in the gardens, wholly frustrated, as I call my dragon, trying to transform so I can fly.

"Why doesn't this work when I want it to? It only works if I need to fight?" I pout. Red scales and steam are about all I can muster under my frustration.

"We all still have a lot to learn." Fang tries to soothe my irritation.

"Kayla needs me, Fang. Like, I should be able to call my dragon as easily as you do your wolf."

Fang stares sympathetically at me. "I understand. I have always felt the triad: the man, the wolf, and the dragon. I would have never imagined the dragon buried deep inside me had a real possibility of emerging. Not until I saw Talen transform into his dragon. I am now eager to feel my dragon emerge. Like you, my command is ignored." I gaze at my mate, realizing he must rant about his dragon as much as I want mine.

"Well, plan A was to fly. So, what's plan B?"

"We can travel the path we took to get here, but I wish you would let me send a messenger to deliver the book. This will be dangerous," he replies.

I stiffen. "I am already in a bad mood. Please don't make me go through this argument again, Fang. I am going to Kayla."

Fang sighs. "Then I will call upon my best men, and we will make the journey to the wildwood. The girls should stay in the women's dorm with their guardians."

I feel torn, not wanting to leave the girls behind, but also, I want them safe.

"I will leave Hudson in charge of the men at the castle. Hudson and Barron will rank above the rest of the men. They will make sure the girls are safe, along with the women." Fang tries to reassure me.

Leaving the babies feels unnatural to me. I reluctantly agree. "I want to go see them before we leave."

We walk to the women's dorms below the castle. I see Barron and Balthazar standing guard outside the dorm's entrance in the main hall. Fang greets the men. They are like family to me now.

Barron holds the door open as I walk in. My heart melts at the sight of the younger toddler boy riding piggyback on Hudson's back. Star is standing comfortably close to help keep the boy balanced.

The mother of the boy notices us as we enter. She grabs her son, adjusting him on her hip. With a smile, she greets us.

"Phoenix, this is our dragon queen, Brooke, and our king, Fang," the mother introduces.

"I am Willow, a witch." She snaps her fingers and twinkles in the shape of a heart fly in front of us. The boy giggles. She lowers Phoenix to the ground to play.

"I am so glad to meet you. I meant to meet you sooner, but a lot came up." I smile warmly, feeling an instant connection with Willow.

Fang looks down at the boy. "He is so adorable."

"I am glad the girls can be raised around him," I smile.

Willow smiles back. "Me too. Children are so rare. I am so glad the dragoons have returned. This gives me hope for Phoenix to find his true mate eventually."

I feel for Willow. "You should have hope for a true mate as well."

Willow smiles, but it doesn't reach her eyes. "Perhaps, but I have not found him yet. It is okay. Phoenix is my soul, the love of my life, and I am so grateful."

I smile at Willow. "My sister has plans to get all the women to meet more men. Hopefully, all men and women will have a chance at happiness. Water dwellers had a union, a true mating between land and water. Several matings are among us here at the castle. There is hope the goddess has found a way to bless us with true mates again."

"I think that opens up mating opportunities no one was considering," Fang says, adding his thoughts.

Willow's eyes light up at the revelation. "These are danger-ous times with the evil that is out there now. With a little help from the goddess, I truly believe things on this planet will be as they should, with love available for all."

Willow smiles, and we all see Gemma and Kit as they hold the sleeping babies and step closer to us.

"Gemma, thank you so much for all your help," I say as I approach Faith and Hope.

"I wanted to hold them before we leave. Kayla is too pregnant to travel, so I need to visit her. Would you be willing to come? She needs a healer," I ask as I sit, holding the babies.

Kit kneels next to me. "I vow I will take care of the girls. Star and I will watch after them like they are our own," Kit says with seriousness.

"I am here to help as well," Willow offers.

Hudson and Barron step close. "I will keep them safe with my life. I vow it," Hudson swears.

"I as well," Barron says.

"Yeah, those men are extremely protective. They will probably become even more so when we leave," I say, looking at the females.

"I truly am grateful to each of you. It is tough to leave," I say as I choke back my tears.

I kiss the girls, and so does Fang as I hand them back to Kit and Star.

"We will return as soon as possible," I say as we walk out.

Near the gate in the gardens, Gemma—the tiny female with the pixie style—joins the small group of men gathering to leave and us. Balthazar stands next to Fang, looking at Gemma and me with concern.

"I am shiften," Gemma says as she flashes her owl-like eyes. "I am excellent with healing magic. I usually help the females here during delivery. I helped with Phoenix when he was born."

Gemma stands firm in her tiny form, trying to convince all the strong men that she means to go. The men start to balk at another female putting herself in harm's way.

I wave my hand to silence them. "Are any of you shiften here with healing magic?" I ask the men, not considering that Balthazar is also a shiften with healing magic.

"I am." The bulky muscled Balthazar steps forward. The man steps up in front of Gemma, towering over her.

*Of course, he is.* He saved Fang and me. For that, I love this giant brute of a man. But that's beside the point.

"Balthazar, officially meet Gemma," Fang introduces.

Gemma stares up and up, meeting the eyes of the huge man's eyes as he stares down at her sternly.

"I can heal females. You should return to safety," Balthazar insists, adamant about keeping Gemma safe. Gemma's pale, sparkly face turns red with anger, but I chime in before she can snap her sass at the arrogant male.

"Balthazar. Healer Balthazar. How many babies have you delivered?"

"I have not delivered babies. Females are too few. They tend to care for their own. However, this is dangerous. It's bad enough you are going. Adding another female to protect weakens our defenses. I am a strong healer. I am confident I will care for our queen with all the skills necessary to heal her and deliver young."

Both Gemma and I bristle at the arrogant man. Fang interjects, saving the male from both barrels as I dish out complaints.

"I think it's handy to have two healers, for the queen's sake," Fang winks at Gemma and me.

Balthazar wants to argue, but something in Fang's gaze tells him to be quiet while he's still ahead of our women's scorn. Balthazar's jaw ticks as he clenches his mouth shut, clearly wanting to argue more.

"What is your familiar?" Gemma asks the colossal man.

He stands proud and lets his form take shape, a giant moose standing tall in answer. Gemma laughs, and the tension eases as they all prepare for the journey ahead.

I tuck the book close to me into a pouch on my back. I glance back at the castle and the guards surrounding it in extra protection, with many men taking extra shifts. I start chanting a quiet prayer for the girls to be safe while I am away.

# The Vampire

I wake up feeling fresh and eager to get my prize. I send my spies to scout with the priority of finding the queens. I want my hands on them all. I will get them. I need their blood. Their solid and robust blood will soon be all mine.

I call on all the witches and warlocks I have. I have them searching for a spell to suppress the dragon fire. Yes, if I can control the effects of that fire, I won't have any weaknesses.

The fire barely hit me at the beach and burned hotter than the sun. The fire will be deadly if I get hit with too much of it, especially without dragon blood to heal me.

Yes! I need to suppress the dragon fire, and I will have my way with the dragons. My single-minded focus is to get my next intoxicating fix of dragon blood.

*"Where are you? COWARD!"*

I grab my head. That incessant water-dwelling female has been out seeking, hunting for me. I was constantly pushing her threats into my mind.

I will deal with her. Put that bitch in her place. I am her god, and she will cry out to me for mercy before I finish with her.

My spies report that she hunts with her pod, another water-dwelling female, and a male shiften. An irritating nuisance I will have to deal with eventually. For now, I want my prize. I will have the queen's blood.

*"Come out, wherever you are, you nasty creep!"*

"Argh!" I roar, grabbing my head. "That bitch will pay for this annoyance," I mutter. She must be getting closer. Her screech is getting louder.

*"I am going to turn you into chum, demon!"* I hear that fish scream again in my head.

I need to get farther away from this bitch to focus on my dragon blood. I must delegate my minions to make this plan successful.

# CHAPTER 31

## Brooke

We march along on our journey to the wildwood.

"You know, Gemma, there are these huge trees on Earth, the planet I grew up on. They are called redwoods," I explain.

"Kayla and I always wanted to go to the redwood forest and drive through a tree." Staring at the trees as we walk, I continue.

"We wanted to camp there, maybe hunt for bigfoot on some silly tour." I'm enjoying my chat with Gemma.

"This world has the largest trees I've ever seen. Kayla wanted a picture of me hugging one of the redwood trees." I point to the enormous trunk of the tree towering tall next to us.

"I bet you could drive a semi-truck through that one. This place is so much cooler than the redwoods. I mean, there's no Paul Bunyan, but still, this place is amazing."

I can see Gemma eagerly trying to comprehend me, but she asks, "What is a truck?" I laugh.

"Well, we have transportation machines we can operate and drive. They take us places on wheels, and it is comfortable and fast. A semi-truck transport is usually bigger because it hauls stuff with a trailer. Trucks are convenient, but the fumes are bad for our Earth. I'm glad this world doesn't have them." I see Gemma's curiosity and try to explain a few Earth things.

"We had many things made with technology that I miss a bit, like TV. But I really wouldn't trade it for what I have now. This world is my home. Fang, my family. The magic in the people here is pure—more animal in their instincts, but above all, respectful of this world and each other."

"I love the 'less is more' vibe of this place. There's plumbing and modern-day convenience, but it's run-on magic. All the comforts of civilized society without pollution. I would be a happy camper if I could only manage my magical abilities—preferably, the dragon on demand." I'm rambling, but Gemma's a good listener and doesn't judge me.

Gemma stares up at me with her tiny pixie self. "I like hearing about your birth world. It's strange," she says.

I glance around at the shield of men surrounding us. "I will tell you more about it sometime. Right now, I can't wait to show you the crystal caves in the mountain pass." Gemma's eyes sparkle with interest.

"I love crystals. They are a weakness of mine. I can use some as conduits to help aid my healing magic." Gemma's excitement flares.

"Then you are going to love this place."

I pick up my pace, excited to have a friend who's as much as I am into crystals. We travel up the pass, looking for the hidden door to cut through the mountain.

"Believe me, Gemma, it beats the cliff edge these fools tried to make us do the last time. Kayla and I just about beat them for that stupid idea. Thank the goddess for the magic of this place. We were able to find the hidden door instead, a much more pleasant path."

Gemma seems tired from traveling hard all day. The

moment she enters the cavern, she hums with energy and excitement. When the crystal hall is on her radar, she practically runs as everyone gets busy making a simple camp on the large platform in the center of the mountain.

A magical glow of crystals gently lights our way. I loved this place as much as the first time I was here. I saw Gemma's face light up with excitement, making this a different experience.

"This place is sacred. An ancient hall, it has the most enchanting display of crystals. See that one hanging up there," Gemma says in awe.

"This is a healing, holy place. I feel a pull to a certain crystal, calling me incessantly." Gemma's eyes flash owl, and she starts to panic, really wanting that crystal.

I look up and see the crystal glowing in a pulse, reminding me of a heartbeat.

Gemma is obsessed. She tears off her clothes, not caring who sees her. She flies her little snow-spotted owl self to her coveted crystal. The crystal is out of her reach as a woman. Now, she tries to rub herself against it as an owl, desperate to touch it in any way possible.

"Gemma?" I call up to her, a bit startled.

Balthazar and Fang frame me as they all watch the fumbling owl.

"Gemma, please come down and let us help you," I beg as I feel Gemma's frantic energy. I feel sorry for my tiny friend. Gemma lands and transforms into a woman in front of us.

Balthazar tries to block her from anyone's view with his massive body, putting himself in front of Fang, me, and the rest of the men. Gemma stares up at his wide brown, concerned eyes. Gemma's own wide owl eyes plead with his.

"It's my totem, the pendulum crystal in the clustering." She points at the crystal hanging up there.

Balthazar's eyes follow her finger, and his shock spreads on his face.

"For their kind, only the most ordained healers are blessed with a sacred totem," Fang explains.

"I have a higher respect for you, Gemma," Balthazar says with a bow.

He is determined to help Gemma. Balthazar continues to block Fang and me. I want to help my friend, so I try to investigate.

"Sire, my queen, please allow me to assist. I know what Gemma needs. Please give us some space," Balthazar insists with his back still facing us.

A demand to back off. He takes off his shirt and hands it to Gemma. I start arguing with Fang, trying to get past the giant moose of a man to get to my friend Gemma.

"Dress, little owl. I will transform, and you can stand on my back to reach it," Balthazar tells Gemma.

Gemma puts his shirt on automatically as the moose drops his pants, giving me a front-row view of the moose's ass. Fang instinctively moves, stepping in front of me to urge me back.

After Balthazar changes, he kneels on his two front legs, letting Gemma use his huge antlers to help boost herself up. Gemma maneuvers herself onto the moose's back. The shirt she wears hangs long, just above her ankles. Gemma is agile and keeps her balance with her bare feet on his furry shoulders.

Gemma still can't reach the crystal she wants as she stretches, arms reaching high. Gemma moves to sit on her knees on Balthazar's back gently. She leans her head to his ear, holding on to his antlers.

"Will it hurt you if I stand on your antlers?" she asks Balthazar.

He stands tall, holding his head as high as possible in response.

Gemma wastes no time climbing him, balancing herself elegantly with one foot on each antler. Her bare feet must hurt as his antlers dig in. Gemma can grab the tip of the crystal.

The moment she touches it, the crystal comes free, falling into her arms.

Gemma loses her focus on balancing and falls. Balthazar changes so fast that he catches her in his arms. He's standing in a honeymoon pose, holding Gemma now. I am confused, even as I watch it all.

Gemma isn't aware of us. She's in a trance as the sacred crystal completes its bond, imprinting with her.

"Oh, my God!" I rush to check on her.

Balthazar twists yanking Gemma away from my outreaching fingers.

"Don't touch her yet!" he growls, sounding as if he's in pain.

Balthazar walks on unsteady legs to lay Gemma down on a bed mat. He settles his blanket over her. Then he sits naked in front of Gemma's sleeping body. He puts his head in his hands, breathing deeply, trying to shake off something.

Fang holds me back from behind, trying to keep me from touching Gemma.

"Brooke, my love, calm down and notice that Balthazar is suffering." Fang tries to calm me.

I have smoke trailing from my nostrils and a peppering shadow of red scales surfacing. Fang keeps trying to reason with me.

Balthazar glances up at us. He is depleted and weak. He places his head back in his hands, ignoring us again.

"Gemma is a blessed healer. Her totem called to her, and now they bond. To touch a totem bonding while it is in the making is dangerous. That pulse and merge of power are painful to anyone that is not part of the bond," Fang tries to explain.

He pulls me into a hug, letting me bury my face in his chest. I am worried for Gemma.

"It is okay, my love. Gemma is truly a rare healer. I have only heard legends of the sacred totem healers. I have never met or known of any in our long lifetime. Gemma is truly bonded with the elements of this world—flesh, stone, air, water, fire, and all the magic."

Fang holds me a bit tighter. "Balthazar was hurt helping Gemma while the bonding was initiated. He will need a moment to mend. It is said she can heal not only flesh but the land, sea, and anything of this world. They are the most powerful of healers. Be happy for your friend. This is a miracle."

"She was so frantic. Her energy was screaming in panic. All my senses wanted me to help ease her," I say. "I'm so glad she is going to be okay. I'm happy for her if this is such a huge deal. I need to calm my nerves."

Fang takes my face in his hands and kisses me. "I can calm your nerves if you'll allow it."

*Oh, I'll allow it.*

# CHAPTER 32

## Kayla

I fall asleep and in my dreams, I hear that telling ringing in my ear. An unfamiliar male voice drones in my mind, giving me a vivid dream.

My clairvoyance shows me something important. I see the goddess, Harmony. She is laughing with her friends—a man and his family.

Somewhere in the past—long ago when Harmony lived here. She was visiting her friends, and they all seemed happy. I feel a nudging, but not that feeling when someone touches me and some other person's energy invades and takes over.

This energy doesn't feel evil. It feels like a knock, a longing for me to hear them. When a being wants to tether a communication pathway from mind to mind, the invitation is gentle and easy to connect to.

This is a muddled communication tethering and the desperation on the other end throbbing at my skull is not easy to contact.

The image of dirt and mud flashes over and over in my head. I feel panic and suffocation.

I know this is not my panic. This is not my emotion. I scan the energy, trying to decipher a threat. The image of the goddess casually hanging out with that man and his family flashes in my mind again. I feel like the man is trying to connect and communicate with me. I allow the rope to connect, sensing that a friend of the goddess wants to talk to me.

*"I am Fabian, a high priest of the goddess Harmony. This is a memory of my family back when this world was well and happy without that vile creature."*

The energy is sad, such an overwhelming sadness. The man sounds muffled and has a monotone voice.

*"I feel the energy of the goddess inside you. I had lost hope, but with you here, I believe you may have the key to saving my family. Please . . .* The man's voice fades, and I wake with a startle.

Having a lingering feeling of loss and sadness. Who is Fabian? This is the first time since arriving that I have been invaded by the energy of another unexpectedly. At least it wasn't evil, like the vampire.

Granted, it was a desperate feeling, and he wanted my help. This guy was close to Harmony. I want to help him. I try to find that rope and reconnect.

Another wave of pain takes over my whole body, and I lose any ability to concentrate.

I need Brooke. Talen holds my hand, supporting me. Sweat breaks out on my forehead.

"I need my sister." I plead with Talen as pain radiates all over my whole body.

Talen swoops me up in his arms and lays me as gently as possible in the hot water of the flower tub that he has drawn up for me. The aroma fills the room, lavender chamomile. The mosaic tile depicting the dragon queen gives off a glow. The crystal lights chime with a dimness. Everything around me is trying to comfort me.

I want to appreciate it, but all I feel is pain. I cry, and pant as hot water tries to ease my contractions. Fear overwhelms me.

"I am so scared, Talen," I croak out through the pain.

"I am here, love. You are doing so well. Do not fear. I am with you." Talen tries to reassure me, but I see he's terrified himself.

"I need my sister." I cry out as another wave of contractions hits.

I feel my armband heat up. My baby girls cry out, worried about me and confused.

I feel Brooke trying to connect to me just as I use everything inside me I can muster to close off my armband from them, not wanting my babies to suffer. The result causes me to pass out, and blackness blissfully gives me a reprieve.

"Talen!" I sit straight up in our bed, awoken from what little sleep I could get.

Talen sits up fast, responding to my sudden cry.

"What is it, love?" he asks as he frantically examines me.

"I felt another hard contraction, and I panicked," I say.

"This one woke me up. Can they come this soon?" Has it only been days since I discovered my pregnancy?

My belly is huge. Angry red stretch mark lines stripe down my belly and hips. I know that my sister Brooke is coming. Still, I'm scared to do this without her. I looked at Talen.

"What do we do?" Talen is lost as he gets me some water.

"Here, have a drink of water. Stay hydrated. Try to be calm and focused. What does nature tell you, your intuition?" he suggests.

I feel an unbearable contraction, and all my ability to think leaves me.

"Don't tell me to be calm!" I growl at him in pain.

Talen's face falls. He tries to rub my back. I grab his hand, yanking it away from touching me. His feelings are hurt, but I'm suffering. I'm not genuinely rejecting his touch. It just magnifies my pain. When my pain ebbs, I try to stand.

"Help me to the treasure." Talen walks with me, holding me as I lean on him whenever a contraction hits. Stopping every few feet, I refuse to allow him to carry me.

"This fucking hurts like hell!" I cry out.

Talen's forehead beads with sweat as he stresses over my pain. I am so overwhelmed with labor pains. I can tell he only wants to help ease my suffering.

"I will never put you through this again. I vow it!" Talen swears, not able to stand my suffering.

"This is not about you right now. So, get—" I take a breath, "over—" I pant, "your—" I moan in pain, "little pity party, tough guy!"

Finally, the dragon inside me takes over the nest of jewels, transforming my body. My tail swishes, knocking Talen on his ass and sliding him six feet along the floor. My dragon whimpers and fire streams out in a puff, searing the ceiling. Luckily, the flame goes out, staining the crystal ceiling black above our heads. I feel my eggs grow even more inside the belly of my dragon.

I feel the urge to push. My dragon bears down, and I lay my first egg. I bear down again and lay my second egg. The pain subsides, and I know my eggs are delivered. Magic swirls through me to my eggs as I incubate them.

I feel a mix of excitement and fear, my childhood comes to the forefront of my mind, and all I want is the best loving home for my children. The only memory of my parents that I have flashed in my head. I was three years old, sitting on the bathroom counter, crying because my finger was bleeding. I somehow had a splinter, glass or something, wedged into my toddler's finger.

My mother was hungover, trying to use a sewing needle to pick the splinter out. Her touch had me feeling nauseous and hungover. I felt her anger, exhaustion, and not wanting to deal with me. The dirty sink, stained with brown gunk, was typical to me. I remember the red blood from my finger being rinsed down the drain under the cold faucet water, running over the stained, dirty basin. My dad came into the bathroom and punched my mom.

They fought and yelled as he dragged her out of the dirty bathroom. He threw my mom on the bed in the next room. I couldn't see them. I was stuck on the cluttered counter, crying and bleeding, helpless, forced to listen to my parents fighting and to feel the energy of their madness.

A loud bang startled me. I fell and broke my arm. The pain was so intense I lost my breath with the long-winded cry I let out. When I could, I finally sucked in a breath. I could smell the unflushed toilet odor. A door slammed and I was left on the dirty floor of a messy bathroom with the sound of my crying and the constant drip of a leaky bathtub faucet.

The neighbors called the cops when they heard the gun go off. Three prominent men in dark-blue police uniforms kicked down our door and found me huddled near the toilet. I was in tears, rocking myself holding my broken arm, and sucking on my bleeding finger. The man seemed like a giant as he lowered his towering form to comfort me and pick me up.

The moment he touched me, I was overwhelmed with his emotions—anger, disgust, and sadness for me. His energy made me feel worse. I was too young and scared to understand clairvoyance or anything psychic. I had only known fear, hunger, pain, and neglect.

That is the first and only memory I can recall of my parents who were drug addicts and estranged from the family. My father shot and killed my mother that day. He was later found under an overpass, dead from an overdose of meth. So, into the system, I went.

My raw emotions have me shaking off that distant memory. I am more comfortable here on this magical planet than I ever felt on Earth. Harmony is home now. I am so grateful to have my children here with Talen.

# The Vampire

I summon my deep-ground-dwelling spiders. I once had my warlocks cast a spell on them. The spiders burrow in the dark caves and migrate out of their hidden holes for mating once in an annual cycle. They usually live off cave mice and bats. Normally, the spiders are the size of a small canine. However, I used the warlocks to feed the spiders my blood, to mutate the spiders, making them into eight-legged giant monsters the size of a horse. These spiders are monsters, and I love that I created another pet. Being a god has its perks.

Feeding them rabbits and small furry creatures, I trained them until I controlled their tiny hive minds. I saddled a few, so some of my minions could ride.

I send them out to get me a queen. I knew these things would come in handy one day.

I allow a few minions to lead on the backs of the spiders that take up the front row. The rest just gather in a mass to follow. I have my warlock mutate up the mating migration, creating a single-minded goal: my mission. The spiders can't mate unless they bring me my prize. It is too easy to mutate and manipulate them, like shooting fish in a barrel.

# CHAPTER 33

## Brooke

In the middle of the night, camped somewhere in the forest, I woke up in pain. My armband burns in waves and waves. Fang is at my side, noticing me feeling my arm.

"Are you in pain?" He asks.

"I feel an annoying burn, and it comes in waves. It didn't hurt like when the vampire attacked Kayla. Something has happened to Kayla."

I'm worried and want to pack up the camp and move faster. I worry about the girls too, knowing they felt the same warning in their little arms.

I am suddenly cut off from pain. Now I am frantic and scared for my sister.

"I know you want to go. We have been pushing all of us too fast, too hard. We need to let them rest for a bit longer," Fang insists.

I want to argue and insist on leaving, everything in my gut screaming at me to go. The loss of pain and that connection just voiding out on me ramp up my anxiety.

I notice Gemma waking up with a wild gaze that makes me scared. Gemma pushes hard on Balthazar's sleeping form, waking him. He stands up fast, alert, and looking around, on guard.

Gemma grabs his shirt with her right fist and holds her totem with her left hand like a sword. Gemma faces me and starts marching toward Fang and me. The sight brings an image of a poodle dragging its owner with a leash.

I want to giggle, looking at that tiny lady pulling this huge man behind her. But my senses set off warning alarms. Gemma is concerned as she drags the moose to us.

Gemma is chanting, profoundly serious in her disposition. At that moment, I feel a wave of dark energy heading right at us. I put my blocks up. I try to warn Fang, but everything happens so fast. As soon as Gemma gets close to us, I hear her vocalized chant and feel her push my mind simultaneously.

*"Get the men to surround us. Get them close to me, or they will succumb"*, Gemma demands in our minds.

"Get up! Fall in!" Fang bellows.

"Surround us close!" I yell.

Men hurry as they hear the alarm. In the outer area of our camp, I see men start collapsing where they stand. They are too far from Gemma. Our camp is sufficiently lit with fire and magic torch stones. The forest beyond our lights is covered in eerie darkness.

I feel evil surround us and eyes on us. Power pulsates, trying to get through the shield Gemma erected around us.

A man in the outermost area of our camp is lying prone where he passed out. He's not under the shield that Gemma erected. A berserker beast jumps into the light, biting the man's leg, taking our helpless warrior back into the darkness in silent horror.

The beasts snatch two other prone men. I feel Gemma's grief as she feels she failed to protect the poor men. I feel my dragon stir. The trigger needed to call her forth is the need to fight. I finally transformed.

Fang also shifts into his dragon for the first time.

Since Gemma is feeding us the power to help us shift, her magic is super amped-up. My red dragon takes up the left, and Fang's black dragon is to my right. I use my tail to sweep sleeping men toward Gemma, putting them under her shield.

Fang blows a small puff of fire to light the darkness, careful not to burn the giant trees down. The flash illuminates a line of people—dark-robed men, reminding me of the death reaper character depicted back on Earth. All these fools need is a scythe.

Fang blows flame again. We see the death reaper guys as they stroll in a formation, the berserkers tearing the bodies of our stolen warriors apart behind them in a frenzy, eager to battle.

*"I want to torch these assholes."* I push to Fang, feeling eager to fight myself, which is not normal. My dragon is taking more control than my peace-loving skin self.

*"Maybe we should munch them and save the forest from our dragon fire.* Fang tries strategizing with me.*"*

*"Oh, I like the way you think."* I snap my snarling teeth toward the darkness in threat to emphasize my desire to rip and tear them apart.

*"Listen to me,"* Gemma interrupts.

*"The essence of all magic is tuned with me, with my totem. I know their intent. The vampire has sent them to cast a spell on you—an attempt to amputate your dragon fire. The vampire has a bloodlust for your powerful dragon blood. These demented, turned warlocks are out on a mission."*

Gemma strains to communicate with us and casts her spell simultaneously.

*"He knows your fire is too risky for him. He needs your fire to be harmless to ensure his safety while he tries to capture you. These tainted warlocks are compelled to use all they know to achieve this goal. I am focusing on redirecting the spell and safeguarding us and the environment."*

*"What the hell?!"* I snap as Gemma continues her explanation and plan.

*"When I say go, blow your hottest, most arduous fire circle outward around us. Trust me. They will be disintegrated,"* Gemma explains in a rush as she multitasks her magic in collaboration with her chanting and connection to this world's core source of magic.

*"Ready when you are, sweetheart."* I encourage you.

A berserker gets bolder, jumping into the light, snarling, and clawing at the ground in challenge to Fang and me. I want to flick it with my claw to watch it fly. Who knew fighting could be so amusing? Instead, I hold steady, waiting for Gemma's command.

*"Go! Go now!"* Gemma screams in our heads.

I huff and puff my flames hard, blowing them out fast as I turn to the left in a circle. I blow my fire in a steady flame. Fang turns to the right in the same motion. We keep our people safe in the middle between us. We blow nonstop until our fires join, like a fiery kiss. We seal ourselves in a ring of fire.

My dragon flame incinerates the warlocks and berserkers. It feels like a triumph to me. The environment and the beautiful trees have no scorch marks. They are free of dragon fire— no burn scars on the bark. I have to blow my flame in a puff to double-check that my eyes aren't deceiving me.

A berserker jumps out at Fang, grabbing his wing. I snap my teeth, chewing that berserker in half to get it off, my mate.

*"Did it hurt you badly?"* I ask.

*"My love, you worry over a scratch. That thing could not truly harm me,"* Fang says with amusement.

We chase after the minions that initially escaped us and incinerate every one of them. We quickly return to Gemma and our men.

I take a moment to sense the nature around us and feel nothing but grateful chimes, the nature and trees confirming we did not harm them. The tree hugger in me is ecstatic. Thank the universe for Gemma.

Gemma explains, "I had to rework the spell they tried to cast. I ensured your dragon fire did not harm the untainted, innocent world. Now your fire will only hurt the enemy."

I am impressed by my new friend. *Girl, you're my new favorite superhero. Gemma the mighty*, I say in amazement.

*"You, indeed, are a sacred one." Fang* complements Gemma.

Balthazar's face is lovestruck, watching the tiny woman, gazing at her wild-streaked hair poking out in various directions.

"That was the most beautiful thing I've ever witnessed," Balthazar says to Gemma.

Gemma, in her excitement, jumps at the burly man. Balthazar catches her and holds her up as she wraps her short legs around his waist as far as she can. Gemma anchors her arms around the man's neck and kisses him delightfully.

I am glad to have witnessed the sweet moment between the new couple. But then, melancholy sadness interrupts my brief joy. We have lost some worthy warriors. I reach out with my senses, trying to detect if there is any more danger.

*"Do you feel any threats?"* I ask Gemma, hating to interrupt the moment.

Gemma takes her time, savoring her first kiss with her huge moose. She finally comes up for air. Balthazar and Gemma are both dazed and satisfied.

Gemma puts her dainty finger to Balthazar's lips. "Wait one sec, okay?"

She tilts her head as if trying to hear, closes her eyes, and focuses while the huge male stands like a statue, holding her tiny body around his waist. The men are busy packing up the camp around us.

"Nope, no more threat tonight," Gemma says confidently. "Now, back to business, moose." Gemma returns to exploring Balthazar's mouth with hers.

I feel that familiar energy of a true mate imprinting bond happening for the couple.

Fang, still in dragon form, gives me a knowing gaze. *"I've noticed a lot of mating lately. In my long life, I have never seen such a blessing."*

He radiates happiness at the change in the air. *"You and your sister's arrival set in motion a rightness in our world."* Fang sends waves of affection and appreciation my way.

I feel the joy of Fang in his dragon form. I am happy for him. I wonder if my dragon can blush. It feels like it, with heat pooling near my snout. But I still have a driving need to get to my sister.

*"I love you too, Fang."* I push all my emotions toward him.

*"If the threat is gone, I want to take advantage of this form and fly. I need to get to my sister."*

*"We need the men organized to meet us at the wildwood,"* Fang insists.

*"I want to bring Gemma and the giant moose with us,"* I tell him and exhale with a huff, hating to interrupt the new couple's lingering kisses. Fang stares at the couple.

*"Better you than me,"* he replies as he turns to engage his men, leaving the task to me.

*"Brat!"* I say to his back, watching him leave me. I hear his laugh in my head as he goes to his men.

*"Um, hey, you two. Um, congratulations and all."* I try tentatively to get their attention.

*" I hate to interrupt a good thing, but I feel an urgency to get to my sister. Will you fly with us to check on her, please?"*

Something must register in Gemma's head that I am worried about because she snaps out of her kissing trance. Unfurling herself from the love-struck drunk Balthazar, Gemma adjusts herself gracefully. Looking up at my red dragon, excitement fills her eyes.

"I would love to fly with your dragons. I'll have to ride with you, though. I don't think my owl can go as fast as you."

Balthazar stands still, with his eyes locked on Gemma. He

moves his fingers to touch his swollen lips, a skeptical, stunned expression plastered on his face.

"Moose!" Gemma snaps her fingers in front of his chest, trying to get him to focus.

"We need to get ready to fly." She smiles excitedly up at him.

"Wait, what? Did you say *fly*?" He stumbles after her, full of anxiety. "Gemma, I am a moose, a land creature. Watching you fly is beautiful, you delicate-feathered owl. However, I am not meant to fly."

Gemma plucks a bark flower from the base of a tree, putting a bloom in her wild pixie hair. Gemma thanks the tree, then turns to look up at him.

"Well, I thought we could kiss more when we get there. But I guess you can walk with the men instead. I'll see you whenever you get there, then." Shrugging her shoulders, she practically skips away from him.

Balthazar changes his tune. "Wait a minute. I could fly. Yes, let's fly."

I'm getting a kick out of my little friend Gemma. She's so cool. Soon, I have Gemma in my claws, and Fang has Balthazar. I leap into the air as the morning sun rises, painting the sky in deep colors of purples, reds, and blues. We fly as fast as we can. I dart through clouds and dodge the floating crystal platforms.

I land outside the barrier shield of my wildwood home in the forest. Fang lands behind me. We both gently set our friends down. I take the form of flesh. Gemma's thrilled with the adventure, smiling cheek to cheek as she digs out dress and clothes for Fang from my bag that holds my stuff. After we are clothed, Gemma hands me the book.

Balthazar is a bit green, trying to regain his bearings and land legs. I look him over, one eyebrow raised.

"Not a fan of flying?" I ask.

Fang chuckles. "I wasn't too hard on him. If he had opened his eyes, he might have enjoyed himself."

Balthazar stares at Gemma. "You're lucky I love you. I would not fly for any other reason."

Stunned, Gemma takes a second to register what the man has declared.

"You love me?" she questions in shock.

An array of emotions flickers across his face.

Love shines in his eyes. "Yes, I love you, Gemma."

Their animal instinct knows without question the emotion of love and the true mate bond they have been blessed with.

Gemma runs into his arms, letting him lift her so they can kiss. "I am pretty sure I love you too, Moose!"

"Pretty sure?" Balthazar asks between kisses.

"Yes!" Gemma confirms.

"If that is the case, then my goal is to make sure you love me back."

I lean in to kiss Fang, feeling love in the air.

"Great! We are all in love." I giggle as we escort them to my first home in the hall. I'm reminiscing as I point things out, telling Gemma and Balthazar how Kayla and I ended up here, getting sucked through a god portal.

"You are going to love our grand hall. We have an apothecary wall and a magic blue door. I can't wait for you to tell me about some of the herbs and what they can do," I say to Gemma, excited to be back home.

Gemma says, "I feel enormous power here."

Talen greets us at the door, stepping outside before anyone can enter. Proud purple eyes shine at us.

"Kayla laid eggs. She is in dragon form," he explains. "I'm worried that her protective instincts might flair up around so many visitors."

"What?" I say, shocked, saddened I wasn't here for that.

Talen gazes at me. "Kayla wanted you to be here too. You would have been if it were possible," Talen says.

"Maybe I should go, just me to start," I suggest.

Fang can't hide his concern. I light up with excitement and

concern. I want to see Kayla. I turn toward my three companions.

"Fang, honey, can you please take Gemma and Balthazar to the meadow and make a fire? I need to see Kayla and her eggs."

Fang hugs me and kisses me reassuringly. He turns to his brother and brings him in for a hug. "Congratulations, brother, you truly are blessed."

Talen takes his brother's hug in solid arms. "Yes, indeed, brother. My words fail me. I am so happy right now."

Fang smiles. He leans in and kisses me gently. "We are fine. See your sister. I'll be waiting." He ushers the new couple to the meadow, retreating from the magic hall.

Talen gives me a knowing look and escorts me inside. I hardly recognize the place as I walk in. The smell of charged sulfur lingers in the air. My sister is in her blue dragon form, curled up in a pile of treasure. She wraps herself around her eggs. It's the most beautiful sight. Talen holds me back from running up to my sister in my excitement.

"Slowly," Talen encourages. I take a deep, calming breath and move slower than I want to.

"Kayla. Oh, Kay-Kay. I'm here. I finally made it," I say softly. Kayla lifts her head and leans in to sniff me.

*"I've missed you. I wish you could have been here, Brooke. I had two eggs. Can you believe it?"*

Kayla unfurls herself to show off her eggs better. The eggs magically glow with a blue swirl, a mist clouding around them. It's remarkable.

I take a tentative step toward the eggs. "Oh, my goddess! This is so amazing! I am so proud of you, Kayla. You did great." I go to touch the closest egg.

*"No!"* Kayla yelps in my head. Smoke streams from Kayla's nostrils as heat waves through the air. Kayla huffed a breath and tried not to let loose her fire.

I snatch my hand back before I can caress the egg. Talen

places his body in front of me, between Kayla and her eggs, making me take a step back for safety.

"I'm sorry," I say solemnly, trying not to feel the pang of rejection from my sister.

A pungent smell of smoke sifts through the air. Kayla's nostrils puff smoke some more. I take a few extra steps back.

*"Don't be silly, Brooke. It's not you. Of course, I want you to be a part of this. I trust no one more than you and Talen with my children. You know that. It's beyond my control. I don't understand having babies this way. My dragon has more control than I do now."*

I pat Talen's shoulder, asking him to step aside. "I completely understand. I will keep my distance and save hugs for later. For now, know I am here. I love you, Kayla. Tell me all about how it happened."

Kayla relaxes a bit as I step back and settle, sitting down to listen. As Kayla fills me in on everything from the vision to the delivery of her eggs, I take it now and enjoy our sisterhood. I tell Kayla about my adventure and Gemma's strength as a healer and magic user.

"Maybe she knows about what to expect when you're expecting hatchlings. How long the incubation will be and so forth," I suggest.

Talen wearily sighs. "It might not be wise to bring Gemma here near Kayla and the eggs. I'm not sure her dragon can stand anyone but you and I, even at a distance."

I continue, not phased one bit by Talen's warning. Dragon or not, I know Kayla. I can help calm her emotions enough to be safe. Kayla would never attack me, ever, no matter her wild side. I know Kayla would protect me, even from her instinct.

"Kayla, Gemma is so magical. I think she can help us. I would never bring anyone near you that I wouldn't trust myself."

# CHAPTER 34

## Kayla

The following day, Brooke and Gemma come into my nesting area.

"I'm Gemma. I know we barely met back at the castle, but I am excited to get to know you better," Gemma says in greeting.

"Brooke wanted me to check on you. I am happy to help if you'll allow it."

I send out waves of appreciation and am comforted by Gemma's presence.

The morning flies by. Talen and Fang become even closer friends with Balthazar, building cradles outside. Talen checks in with me and keeps me updated since being away from my side is difficult for Talen and me both.

"You are so beautiful in your dragon form. I never imagined I would ever see one in real life." Gemma compliments me.

I feel genuine respect for Gemma and am eager for her friendship. My dragon seems content enough to let Gemma enter my nesting grounds. I recognize my sisterhood and life-lock connection, instantly feeling at ease with Gemma. Accepting my dragon's invitation, Gemma keeps her distance and walks closer to Brooke.

Gemma is just about to explain how long the incubation lasts and what to expect when dread swamps us all, a sudden surge of fear coming from my girls. Hope cries out in terror in my head.

I see through Hope's eyes my worst nightmare, and I am helpless to intervene.

Barron and Hudson escort the women with the babies to the gardens. They stand at the goddess fountain because they insist Phoenix needs to make his wish at the wishing well. His mother, Willow, and his visiting father, Pax, enjoy watching the boy playing under a colorful sky. The blooming flowers of the garden make it a beautiful day to enjoy.

Out of nowhere, warriors sound the alarm. Hope, wide-eyed and startled by the energy of panic and fear, sees the spider monsters attacking the people. Chaos. Everything is moving too fast for me to understand what Hope is seeing. I glimpse berserkers on the backs of the first wave of giant eight-legged creatures. Hudson grabs Hope, and Barron grabs Faith. They take the babies from Kit and Star.

I see things through my baby girl's eyes—her confused, frantic fear making it hard for me to decipher what kind of attack is threatening my child. Since Hudson holds her, I siphon Gemma's magic to tap into Hudson instead of Hope so I can concentrate inside an adult mind. I can hear and feel Hudson as he runs, holding my Hope as fighting erupts everywhere. Hudson's tactical training has him calculating and staying in control, so my ability to decipher the battle is evident now.

Willow and Pax try to save their son. The boy, Phoenix, had been playing next to Hudson and Barron when this started. His mother, Willow, runs behind Hudson, trying to save her son. A warrior fights off a berserker on a spider that is fast on its heels.

Swarms of the creatures come in waves, covering everything with a blanket of furry, brown-legged spiders. Pax fights several of the creatures at once, trying to give Barron a chance to save Faith.

Pax becomes a bear, fighting for a path for his son and my babies to get back into the castle. Venom pours into Pax's leg as a spider bites him. Pax roars and fights, even as he takes his last breath and starts to liquefy from the venom.

Willow screams and tells her son, "Close your eyes, Phoenix. Mommy and Daddy love you. Go with Hudson but close your eyes. Just close your eyes until you are safe." she insists in a motherly tone.

Willow compels him with her magic as a spider sinks its fangs into her back. To hold off the creature with the last of her magic, Willow tosses her son to Hudson.

Hudson catches the boy. He holds Phoenix in one hand and Hope in the other. He runs hard and fast and feels the power of Willow. She uses the last of her magic to clear a path to the castle door. Hudson glances back as he punches his way to the doorway. Sheltering the two children in his arms, he sees Willow liquefy.

He sees Barron, who roars as he holds Faith, trying to protect her while trusting the soldiers to fight off the monsters. As their mother, I can witness the battle through the eyes of Hudson. He's horrified as a spider bites Barron's back. Barron tries to pass Faith to the warrior next to him before he falls.

Hudson howls in horror as a spider quickly rolls Faith up in her silk threads and carries Faith away in a comfortable retreat over the other spiders. He wants to fight his way to her, but he must get Hope and Phoenix safe.

The spiders and the minions retreat fast now that they have Faith. Once Hudson has the two children safe with Kit and Star, he howls a defeated cry as he transforms and runs after the retreating spiders.

I am losing my sanity, watching in horror.

I feel hopeful, so I leave Hudson and connect to Hope,

trying to send her my love and promise that I will save Faith. Star and Kit hold two hysterical children. Several other women huddle around in a safe room. A few warriors stand battle-ready, locked inside with the women and children.

The women sing a healing, calming song in a soft melody, trying to help calm the terrified children. Kit raises her head enough to lock her tearful eyes onto Star's as she rocks back and forth helplessly, trying to protect and help calm Hope.

Hope is transforming, her skin rippling with scales. Hot smoke leaves her nostrils. Star steps forward with Phoenix in her arms. Kit sends Hope her energy, trying to coax her to calm down.

Hope takes the form of her dragon. A tiny dragon jumps out of Kit's arms and waddles to the door. She's too tiny to blow a significant flame. Hope in her baby dragon form is purple and pink. Dragon smoke fills the room, along with fire. The vent in the ceiling takes the heat and smoke away, sucking it out fast.

A couple of soldiers are burnt by the baby flame as they reach for her. Kit and Star desperately try to calm the baby dragon. Phoenix walks up and wraps his tiny arms around the angry baby dragon. The moment he touches Hope, she seems to calm.

Phoenix sits, holding a baby Hope. Gemma sends a spell to sedate Hope as she relaxes and returns to her skin form—the boy sniffles, sad about his parents. Willow's lingering magic is keeping Phoenix somewhat sheltered from the trauma. The boy rocks back and forth. Both children support each other in a way that no adult can manage.

# CHAPTER 35

## Kayla

Gemma, on instinct, uses her totem crystal and all the magic she has to try to control my blue dragon and Brooke's red dragon. Brooke transformed instantly after the cry of my frantic babies boomed in our minds.

Gemma sends her voice to reason with me.

*"Trust me, dragon, to watch over your eggs. Trust me so you can attend to your young in need."* Gemma points to the blue eggs, trying to break through my madness to remind me to be mindful of their delicacy.

*"Trust me to keep your eggs safe, dragon mother,"* Gemma pleads with me. She repeats herself until her magic helps to calm my panic.

The raging inside me subsides enough for rational thought to take hold. I focus on my daughters, realizing I have to get them.

I am calm enough to focus on Gemma.

"Let me help you transform to your skin form so you can exit. Then you can transform again and fly to your daughters."

Brooke is still in battle mode, almost completely gone.

Gemma and I have to push hard to get Brooke to be calm enough to focus. Without Gemma's aid, all this would be impossible. We leave the great hall as two naked women. Gemma stays connected to me as she sends me a constant image of my eggs. Gemma lends me her energy to help keep my babies calm. Fang and Talen had already left and transformed the second Hope cried out.

Balthazar takes guard outside the hall door.

I encourage Hope to stay calm and safe. Without Gemma keeping me sane, I would be all dragon, with wildness out of control. I send Hope love and comfort. It's maddening not being able to connect to Faith.

Gemma helps me to give Hope a soothing wave of energy. Gemma sends her energy to help us all remain as rational as possible. However, she focuses mainly on me.

I touch the minds of the other three dragons, and madness overwhelms me. I know Gemma focusing on my eggs uses as much strength as she had used to incubate them and even more strength to keep me sane. This female is so gifted. I owe more than I can ever repay for this help.

Talen blows flames as he flies. He's raging. He has a single-minded focus on reaching out to his daughter Faith. His dragon is in total control. Fang flies over the castle grounds, burning the gardens as he makes a firestorm with his rage. We continue to fly, following the trail the herd of spiders made. The fast-moving creatures are already far east.

Brooke sets loose her dragon's fire onto countless swarms of mutated spiders. I watch them burn, their bodies popping in the heat. Fang blows his fire as we all land near the opening of a cave.

We are excessively too large to enter it. The madness in the minds of the dragons around me has them stuck in dragon form. Talen blows his fire in the cave as hard as possible, trying to burn all the foul things.

"*Release my child!*" He roars as he sends a menacing push outward with his command.

I desperately reach out to connect with Faith. I can't feel her. Gemma sends me reassurance that my child lives. She's only unconscious, knocked out from the dose of spider venom. My sanity is on the edge, even with the aid of the sacred one.

Brooke roars and claws at the ground, trying to dig her way inside the cave. Fang flies in a circle, spitting fire, looking for another way into the cave. Rage doesn't describe the waves of energy radiating off these dragons. Nature itself seems to tremble in fear as a reaction to us angry dragons.

Gemma grows weary, but I feel her determination. Gemma holds me steady as the day fades into night. The deep colors of twilight fade into stars as the dragons continue to rage—clawing, digging, and flying in lunacy to get to Faith.

I feel the stirring of the vampire as he wakes during sunset. Fearing for my daughter and fighting my madness, I use Gemma to help me transform. Naked, I go into the cave. Talen rages and blows fire into the cave. I feel the flames licking my skin in a soothing caress. I walk in fire. I see the flame colors as I walk through the flow of dragon fire unscathed.

I use all my senses to find my sleeping daughter. Seeking Faith out, I move deeper and deeper into the bowels of the vampire's lair. I walk past the reach of my mate's flames.

Berserkers attack me. One tear into my side with his oozing sharp claws. I must retreat into the safety of Talen's flames to escape them. My side is damaged terribly. I feel Gemma jolt as her magic is affected by my weakness.

My blue scales surface and I feel my madness returning.

"*Leave the cave.*" Gemma sends me a compulsion.

I retreat outside the cave, where rage transforms me again into my dragon. With my side sliced open, my blood spreads freely.

Berserkers come after us from all around. We swoop, burn, and tear apart these beasts in a wild rage. I feel Gemma and all the women who helped me before sending me their magic through the life-lock to help me regain my sanity.

I transform again, still bleeding a little. I know I need to get to my Faith before the vampire does, so I run back into the caves. I go down farther, letting my intuition guide me to my daughter.

This time, the berserkers aren't there. I come across a man made of mud, and he feels familiar, but I don't care. I ignore the warlock who appears out of the mud as I pass him in search of my child.

I finally find my precious Faith wrapped up in a spool of webbing, cocooned like a moth.

A spider strikes out at me as I approach my baby.

I hiss in my skin form. I partially change and blow out my dragon fire. My dragon's wrath gives me whatever I need to save my child. The spider disintegrates. I run to my daughter and tear open the sticky webbing that traps Faith. I hug her close to me and turn to leave this evil place.

"I get two for the price of one!"

The vampire's cringy voice pierces my ears as I fight the raging madness of my dragon trying to take over. I stop in my tracks as I register the threat of the vampire close to me.

I narrow my vision, scanning my surroundings. I can see the mud-shaped man standing stuck on the dirt wall, watching me sadly. The vampire walks out of a cave hole, circling this space to position himself to strike.

The vampire is salivating as I stand naked and bleeding, holding my baby.

Grateful my baby is asleep for this, I glare at the vampire.

"Don't you dare take another step closer," I command with a calm, intense tone.

The vampire laughs. "Aren't you cute?" he responds, not aware of the danger he's in.

"I am your god, and you will obey me like my little pet."

Gemma and all the females lend me a surge of power. If I'm not mistaken, the mud man sends me his energy too.

The vampire lunges, driven by the frantic desire to consume my blood. I partially shift as blue scales take shape on my skin. I hiss and blow my dragon fire at the vampire.

Even with his vampire speed, my fire floods the caverns. The vampire feels the burns all over his body. The coward retreats through a vein of the cave that opens into the forest.

I carry Faith, blowing fire in every direction, eliminating any minion or creature that the vampire has hidden in his horrible lair. I finally walk upward into Talen's flames. I gaze at my baby sleeping in my arms. The red and orange flames embrace us. She is so beautiful. I'm so happy to have my baby back.

Brooke and Fang frantically chase the vampire. Minions explode out of the caverns like an ant hill being flooded. The vampire makes his escape down another vein in the cavern's system. Brooke and Fang start to destroy the scattering minions.

Out into the starry night, I meet my raging mate. Talen inhales the scent of our daughter and me deeply. I send Talen an image of my eggs, and his crazed dragon calms down slowly. The man finally gets some of his senses back.

Now that his stolen daughter is safe, Talen scoops us in his claws and gently carries us back to my nest. Talen whispers a push of encouraging words to soothe our baby and me as he flies.

Brooke and Fang fight with wrath as they blow fire at their targets, the dragons relentlessly pursuing the vampire while fighting the tainted minions. Fang blows fire into the mouth of the cave the vampire entered. Brooke flies in a circle, seeking out other entrances. I nudge Brooke's mind.

"Get Hope." I send Brooke images of Faith safely sleeping in my arms.

Gemma and the females focus on Brooke, trying to help her regain her sanity. Brooke starts to calm her mind as her dragon retreats, letting the woman think more clearly.

# CHAPTER 36

## Brooke

send Fang images of Faith and Hope. *"I am going to get Hope and take her to Kayla."*

Fang's madness swirls in his dragon mind as he hunts the vampire. I fly to him, landing next to him as he blows more fire into the cave. I push at his mind to get his attention. Fang reluctantly responds to me. I send him my love and pride in his determination. I send him love until his mind calms and his madness retreats a little.

*"I need to take Hope to Kayla,"* I say as I send him images of Faith in Kayla's arms. Fang finally understands.

*"Yes, reunite them. I will stand guard and keep this creature trapped here for now."* Fang settles his dragon form near the entrance to the cave, allowing his dragon more dominance than the man.

I nuzzle his head with mine, sending him a mental kiss. I leap to the skies, flying toward the castle. The battle has raged all night. The smoke and fire make the sky colorful as I land in the charred gardens of the castle. Many men stand guard, making a wall of flesh blocking the castle entrance, all on alert.

My heart melts at the wave of energy. These men are tired and defeated, yet still determined to fight and protect with everything they have. They're genuinely honorable men. As my red dragon finally lets my flesh take form, a warrior hands me a shirt. I thank him and ask him to take me to Hope. Men step aside to create a pathway as I enter the castle and take me to the dorms.

I am wrapped in a tight hug as soon as I walk through the gate. Star holds me tight. Slowly releasing me, Star sobs. I take a deep breath and urge my dragon to remain calm as I hear the significant trauma and loss the spiders' ambush inflicted.

I cry, too, as I hear about Willow and Pax. The guardian, Barron, died trying to save Faith. I cry for him.

"Hudson ran after the spiders but hasn't returned," Star says through sobs. "Some soldiers are still tracking him and the spider army. Most of us are in the kitchen, trying to help Stan and his staff cook."

"Feeding all the warriors helps us to feel like we are helping in some small way," Kit says.

The ladies escort me to where they keep the children.

Star explains, "We gave them tea to help sedate them. They were traumatized."

Kit says sadly, "Poor Phoenix. He's now orphaned."

I open the door to see a colossal wolf lying around two sleeping children, his sad eyes gazing up into mine.

I can feel his guilt and sadness leaving him in waves.

I kneel as I whisper, "You fought worthily. You did your job. You helped to protect Hope and the boy. I am sorry about all the losses. Thank you for taking care of the children. We burned all the spiders, and Kayla has Faith safely with her now." I send him an image of Faith and an image of the eggs.

Something in the wolf changes, and some of his energy calms.

"Kayla wants her daughter," I say softly.

I stare down at the two children. I see the boy, his face red and nose snotty from crying. My heart melts for the boy. I send Fang an image and am waiting for his response.

I feel a trigger as I see the boy—the universe is telling me this child is mine now.

*"Take the boy, my love. We can raise him as our own from now on."* Fang sends me love and empathy.

"I am adopting the boy," I declare. Star is a bit shocked. She smiles a sad smile.

"Yes, he will need love and a lot of nurturing to help him with his grief. This makes sense." Star accepts my love for the boy and sends me encouragement.

"I need to take Hope and my new son to the wildwood." I glance at the wolf who is attached to the children.

"Move away, wolf. I need to fly them to the wildwood. I will return to search for Hudson. We can gather the other men. If you want to go to the Wildwood, travel there, and you can help guard our children. While I am gone, get some sleep. You need it."

I see Star confirm she will ensure the wolf rests. Star agrees adamantly that she will insist. She picks up the sleeping boy.

"The sedative will most likely have them sleeping until lunchtime," Star explains.

I inhale Hope's scent as I lift her into my arms. We make our way to the outside of the castle. Kit takes Hope from me so I can transform. I can change form at will now, thanks to Gemma's little kick-start to boost my abilities.

Kit places Hope gently in my outreached claws. Bundled in a blanket, Hope sleeps now. Star places the bundled boy next to Hope, and I gently cage them securely in my claws. I hold them close to my chest. I send a wave of gratitude to the universe and take flight, bringing the children to our home in the Wildwood.

# CHAPTER 37

## Kayla

I watch my sleeping daughter as I sit in dragon form near my eggs. A tight tension relaxes as the group I am waiting for enters my nesting area. Talen, holding Hope, brings our daughter up to my muzzle to let me smell her and know she is safe and well.

Talen lays Hope down next to her sister. Brooke takes a boy from Balthazar's arms and carries him to me.

"I adopted him, Kayla. His parents died trying to protect him and your girls."

My heart hurts for the boy, losing his parents. I accept the boy and send waves of love to him and Brooke.

*"I know our past. You are a fantastic aunt and sister. You will be an amazing mother, Brooke. I am here to help, and we will give him all the love he needs."* I offer my support.

As Brooke lays the sleeping boy next to my babies, Gemma speaks up.

"I can help erase the memory in the children's minds. Hide it from them so they won't have nightmares and suffer."

I am shocked, wishing foster kids on Earth had an option like that. I know I could have done without my memories of childhood trauma. Brooke and I both could have.

"You can do that?" Brooke asks.

"Should we do that?" Talen asks.

I send Gemma my gratitude. *"Yes, please. It's bad enough we, as adults, have to live with the sorrow of it. Why have that implanted in their little minds?"*

Talen agrees after thinking about it. Brooke watches Phoenix.

"I want to spare him as much pain as possible, but I don't want to take away the memory of his parents."

Gemma hugs Brooke for comfort. "No, I would never take that from him. I will make it so they remember only the day before and are placed in bed for the night. We can explain things to them in a way they will understand. They will still be sad but won't witness the battle."

Brooke stares at Gemma and nods her agreement.

*"Are you up for this, Gemma? You look depleted,"* I ask.

Balthazar, who stands next to the door, keeping his distance from my dragon, comes farther into the great hall. Taking Gemma in his giant hands and making her face him, he probes her with his own magic and concern lights up his features.

"Yes, I can do this one last thing before I rest and recharge," Gemma says before Balthazar speaks.

Balthazar clearly does not like this, but he steps aside, knowing Gemma has her mind made up.

"You will use me and my magic to assist you," he demands.

"Take what you need from me," Brooke adds, taking Balthazar's hand and facing Gemma.

"And from me as well." Talen takes Brooke's hand.

Gemma smiles at them all as she merges some of their magical energy with hers and reaches into the minds of our children. She takes away the trauma of the battle from their little minds. When she's done, she collapses into unconsciousness. Balthazar catches her in his arms and takes her to the bedroom to recover.

I feel the familiar ringing in my ears—Fabian's monotone voice drones on. *"I sense a sacred totem. I need the sacred one."*

The thought of Gemma pops into my head. But I shake it off.

*"Please, Fabian, not now."* I force a wall up and am unwilling to connect with his sad, desperate energy. That ordeal will have to wait.

# CHAPTER 38

## Brooke

I take Gemma in my claws and fly back to my mate, Fang. He perches on guard, waiting for the vampire. His mind is almost still feral. My friend Gemma has been using so much of herself to help. It was hard to get her away from Balthazar to have her help me figure things out now that we have the vampire somewhat trapped.

Gemma helps me put Fang into a deep sleep since reinforcements from our men and the water dwellers are all rallied near the cave—Rina and her mates, along with many determined, battle-ready shark-like warriors. They all admire Fang in dragon form.

He is strong and intimidating. I am both proud and worried. I don't know how Gemma did it, but I am grateful she got him to rest.

Rina, Jag, Gemma, and I decide to go into the cave and see if we can track the vampire. The sculpted man appears to us the moment we reach his resting area. I feel the ancient being, and his tormented soul saddens me.

*"Sacred one, I have waited so long for you. I almost gave up hope."*

We all hear the words in our minds. I feel for the mud man as I sense his long-lived agony.

*"I sent my mate and my daughters to a god portal. They are in stasis there, waiting for me to get them. The vampire wanted me, as my blood would power him beyond anything else. The goddess herself gave me my power. I sent my family away before the vampire could use them."*

This dilemma demands my attention as Fabian sends a desperate compulsion to Gemma and me to save his family.

*"I then cast myself prisoner here, so the vampire could not use my blood or my power. I have not died because my family is still alive, frozen in stasis. I will bless you, sacred one, with all my knowledge if you find my family in this world."*

Gemma examines the spell the warlock has woven. Fabian's power had once been so close to godlike that we are astonished. Images of the past play in our minds. We aren't strong enough to free the warlock.

I am sad about that. The warlock gives me the names of his mate and daughters.

Gemma knows we can free them from the portal. Gemma speaks aloud to Fabian in mud form.

"I cannot free you. You vowed, long as the vampire lived in this world, you would not let blood flow through your veins. You've made an unbreakable covenant with nature."

The warlock already knows his fate is sealed.

"We can bring your family back." She smiles at him, promising to free the females.

The sculpted man sends us his gratitude and warm energy touches us. He retreats into the wall again.

I follow Rina and Jag to continue our search for the vampire.

We make our way to the deepest bowels of the cave system. Rina jumps into the seawater, searching. She pops back up.

*"I need all of you to leave so I can call my water."*

Trusting the female, I follow Gemma and Jag as we make our way out of the cave. Rina calls the sea. Her waters rush in like a funnel, digging in the dirt to suck this creep out.

*"You're about to enter my arena now, chum!"*

We all hear her send the threat to the vampire. She's battle-ready as the water spits the vampire out from his hidden place into the sea.

Jag and Coral jump into the seawater. Rina swims toward the burned beast and tears into him with her claws, fin, and shark teeth snapping.

She tears the vampire's burnt hand from his body. The hideous thing manages to bite her. The acid venom burns inside her whole body. Coral reaches her as the vampire swims off. The vampire flees deeper into the darkness of the sea.

The water's surface turns as the grand octopus's mother throws the vampire up in the air, his skin smoking. She catches him in her suctions and retreats deep into the sea with her prisoner.

Gemma wakes Fang and calms his mind, allowing the man to regain control. We fly to the wildwood, wanting to be near Kayla. Gemma is wholeheartedly invested in saving Fabian's family.

I worry for my sea friends, but they know how to find us. I'd feel a whole lot better knowing that sick bastard is nothing but ash. For now, this battle is done though, and we will have to wait on reports from the water dwellers.

*Kayla is going to be so overwhelmed.* I think as we land.

# CHAPTER 39

## Kayla

I am momentarily happy to see my family back as they walk past Balthazar guarding the door.

*"Oh, Brooke, I am so glad to see you."* I send her my love and glance at Fang as he rushes toward the children. I feel a stress radiating from all of them.

Fang picks up the boy after giving a gentle kiss to each baby girl. The boy giggles as he plays with Fang's Viking-styled braids.

"I know a lot is happening right now, and things are all over the place," Brooke says as I adjust my dragon to sit up a bit taller and wait for more bad news.

"It's bad news. But we have good news too, Kayla. It's more bad timing, really, but I think if we continue to wait for better timing, there may never be a right time," Brooke continues.

*"Just shoot straight with me, Brooke. Come out with it."* I am stern.

Brooke, sensing my sudden anxiety, approaches me slowly. "Kayla, we know how much strangers affect your anxiety, and your dragon is protective right now. With your vision, the goddess clearly wanted us to bring females through the door, not only yummy Earth food and things for convenience."

I huff. "*Obviously, Brooke, but are you seriously suggesting we start the female delivery line while I am nesting?*" I respond, very much annoyed.

"Of course not, Kayla, but we may need to be a bit flexible if your dragon can stand it. For five women, a family—a mother and her daughters."

Gemma interjects, trying to explain. "They were like family to the goddess herself when she lived here. They have been trapped in stasis. Now that we know of them, with everything the goddess has given us, I thought, once you knew, you wouldn't want to wait for a second longer to get them free either." Gemma pleads, still compelled by Fabian.

"But actually, I don't want to free them this second. I want to take a couple of precautions. First, I want you to feel comfortable. I want to prepare for their potential panic because they were sent away fast, and many lifetimes have passed since then. When they get here, in their minds, they will have just left a battle with the vampire."

"We will need to take a few moments to explain to them. The shock may be too much for them. I want you to keep your nesting dragon calm," Brooke says.

That ringing in my ears surfaces, and Fabian's voice drones in. *"Please!"*

I feel his desperation and compulsion. My past vision of Fabian surfaces. The goddess sends me warmth.

*"It's time."* I gently whisper in everyone's mind. I know the goddess is close with this family, and I'll do anything to show my appreciation for the life and family I have now.

I push down my anxiety. I'm already highly stressed about having a crowd after the trauma of saving my babies. My dragon is protective and fighting me with my reluctant acceptance of everyone so close. I take a minute to process this myself.

*"When do you suggest we do this?"* I ask.

Gemma tentatively says, "Tomorrow."

If dragons could roll their eyes, I would have.

*"Okay, I will work on my nerves and try to accept five new people near my nest and children. Of course, I will do this for the goddess,"* I say in my mind, wondering what can happen next. I'm hoping my anxiety can relate to all this.

I want to keep my children safe and close, shelter them from anything else that might be traumatic. I watch my sister and Fang as they have a painful sensation with Phoenix.

The boy learns of his parents' bravery and their death. He cries, missing his mother at a young age and having difficulty understanding death. Brooke and Fang love and hold the boy until he finally falls asleep.

I will make sure to love my new nephew so much. He will have all the family he needs from now on. This is all so incredibly overwhelming. My heart breaks for him, and guilt eats at me because I am grateful, I have my babies safe, and they have Talen and me. My anxiety and frazzled nerves are small compared to that poor boy's loss.

By the next afternoon, Balthazar and Hudson stand as shields in front of my eggs while I huddle my baby girls in their cradles and the boy under my wing. My dragon scratches the surface with unease.

Brooke makes another wall behind Gemma as she writes five names on the enchanted page. She knocks three times on the blue door. Brooke steps back until Fang's bulky body stops her.

The door swings open. My heart starts to pound. I hug my young even tighter. Color blurs as an image distorted falls to the floor like a slinky. In moments, the image stretches to form a still, translucent picture. The picture becomes clear and solidifies, showing five women—terrified, solid, like wax museum statues.

I feel their energy. A feeling of fighting and terror tears through my nesting area the moment the five women become whole and alive. The blue door slams shut. My nostrils flare, and steam puffs out.

Chaos and screaming fill my lair.

"No, Daddy, don't!" Helena yells.

Simultaneously, Theodora screams, "Get off me, you demon!"

I know each female by name, recognizing them in some magic way from the vision the goddess and Fabian once shared with me.

"He bit her, Mommy!" Sybil yells.

I see Margery lunging. "I will kill you, monster!" she roars.

Cordelia, their mother, screams. "Noooo!"

Theodora grips her arm and falls to the ground in pain from the vampire bite. This is way too much all at once for me. I lift my snout and blow a puff of flame at the ceiling, trying to calm my dragon and nerves.

"Things just got more complicated," Brooke announces.

Gemma takes her totem and tries to reassure the females.

"Calm, you're safe. We are here to help. We are friends." She seems shocked at the resistance to her magic.

"I don't know how, but these witches are the most magical ladies I have ever felt the energy of," Gemma mutters under strain.

Brooke charges the female who is about to jump Gemma. Balthazar pulls Gemma behind him, and close, Fang runs into the fray with Brooke.

"*Stop!*" I yell in everyone's minds.

Recognition of my dragon's command must affect these witches because they stop fighting. Confusion replaces the terror for everyone except for Theodora, who is wholly focused on the pain often.

"Let us help you." Brooke offers her hand to the injured girl.

Gemma steps around her huge moose and goes to the family of females.

"Kayla was bitten once, and we helped her. We can purge the venom before it's too late."

Cordelia is terrified for her daughter as she cries. "How?"

Talen says, "I sucked the tainted poison out in the shower, and the females helped, sending their magic to help purge it out. The goddess healed me, Kayla, and our exposure to the venom by boosting the efforts of the healer's ability."

Gemma interrupts Talen. "There's no need to call upon the goddess. I can order the venom to leave. I am the new sacred one."

Gemma stares into Cordelia's eyes and asks her permission to help Theodora. "Please."

Just then, Jag and Coral burst through the door.

"Help! Please," Jag yells as he carries Rina's limp body into my nesting area.

I let loose another puff of fire toward the ceiling, trying to control my anxiety. More are in my nest, with trauma and fear rolling off them.

*"Goddess, give me strength here. I am losing it,"* I pray.

Talen rushes to Jag and his mates.

"Give her to me. Please stay back," Talen insists in a panic.

Jag has to hold Coral back as he says, "Anything, please. Just save her."

Coral's cries have my nerves on high. Talen lays the water dweller down next to the other bite victim.

Gemma chants hard, sweat beading on her forehead.

I start sending my own magic to help. The females sense my worry from a distance, and I feel them through our life-lock magic as they chant, lending Gemma, Brooke, and me. Everyone is chanting and offering aid. The blackness seeps out of Rina's arm first. A slow drain seeps from the sister, Theodora. She's been stuck in limbo for so long.

"The bite has been in her arm for centuries," Gemma croaks out, feeling the strain of healing both females.

Gemma is a saint in my eyes. I watch her straining to heal both ladies. Gemma finally succeeds. Balthazar is there to catch his mate as she falls, exhausted from her healing efforts. He takes her to the bedrooms.

Sybil responds before her mother can. "Thank you for saving my sister," she calls out to Balthazar's back as he takes Gemma away.

"We are all alive, and that is what matters most." Helena lies next to Theodora, wanting to watch over her as she recovers.

Fang lays down furs as a pallet for the females. My nerves are shot, and I'm struggling to remain calm.

"Please, ladies, know we are here to help you. We are your friends. I know you must have many questions, and we will answer them all for you," Brooke says.

"But you also must know that you are currently in my sister's nesting area." Brooke points at me.

*"You are not helping!"* I push at Brooke, hating all those eyes on me.

"Her eggs are due to hatch anytime now. We have three small children here. With all the commotion, our tussle has stressed momma dragon. We will accommodate you, but we also need my sister to accept your presence here," Brooke insists.

I feel Cordelia send out a calming energy as the females start to understand. Brooke wants to check on the children, but I am too stressed to let her come close. Instead, Brooke, Fang, and Hudson decided to take the women out of the building to give me my space. Fang carries Theodora out on her furs as Helena hovers close by.

I finally let out a sigh of relief. Glad to have my nest to myself, I snuggle next to the sleeping children and my eggs, finally feeling calm. I feel the strong witches send me power. They help my anxiety, and I feel at peace.

*"Thank you, my dragon queen."* I hear Fabian softly whisper and I sense his total happiness.

A wave of relief washes over me.

# CHAPTER 40

My eggs start to move and crack.

*"Talen! Brooke!"* I call.

My panic has everyone coming to me.

"Oh! Wow, now?" Brooke realizes it's time to deliver the hatchlings.

Snapping herself into action, she does what she does best and starts getting things ready. "We got this, Kayla. I'm on it."

I feel my dragon relax as I take the form of a woman.

"Talen, they're coming." My voice cracks with emotion.

Talen wraps me up in a robe and kisses me. His pride and joy radiate from him. "Yes, my mate, it is a blessed day."

"Talen, are we ready?" I'm scared and nervous.

Gemma has Balthazar and Hudson bring in the hand-carved cradles and place them next to my nest of gold. Brooke runs to inform the females the hatching is happening. She has them help her carry supplies from the closet she has been storing in preparation.

Talen pulls me in for a hug, kissing my forehead tenderly.

"Yes, Kayla, we are ready. Besides, Brooke has probably thought of everything." He laughs as we watch everyone jump into action in preparation.

Sybil, Margery, and Cordelia get hot water as Gemma adds blankets to cushion the cradles. Brooke shows Gemma how to mix the formula.

The first egg breaks, and I breathe, excited to meet the first baby. "Mommy's here, little one," I coo, reaching for my egg.

Talen and I help the first egg hatch, pulling out a baby girl.

"She is so beautiful," I say through tears as I kiss my newborn daughter. I imprint on her and pass her to Talen, who takes her with trembling hands as he, too, imprints.

"She is perfect," he says as he turns to show off our slimy new baby girl.

"It's a girl!" Brooke says excitedly.

"Told you," Fang agrees.

"She is perfect," I say through tears.

Phoenix coos, "Baby!"

Brooke takes my baby girl from Talen. As soon as Brooke grabs her, my baby wails and cries.

"It's okay, baby girl, Auntie BB has you."

Brooke bathes my new baby girl, diapers, and dresses her. After wrapping my baby up, Brooke lays the new baby down in the sacred wildwood cradle. The wood sings a soft vibration, the song of the trees, as it lulls my baby to sleep.

I call out in shock while reaching into my egg. "No way!" I pull another baby girl out of the egg.

"Twins again," I say in awe, looking at my new baby girl.

Talen reaches down into the second egg that cracks open to grab our third child. "Triplets!" Talen announces with pride.

I am shocked, somehow expecting my eggs to carry only one infant each. I don't know why I assumed that since Faith and Hope hatched as twins in one egg. Maybe this is normal.

Either way, I am happy and scared. It took both Brooke and me to care for Faith and Hope, and having Talen and

Fang, and the guardians ended up being such a help. Now I have Faith, Hope, and two more sets of twins.

"How will I be a decent mom to so many all at once?" I say.

"Kayla, you are a good mom. We have help. You are not alone in this," Talen says, sending me waves of love. "See our babies."

I gaze into my girl's eyes, my anxiety replaced by love. "I love them so much," I say.

We both imprint before handing my second baby girl over to Brooke.

"Boys!" I say as I help Talen pull the second set of babies out of the last egg.

Brooke takes the first boy and hands him to Cordelia to wash as she washes the second.

"Handsome little fellas," she says, feeling the moment's joy.

The boys wail until they are dressed, bundled, and laid together in their cradle. The wood lulls them to sleep. We've found a rhythm for cleaning and dressing and feeding them.

I admire the three cradles holding three sets of twins. Four girls and two boys, the boys are looking so much like Talen. My new set of girls has my dark skin and hair, contrasting with Hope and Faith, who are so pale with blonde hair. Somehow, it reminds me of Brooke and myself. Perfect. I'm so in love with all my children.

The boys take after their dad, with his tan skin and purple eyes. Everyone who helped me vows to support us and help care for the children. We bonded even more during this, and the support and feeling of a genuine family are endearing to my soul.

I let go of that traumatized child I once was, and something inside me heals what was broken. I finally feel whole. I finally feel safe and secure, knowing the people around me can be counted on.

"We need to name them," I say as Talen and Fang admire the babies. I walk up to my boys. "Brooke and I loved this show. It had two brothers as the main characters, Sam and Dean. I want to name them Sam and Dean," I say to Talen.

"Sam and Dean it is," Talen says, grinning ear to ear.

Brooke bounces, her beads clapping together with a jingle. "I love it too, Kayla." She winks at me as if we share secrets only Earth girls will get.

I walk to my new baby girls. "I want them to be fiery and sassy. I want to call this little one Ruby." I pick her up, snuggle, and kiss her before I hand her to her father.

"Hello, my beautiful Ruby," Talen says as he kisses her forehead.

I pick up my other daughter. "I like Ember for her."

Talen leans over and kisses her too.

"Hi, little Ember," Talen coos.

We all sit in a pile of furs and chairs, proud of our make-shift nursery. The ancient witches, Brooke, Gemma, and our selected guardians and mates make up my new family dynamic. I soak up the moment of tenderness as we all do our part to care for my newborns.

*"Thank you for all of this."* I thank the goddess.

These females send me constant reassurance and magic energy to help me stay anxiety-free so that I can bask in this milestone moment. I love them each for their efforts.

Hudson rushes inside, interrupting the moment.

"Sire, you have to see this."

Talen hands Ruby to Brooke, and he and Fang rush out the door, worried.

"Kayla, come. It's safe. You must see!" Talen calls back to me.

"Grab the babies," I say to the ladies behind me.

I hold Ember in my arms as I step outside to join Talen and glance up. A flock of gray dragons swarms the colored sky above. It's stunning. I feel waves of love and congratulations sent to us for our new babies.

The dragons radiate happiness at being able to become dragons, as they should be.

# CHAPTER 41

## Kayla

## One year later

We're standing by Harmony's blue delivery door.

"Ready?" I ask, looking at Brooke while our mates stand close by us.

"The universe says it's time," Brooke says.

I write "true mates" on the enchanted page of the book, and then I knock three times.

"I am so excited to start this finally," Brooke says, eager to see a true mate.

"This is a fitting way to start the celebration," Fang agrees.

Talen holds my hand. "I am so proud of you." He kisses my hand in encouragement.

The door opens, and an image comes through, stretching like a funnel, landing like a slinky on the ground, showing a distorted image that finally solidifies into a woman with curly dark hair. She's sitting in the air with her hands cuffed behind her back, a silent scream, and a sight of fear on her freckled face.

The woman, now solidified and alive in a new world, screams.

"Nooo! Tommy, drive!" Her scream cuts short when her ass hits the floor.

Dazed and confused, she rolls to her side and scans around to see us standing over her.

"Did the train hit us? Am I dead?" the female asks.

Brooke helps her to her feet.

"No, honey, you're not dead, but we have some explaining to do," Brooke says.

I smile warmly at the short, curvy female. "Here, let's see if Talen can get those things off. What is your name, sweetie?" I ask.

The curly-haired, green-eyed woman replies, "Lucinda."

She's still in shock. She's wearing dark jeans and cowboy boots, with a fitted purple shirt that reveals her healthy cleavage. Lucinda stands numbly as Talen releases her from her cuffs.

Her eyes widen at the pile of gold and treasures behind us. "This is unreal. I must be drugged."

Brooke giggles. "I know it seems crazy, but it will make sense soon, I swear. Where are you from, Lucinda?"

I carefully offer her a goblet of water, mindful not to touch her.

"Here, drink. You are safe," I encourage.

Lucinda feels a bit calmer as she begins to relax.

Brooke and I send her calming energy. Lucinda starts to tell her story.

"I finally had enough of Tommy. I got too hot and heavy with him. I thought he was my hero. I lost my adoptive parents in a crash two years ago. I don't have any other family. We had moved around so much, with my father working for the government. Making close friends wasn't an option. When I met Tommy, I was at a grief counseling group. I thought it was love at first sight and my step toward healing. But he was a control freak, an abusive asshole. I finally found a women's center to escape to." Lucinda takes a deep breath.

"I suffered six months of being held under his thumb before I could escape him. But Tommy, eventually, he found me in a state away." Lucinda sniffles, getting emotional.

"He used a Taser on me in the parking lot. I was closing my trunk full of groceries when he attacked. He cuffed me and threw me in the back seat. When I came to my senses, we were on railroad tracks, and a train was about to hit us."

Fear shines in her eyes as she continues her story.

"I thought I was going to die. I think I did die." Lucinda pinches her wrist. "Ouch! Yep, that is a real pain."

Brooke gives me a knowing smile.

A giant gray wolf and brown bear run into the hall. Lucinda jumps in fear.

"Do not fear, Lucinda. They're friends." I try to soothe.

"If you say so," Lucinda says, unsure as she stares at the bear.

"Have you ever seen Star Trek?" I ask.

"Who hasn't?" she replies.

"Well, the easiest way to explain it is Scotty beamed you up here."

Brooke laughs. "I don't think that will help, Kayla."

I shrug and let Brooke try to explain. "You see, Lucinda, you are no longer on Earth." Lucinda still is perplexed.

"You are close when you had an afterlife in mind," Brooke continues. "There are gods and goddesses. The goddess of this world was pulled out of here by a bigger god the day an evil creature came to this planet. That bad guy came here and mucked up some stuff, and long story short, there are too few females here compared to men. " Taking a breath before continuing.

"The goddess chose you. She is sending compatible females from other worlds to live here and help restore balance. She promised only to take the unattached females from those other worlds, and it is our job to welcome you and make sure you acclimate and love your new home here. We cannot send you or any of the new arrivals back. This is a one-way ride," Brooke explains.

Lucinda is trying to understand. "So, I'm not on Earth anymore?"

I smile. "No, sweetie. This place is full of magic. You will dig this place if you love *The Lord of the Rings*."

"Really? Magic?" Lucinda questions.

"Yes," Brooke insists.

"You will have magic too. Things are more about intuition and gut instincts here. Just roll with how you are feeling. Don't be too surprised when people shift from skin to animals and other things."

"Will I be able to shift?"

Brooke laughs. "Yes, eventually, you will understand your inner magic."

"The adrenaline junkie in me has me loving this place. Can I skydive here? It's one of my favorite hobbies," Lucinda asks.

"I admire how well you are adapting to this. I was a wreck when I first arrived," Brooke says.

I like this new woman. Something about her feels right. "We don't have parachutes here, but you will enjoy our sky. We can fly," I say.

"Hell yeah, you already know!" Lucinda lights up with excitement.

"Don't be too surprised when you turn into a dragon," I say.

Lucinda's eyes go wide. "Really? No kidding?" she asks.

"I don't know if you can change immediately. It took Kayla and me a little time before we could transform," Brooke explains.

I motion for Lucinda to follow us outside. "We have an event tonight. Do you feel up to joining us? If you are not too overwhelmed, we can fly you there after we transform into dragons," I offer, sensing Lucinda is adjusting with ease.

Lucinda grins ear to ear. "Hell yeah, let's roll!"

Brooke holds Lucinda in her claws as we fly to the castle. The new female certainly is embracing this new world with joy.

We land, and the festivities are in full effect. Brooke chats with Lucinda, going more in-depth about things. I hold Talen's hand as we make our way to the wishing well, the goddess fountain. Females from all over show up, excited to meet and mingle with men and see if they can find their match. The ratio is still off by a lot more men than women.

The buzz in the air is full of excitement and hope. Lucinda is watching—wide-eyed, excited to be here—when she catches a man's eye.

"It's started," I say as we all feel the energy of imprinting.

"I haven't gotten to explain that yet," Brooke says, worried it is all too much too fast.

Lucinda runs up to the man. "Hi, I am Lucinda. What just happened between us?"

The man hits his knees. "Lucinda," he says in a daze of wonderment, love shining in his eyes.

"I better try to explain," Brooke says, rushing over to Lucinda.

I get the feeling, though, Lucinda is quick to catch on to things and will be just fine.

I turn to Talen, wanting to escape with him to my favorite place.

Leaving Brooke to take over and introducing Lucinda to our world, I take flight with Talen.

"I can't think of a better place to celebrate."

I fly back toward the Wildwood fortress. I find my favorite sky crystal pedestal and land, shifting back into my skin.

I feel like a goddess as Talen gazes at me with hunger. I run and tackle him, greedy for his touch. I kiss him as he lies back on the crystal bed.

"You are so tasty with the stars twinkling behind you," he says as I sit up and lower myself on his cock.

I moan his name. "Talen."

He bucks under me, repeatedly thrusting. His insatiable pumping up into me, stimulating my body in all the right spots. My clit throbs and my orgasm is building.

"Oh, we aren't done yet." He flips me over to lie on my stomach as he starts a slow, steady rhythm. A thrill washes over me.

I feel the floating crystal cloud add magic to our moment. Looking through the platform to the land below has me feeling nothing but bliss on the edge of Talen's electrifying rhythm, his cock filling me deeply, his mouth licking and kissing, sucking on my neck.

I relish his veracity. I will never tire of this intensity.

"Oh, Yes! Just like that, don't stop. Please don't stop!" I beg in my ravenous state as he sends me over the edge in a tantalizing orgasm.

Talen makes love to me all night. We hold each other as colors start to streak across the skies.

"You are the most beautiful woman."

Talen drives me nuts when he whispers in my ear, causing goosebumps. Those damn butterflies. I squeeze his shaft as he sends me over in pulsing waves.

"Talen, you are my handsome mate. I have been truly blessed with you as my true mate."

We kiss each other gently under the stars.

# CHAPTER 42

## Kayla

Under a starry, crisp night sky, many years after having my babies, it's finally time. I burned the vampire so badly all those years ago that he tried to hide and rejuvenate. My family and friends fought him after I battled him to get my precious Faith back.

Rina got the vampire out of his hiding, and she viciously attacked him, injuring him even more. My dear friend almost died from his venom. Thank the goddess for Gemma and her healing ability.

The great octopus snatched the vampire up the moment he swam down to the deep dark of the sea after his fight with Rina. She's held him captive ever since. He drowns over and over, every day and night. His bite doesn't work on the octopus. One of her hatchlings guards our castle shores. My children adore her as I cherish the Grand Guardian octopus.

*"I told you, bastard, that you messed with the wrong momma."* I send out a mental push, hoping the vile thing can

comprehend me. I don't feel sorry for that vampire. Not one bit.

Now he has had years to suffer the great octopus' justice. The grand guardian brings me pearls and sea gems frequently, always seeking forgiveness for taking me. I send her love and forgiveness, but she insists on bestowing gifts.

Tonight, we all gather at the seashore, united as land and sea people, to rid our world of that evil vampire finally. This has been a long time coming. The goddess has gotten better at communicating with me.

I guess the time on our planet is faster than the time passing up in the realm of the gods. So even though Harmony has been gone for only minutes up there, it has been centuries here for us. For those few minutes, Harmony was pissed off at her true mate.

Tonight, though, she will fix it. She is having her mate retrieve the vampire he made.

So here we are, waiting for this moment. We cheer as one when the grand octopus throws the vampire on the beach at our feet.

I hold Talen's hand in my excitement. The vampire lies there, soggy and gross. He coughs out water. Weak and nasty, he tries to stand.

"But I am a god here," the vampire says weakly with fear as he feels the hand of God reaching for him.

We all hit our knees as a bright light lights up the night sky. The glowing hand of a god comes to our planet. It uses two fingers to pinch the vampire and take him out and away from us.

We raise our bowed heads, stand, and cheer.

*"Thank you, Harmony."* I send her my gratitude for the unique gifts she has blessed me with, my beautiful home on this planet, worlds away from Earth, and my horrible life there.

My heart melts as Fabian appears in front of Cordelia. He's whole, in the flesh once more.

We all cheer again, and then the festivities start.

I see my grown children jumping up and cheering with all who gathered to witness. I see my family and feel the hum of goodness wash over us now that evil is finally cast out.

I love all these people. I trust them and am so grateful my heart has healed, and my faith is solid and whole. I no longer hold hate in the forefront of my heart.

I glance at Brooke with her grown son, Pax. She hugs Fang excitedly as her pregnant belly fills the space between them.

I gaze at Talen with tears brimming my eyes as I melt at the love shining back at me. I kiss him tenderly. As we slowly pull apart, I softly whisper, "I love you with all I am, Talen."

# THE END

# EPILOGUE

## Harmony

Hecat pulled the vampire out of my Eden. He put him in a sphere where time equaled that of Harmony.

"What a vile creature, that vampire. How could you make such a thing?" I say in disgust.

The vampire has to live out a hell of the torment of a thousand years, never getting a reprieve—all the time it takes to continue my argument with my arrogant Hecat.

Moments in the time of the gods pass as if the vampire is an afterthought. My Hecat waves his hand, and with only a thought, the vampire is unmade, unable to live in any afterlife.

"I will miss living among them," I say.

Hecat takes me into his arms and kisses me apologetically.

"I hate that you are sad, my love, but I am glad I grabbed you and finally found my heart," he replies.

I gaze upon my little world and see love among my people. I am glad that my little Eden's balance and Harmony have been restored.

"You should have never messed with my dad. Going after Lucifer was a bad plan," I insist.

"I wanted to fix the problems that Lucifer caused for the great creator," Hecat explains.

'You were trying to get my dad's attention, you fool. You need to apologize to Lilith and Lucifer." I glare.

"My mother must have known you would rile my dad's nerves when she made you my true mate," I say, knowing my mother loves to tease and taunt my dad.

"If you want to impress my father, you must make me happy. I am a daddy's girl. You're lucky he is willing to give me females for my men."

I see all the planets with life Hecat created in his universe. "Why have you made so many?" I ask.

I made my Eden and lived among them. I could not imagine having so many worlds left abandoned. I am Harmony. Some call me Karma. I have to have balance. Hecat creates to gain power, impress my father, and make all these planets willy-nilly. He's arrogant and does not care for his people correctly.

"Now that we have fixed my little Eden, you need to make it right with my dad. Start your groveling, Hecat. I will not let you lie with me until you fix the universe you've created."

Hecat laughs. "As you wish, my love. Your happiness is all I desire."

I watch all the planets along the path of Hecat's creations.

"Tell me about this planet here, with the purple men. Why are they in such turmoil?"

"That is my planet Laverian. I made that world too close to the god Kato's planet. Kato named his planet Azure. Kato thought it fun to battle my world. I haven't checked on it in a while. I have been busy with my other creations. I lost interest when Kato wanted to play with it so badly," Hecat explains.

"This is exactly why you need to stop creating for a while. We are going to focus on what you've already made. I want to fix the balance in Laverian," I demand.

Hecat, eager to please me, holds my hand as we zoom in for a closer evaluation of the planet Laverian.

# About the Author

TANYA STEVERDING was born in 1977 on March Air Force Base in southern California.

She currently lives in east Texas, where she enjoys spending time with her family and beloved grandchildren. When she's not writing, she is crafting or painting. She's also an avid reader and fan of paranormal romance and the young adult genre. Tanya also enjoys traveling in her RV and bringing her pack of toy poodles everywhere. The forest in the mountains and the ocean are Tanya's favorite places to visit. Creating worlds of fiction for her readers has been a dream come true.

# Acknowledgments

Special thanks to my support system. Especially Amy Briggs for last minute edits. https://www.amybriggsauthor.com/editing-services

The write-publish-sell assist team, Alexa Bigwarfe, Cayce Lacorte , Raewyn Sangari, Nancy Cavillones, and the rest of the team that helped me throughout the launch campaign.

https://katbiggiepress.com/write-publish-sell/

My daughter Alexandra Garcia for her marketing and administrative assistance.

My mother and father have read this story's very first draft and have been my biggest fans.

My husband, who's my muse and gets my creative juices flowing. He always wants to see me achieve my goals.

My personal book team.

Thank you all from my heart.

You are valued and appreciated.

Continue spreading Kindness.


Your humble author,

Tanya Steverding

https://linktr.ee/tanyasteverding
Please join my newsletter for updates.
Follow me on social media.

www.ingramcontent.com/pod-product-compliance
Lightning Source LLC
Chambersburg PA
CBHW031031310726
48969CB00007B/1945